The Ominous Trail

J.C. Fields

D1225831

Publishing Coordinator – Sharon Kizziah-Holmes
Cover Design – Jaycee DeLorenzo

Paperback-Press
an imprint of A & S Publishing
Paperback Press, LLC
Springfield, MO

ISBN -13: 978-1-956806-94-6

PART ONE

ACKNOWLEDGMENTS

As an independent author, it falls on my shoulders to put together the best team possible to ensure the success of my novels. With this new book, my 11th, the team is working like a well-oiled machine. My gratitude and thanks go out to each of the following:

Sharon Kizziah-Holmes, owner of Paperback Press, thank you for your undying support. We fight like siblings, but in the end, there is no one I count on more to support my writing endeavors than you.

My critique group, Shirley, Sharon, Lori, Michael and Conetta thank you for your honest and sometimes brutal feedback when I submit material.

The editorial team, Kate Richards, Nanette Sipe, Shirley McCann and Tina Vyborny help make my novels more readable and, hopefully, more enjoyable.

Jaycee DeLorenzo, my cover designer extraordinaire. It is a joy working with someone possessing your level of talent.

Dr. Clarissa Willis, the newest member. Thank you for taking me on as a client. I am looking forward to your success as you take *The Michael Wolfe Saga* to Europe.

Paul J. McSorley, returns as the voice of Sean Kruger. Paul is also the creator of a successful YouTube Podcast called *Fear From the Heartland*, which I am privileged to be a contributor. I believe much of my success has been the collaboration between the two of us on my novels and short stories.

And again, last but not least, my wife Connie. She is my rock, the love of my life, my best friend and my greatest supporter. She keeps me grounded and on track. I cannot imagine where I would be without her.

DEDICATION

For Connie, Sean, and Ryan.

OTHER PUBLICATIONS
By J.C. Fields

The Sean Kruger Series
The Fugitive's Trail
The Assassin's Trail
The Imposter's Trail
The Cold Trail
The Money Trail
The Dark Trail
The Virtual Trail

The Michael Wolfe Saga
A Lone Wolf
The Last Insurgent
A Matter of Payback

CHAPTER 1

Chicago, IL
Early Sunday Morning

At exactly 3:14 a.m., as expected, the security door on the left side of the building's back loading dock clicked. Two men, dressed from head to shoes in black, their faces obscured by balaclavas, stood there. The shorter opened the door with his gloved hand. Lowering their night-vision goggles, they slipped inside. Before them lay the open expanse of the museum warehouse receiving area. They hurried toward the staircase located on the far west wall. Both knew the layout of the building by heart, having taken the journey numerous times via virtual reality.

Each man had trained for this night's incursion separately in discreet locations and would not be able to identify their partner. Communication was to be by hand signals only, negating the ability to identify the other by voice.

The intruders knew what to do. The shorter one carried a backpack, and the taller man carried a tool kit containing the necessary utensils to gain access to the display cases targeted by their employer.

Both men were lean and fit, which allowed them to ascend the stairs two at a time toward their destination three floors above. When they emerged from the stairwell on the designated floor, they bypassed three glass-enclosed display cases containing historic crown jewels on loan from England and hurried to their targeted exhibitions. The night-vision goggles gathered ambient light from the windows and exit signs, which allowed the taller thief to see details within the cases. Using a tool from his satchel, he opened the unit and handed specific items to the man with the backpack.

With the reception of each article, the shorter man handed his partner an identical copy to replace the stolen item. Once completed, the thief moved on to the next piece on their memorized list.

Repeating the process, the thieves removed and replaced thirty high-value necklaces, bracelets, and rings. Their instructions were to ignore any item they did not have a replacement for, regardless the value. This intrusion targeted specific diamond objects only.

At one minute past 4 a.m., their task completed, the two returned to the staircase. They descended to the ground level where they exited the building through the same door originally used for access. Once outside, the shorter man sprinted toward the alley behind the museum, while the taller one waited to make sure the door locked. When he heard a click, he, too, raced toward the alley.

After their exit from the museum, one headed east, the other west. Both hurried toward parked sedans they used to drive to the museum's location.

An hour later, the man with the backpack, having parked the automobile in the same slot where he had found it on a used car lot, exited the automobile and locked it. He calmly walked to an awaiting SUV with a driver and slipped into the passenger seat.

As the man behind the wheel accelerated, he said, "Where're the keys?"

The thief handed the set from the borrowed vehicle to the driver.

The man glanced at his passenger. "Any problems?"

"Piece of cake. Just like we practiced. In and out, no problems."

"Did you see your partner's face?"

With a shake of his head, the man wearing black placed the backpack on the rear seat. "Nope."

The two rode in silence for several minutes. Finally, the passenger asked, "How much was all that ice worth?"

Keeping his eyes on the road, the driver grinned. "Haven't got a clue. Our employer never told me."

The man in black nodded. "Just curious. Some of those stones were huge."

A traffic light changed, and the driver slowed the car to a stop. Glancing at his passenger, he withdrew a small, suppressed pistol from a shoulder holster. He raised the weapon, pointed it at the temple of his passenger, and pulled the trigger. A subsonic 22 caliber hollow-point bullet entered the skull, causing his now-lifeless body to slump against the passenger door.

***

The 1972 Chris Craft Catalina slowed as the sun reached its zenith in the eastern sky over Lake Michigan. Waves were shallow as the boat rose and fell in a rhythmic cadence. Alone in the thirty-one-foot vessel, the pilot shut off the engine and prepared to complete his assigned task. Two bodies, both clad in black clothing and weighed down with sandbags tied to their chests were lowered into the deep waters halfway between Chicago and Ben Harbor, Michigan.

After watching the second one sink beneath the surface, he returned to the cabin, started the engine, and accelerated toward a dock in Ben Harbor.

***

Monday morning arrived and, at eight thirty, retired Chicago Police Detective Bob Haskins began his rounds. His job, to make sure all the exhibits were ready for the crowds who would enter the museum at 10 a.m.

On the third floor, nothing appeared out of the ordinary as he checked each of the display cases. In the middle of the room, he discovered one of the access panels to a large display unlocked. Leaving it alone, he surveyed the jewelry on their pedestals and at first found nothing out of place. Until he noticed a necklace slightly off center on its pedestal.

He took a picture of the item with his cell phone and then used his handheld radio.

"This is Haskins, I need the curator to the third floor."

"What's wrong, Bob?"

"Not sure. Is Margaret here yet?"

"Yeah, she just walked in."

"Send her."

"She hasn't had her coffee yet. You sure?"

"Yes, I'm sure."

Ten minutes later, Margaret Ross frowned as she examined the pedestal with the out-of-place necklace. "Bob, you said the access door was unlocked?"

"Yes, once I discovered it open, I started checking to make sure everything was still in the case. That's when I saw the misalignment of the necklace."

She wore white cotton gloves as she reached for the multi-diamond-faceted piece. "Is it all right if I examine it further?"

"Yes, I've photographed it from numerous angles."

She removed the necklace and held a jewelers' loupe magnifier close to one of the stones. She studied it for several seconds then turned to Haskins. "Call the police. We've had an incident."

CHAPTER 2

Two Months Later

With a stainless-steel insulated coffee mug in hand, Sean Kruger entered his home office and opened the blinds on the room's window. Taking a sip of coffee, he surveyed the front yard and saw two squirrels chase each other up a giant oak tree just outside the window. The tree occupied a third of the view, but it also provided shade during the hot summer months in this part of Missouri.

Chuckling at the antics of the squirrels, he sat in the office chair and powered on his laptop. The sound of car doors slamming outside caused him to turn back to the window. His mirth at the squirrels quickly dissipated as two men walked away from a black Ford Explorer down the sidewalk toward his driveway. Once there, the taller of the two consulted a cell phone he held. He looked toward the house and then back at the cell phone. With a nod, both men proceeded to approach the house.

Not recognizing either man, Kruger stood, opened the top right-hand desk drawer, withdrew his Glock 19, and headed toward the front door. As he arrived, the doorbell sounded.

Opening it, he kept his hand holding the gun hidden and observed the two men from the vehicle. A full glass storm door separated him from the men on the porch. "Can I help you gentlemen?"

The taller of the two asked, "Is this the residence of Sean Kruger?"

At this point, the glass door remained locked. "What's this concerning?"

The shorter man smiled and offered a business card. "We apologize for the earliness of the day, Mr. Kruger. We are with Tucker, Neal and Spencer, Incorporated. I'm Nathan Tucker, and this is my partner, Robert Spencer."

Kruger remained quiet.

The taller man spoke. "We are an insurance company and would like to hire KKG to investigate a theft. May we come in to discuss the particulars?"

After studying the two men, Kruger reached for the lock on the storm door and opened it. "Please, come in. Let's go to the kitchen. There's a table we can use." With a practiced move, he tucked the Glock into the belt of his jeans at the small of his back. With his sweatshirt covering the weapon, he led the men toward the breakfast nook.

He gestured toward a glass bistro table, and the two men each claimed a chair.

"Would either of you like a cup of coffee?"

Both men nodded as they removed their suit coats. The man named Tucker placed a folder on the table before they hung their coats on the back of their chairs.

After Kruger placed a mug of coffee in front of each man, he sat across from them. "Can I get you anything to go with your coffee?"

Both men shook their head and studied their host.

"Now, what can KKG do for Tucker, Neal and Spencer?"

Spencer started the conversation. "I take it you are Sean Kruger."

"You would be correct."

"We understand you are the head of the fraud investigation department with KKG."

Kruger nodded.

"And you have over twenty-five years with the FBI."

"Yes."

Both men relaxed, and Tucker offered his business card. "Once again, we apologize for intruding on your privacy, but we did not want to meet at your office."

Taking a sip of coffee, Kruger tilted his head. "Why?"

"The nature of our visit is highly confidential. We would prefer to keep our conversation as private as possible."

A nod was Kruger's response.

Tucker withdrew a photo from the file in front of him and placed it facing the retired agent. He then tapped it. "That is a picture of a diamond necklace with a total weight of twenty-four carats. It is valued at a little over five million dollars."

Putting half-readers on, Kruger studied the picture. "I'll take your word for it."

The man drew another picture from the file and laid it on top of the previous one.

Kruger picked up both photos and compared them. "They look identical. Which one is fake?"

"The picture you hold in your left hand. It is pure cubic zirconia. It is a high-quality fake and worth less than a thousand dollars."

A slight smile came to Kruger's face. "How many?"

Spencer returned the smile. "Very good, Mr. Kruger. Thirty in total."

"Total value of the missing diamonds?"

"They were insured for over one hundred and fifty million dollars."

Kruger whistled as he stared at the two pictures he held in his hands. He looked over his glasses at the two men. "Let me guess; someone substituted exact replicas of the stolen jewelry. How long did it take you to discover the theft?"

"Almost immediately." They were taken from The Field Museum in Chicago sometime between closing on Saturday night and when the museum opened on Monday. The museum was closed to the public on Sunday due to Easter."

"What do security tapes show?"

"Nothing."

Frowning, Kruger removed his glasses. "Excuse me?"

"They show nothing. They were turned off. Someone hacked into the museum's security system and shut the cameras down in parts of the building."

"What about the doors?"

"They were all locked."

"Windows?"

"All intact and locked."

"How'd they get in?"

"No one knows. The police assumed since the security cameras were compromised so were the locks. The cameras and the locks are controlled by the same system."

"Any fingerprints?"

"No."

"Figures. What else did the police say?"

"Not much. They have basically told us that due to the lack of evidence, they are unable to justify placing additional resources on the case."

"I take it that means no persons of interest?"

"None, whatsoever."

Standing, Kruger went to the coffeepot and poured more coffee. He stared out the window above the kitchen sink and sipped the brew for a few moments. Turning, he leaned against the cabinet. Both Tucker's and Spencer's eyes were locked on him.

After taking another sip, Kruger asked, "Are you wanting to hire KKG to look into this incident, gentlemen?"

Spencer nodded. "Only if you are the one doing the looking."

"Myself and another."

9

"We must insist on confidentiality."

"Trust me, the individual I am thinking about is beyond discreet."

The two men looked at each other and nodded. Tucker said, "Very well. Does that mean you will look into the matter?"

"You haven't asked about our fees."

"We didn't pick your company after a simple Google search. We've had numerous recommendations from very highly placed individuals within the US government."

Hiding his smile with a sip of coffee, Kruger returned to the table and sat. "I'll need all the information you can provide."

Spencer pushed the file across the table. "This is what we have."

"I'll need it electronically as well."

"No problem." The man paused for a moment. "We'll need daily updates."

"Then, I am no longer interested."

"What does that mean? We need to be on top of your progress."

"Not on a daily basis. Gentlemen, I have a few other projects on my desk at the moment." He paused, his eyes shifting from one to the other. "Since Easter, two months ago, it appears something has occurred to push this little incident to the top of your problem pile. Want to tell me what that something is?"

Tucker folded his arms. "The investigation is in a very critical stage at the moment. We need it cleared up as soon as possible."

"Mr. Tucker, looking into something like this will take more than a few hours or days. From what you've told me, there is a possibility it will never be solved. If the police are struggling, there may not be a lot to go on. But I will look into it, if I'm not micromanaged. Now, I will ask again, what happened to create the sudden urgency?"

Spencer clasped his hands together and studied the tabletop. Tucker let out a sigh and then looked at Kruger. "The CEO of the company that owned the diamonds is demanding we settle the account."

"How demanding?"

"Threatening litigation."

"Okay, tell me the complete story."

***

Tucker and Spencer left two hours later. Standing on the front porch, Kruger watched the black Ford drive off. When it disappeared from his vision, he walked across the street and rang the doorbell on the house directly across from his. The door to the Diminski residence opened thirty seconds later. JR waved Kruger in. "What did the two suits want?"

"They've got a mystery on their hands and want me to look into it."

"Thought you got paid for that now?"

"I do. And you will as well."

"I've got a job, Sean. Getting the building rebuilt has everyone working out of their homes."

"How much longer?"

JR shrugged. "Couple more months. The contractor is having difficulty sourcing some of the wiring we need. What's the mystery?"

"A hundred and fifty million dollars' worth of diamonds were stolen from a museum in Chicago. Security system was hacked and shut down during the burglary and all the diamonds replaced with exact duplicates, made from cubic zirconia. The only reason someone discovered the theft was due to one necklace being out of place."

"Huh."

"I see the wheels turning. You're interested."

"Maybe."

"What if I told you even the Chicago police can't find any

clues?"

A smile grew on JR's face. "You know what buttons to push, don't you?"

"Yes, I do."

CHAPTER 3

Southwest Missouri
Monday Morning

Aviation fuel fumes permeated the old hanger on the commercial side of the Springfield Branson National Airport. The remodeled building served as the headquarters for KKG Solutions and was also where the company kept their leased private jet. Dressed in jeans, an untucked polo shirt, and with an empty stainless steel coffee mug in hand, Kruger entered the small conference room used by the partners for briefings and their regular Monday morning planning meetings.

Benedict "Sandy" Knoll looked up as Kruger entered. "Mornin', Sean. Jimmie will be here shortly."

"Mornin', Sandy. What's on your agenda this week?"

"I'm flying to DC tomorrow. Pentagon is opening bids for State Department security. I've been told we're the leading contractor, and I need to be there to finalize the agreement."

Kruger nodded. "Told officially or from one of your buddies?"

Knoll smiled. "Let's just say the guy who assigns

contracts also owes me more than a few favors."

With a chuckle, Kruger strolled to the Mr. Coffee they kept in the room and poured the liquid into his mug. "We have an interesting opportunity I need to discuss with you and Jimmie this morning."

"Really, what is it?"

"As soon as he gets here."

Fifteen minutes later, all three principals of KKG Solutions sat around the table. Kruger started the meeting. "We have been asked to investigate a possible insurance fraud case in Chicago."

Jimmie Gibbs took a sip of coffee. "Sounds good. What are the details?"

"Diamond jewelry, valued at one hundred fifty million dollars, disappeared from the Field Museum over the Easter weekend. The heist was well thought out, everything replaced with exact replicas made from cubic zirconia. The only reason the substitutions were discovered was due to one necklace being out of place on its pedestal."

Gibbs whistled. "Hundred and fifty mil?"

Kruger nodded.

"Did you tell them we charge 10 percent for insurance fraud?"

"I did."

"And?"

"No problem. However, what I haven't told you yet concerns the sheer lack of evidence."

Knoll looked over his glasses at Kruger. "Has that ever bothered you before, Sean?"

"No, but this one does give me pause."

"How so?"

He proceeded to tell them.

When he finished, Knoll said, "You're planning to look into it anyway, aren't you?"

"Yes."

Gibbs stood and headed toward the coffeepot. "Do you

realize if you solve this, you'll have brought in the biggest contract we've ever had?"

"Don't spend the money, yet, Jimmie."

"I wasn't. But I trust you'll figure it out."

Looking at Knoll, Kruger asked, "Can you have the pilot drop me off in Chicago on your way to DC?"

"He'll be happy to. How long do you plan to stay?"

"Don't know yet. No more than a few days. Why?"

"Just let him know. He's going to stay in Washington until I'm finished."

Kruger nodded thoughtfully. "I want to bring JR into the investigation."

Both Gibbs and Knoll said in unison, "Great idea."

***

Later, Same Day

Stephanie Kruger sat on the side of the bed as her husband packed for his trip to Chicago. The habit of talking to him while he packed had been cemented into their routine during the final years he spent on the road for the FBI.

"Do you realize this is the first time you've been in a hotel for more than one night since you retired?"

"Also, first time in a hotel since retiring, without you. Not looking forward to it, either."

"But…"

"Yeah, there's a however left hanging."

She smiled and folded her arms. "Let me guess, you're looking forward to the challenge."

He chuckled. "You know me too well, don't you?"

Standing, she went to him and put her arms around his waist. "Yes, and I am very grateful for that."

He returned the embrace and they remained quiet while holding each other, each lost in their own thoughts. Finally, she looked up at him. "When do you think you'll be back?"

"Probably late Thursday. Since we have our own jet, I don't mind flying anymore. Much easier, and we can determine our own schedule. One of the reasons I haven't had to spend any nights away from home. Day trips are super easy."

She returned to sitting on the bed. "I have some news from work."

He stopped packing and studied her. "Good news or bad?"

"Very good."

"Well, don't keep me in suspense."

"I was made an associate professor and given tenure."

He chuckled. "That's not good news, that's fantastic news. Congratulations."

"I knew I was being considered for it but hadn't heard anything for several months. Then, this afternoon, President Small stopped by and told me the news."

"That's impressive. The university president told you himself?"

"Yes. It seems he also wants me on an advisory board."

"Uh-oh. Beware of campus intrigue."

"What's that supposed to mean?"

"Advisory boards are usually boring and full of drama. Just be careful."

She chuckled. "You know I don't like dealing with drama."

"I know, but it is inevitable at a university."

"Sean, I haven't seen any yet."

"How many advisory boards have you been on?"

"You're kidding, right?"

"Nope."

"What should I tell the president?"

"Accept his invitation. Once you have your tenure contract signed, then you can conveniently have other pressing matters to attend to whenever a meeting gets scheduled."

She frowned. "That seems a little dishonest. Accept his invitation and then not go."

"Like I said, go to a few. If there's no drama, keep going."

With a nod, she sighed. "What are the odds?"

"That drama will occur?"

"Yes."

"There are no odds. It's inevitable."

CHAPTER 4

Chicago

Kruger shook the hand of Chicago PD Detective Peter Barnes before being escorted to a conference room. Barnes studied him for a few moments. "You look familiar."

With a sly smile, Kruger nodded. "April, 1997. I was a new profiler for the FBI and helped on a serial murder case of three Chicago area women."

"Now I remember. The security guard who dumped their bodies in Wolf Lake."

"Yeah, that one."

"I'll be. I was just a patrolman then. The detectives were impressed with how you conducted yourself. You didn't act superior to everyone else. We've had a few real assholes with the FBI come through here."

"There are more good agents than bad, Detective."

"Call me, Peter."

"I'm Sean."

The detective gave Kruger a smile. "You were one of the reasons I became a detective."

"Glad I left a good impression."

"So, you're retired from the FBI now?" Barnes studied Kruger's business card a little closer. "You working for an insurance company?"

"No, my company was hired by one to look into the jewelry theft at the Field Museum last Easter."

Barnes laughed out loud. "Good luck there."

"I understand there's a shortage of evidence."

"None would be a better description. They still wouldn't know about it if one necklace hadn't been misaligned on a display pedestal."

"Were the replacements that good?"

"Yeah, follow me. I'll show you the crime book."

After studying the pictures of the crime scene, Kruger brought his attention back to the detective. "How did they gain access to the museum?"

"We don't have proof, but we suspect an employee of the museum gave access to the building's security system to someone on the outside. The system controls both the cameras and the locks on the access doors. There's a gap of three hours, the night of the robbery, between two and five a.m. on the security camera videos. We think whoever shut down the cameras also unlocked the rear door next to the loading dock."

"Why that particular door?"

"Closest to the rear stairwell. Easy for the intruder to gain access to the third floor."

Kruger looked again at the photographs and then at the diagram of the third floor that marked the display cases where the fake jewelry was found. He returned his attention to Barnes. "I notice only certain display cases were accessed. Any thoughts?"

"Another reason we think this is an inside job. Only pieces owned by Goldmax Industries."

"Know anything about them?"

"They're a South African based conglomerate who started out as a diamond mining company. They've recently expanded into sourcing industrial metals."

"Huh."

Barnes continued. "I did a little digging on them."

"And?"

"They're one of the leading companies in the world mining lithium for EV batteries."

Raising an eyebrow, Kruger studied Barnes for a moment. "So, they don't just mine diamonds?"

"Nope. The company is fairly diverse from what I found. The diamond collection was a pet project for the company's owner. He openly admits the other mining operations pay for his obsession with diamonds."

"What's his name?"

Barnes folded his arms. "Walter Wagenaar. His corporate headquarters is in Johannesburg, South Africa. He showed up here about a week after the robbery and had a meeting with our chief of police."

"How'd that go?"

"I wasn't here at the time. I'm told it got heated."

Kruger wrote in a small notepad he kept in his sport coat pocket. "Has this Wagenaar fellow been back?"

Barnes shook his head. "Not to my knowledge."

Referring to the crime log again, the ex-FBI agent pursed his lips. "I need to see the museum firsthand. Could you meet me there?"

"Sure, when?"

"Now, if it's convenient."

"I'll meet you there."

Ten minutes later, just before starting his rental car, Kruger pushed a speed dial on his cell phone. A familiar voice answered on the second ring.

"What'd you find out?"

"JR, I need you to do a deep dive on a company called Goldmax Industries and its CEO Walter Wagenaar."

"What am I looking for?"

"I don't want to prejudice your search. Just find out what

you can."

"Got it. I'll call when I'm finished."

After ending the call, he input the museum's address into his cell phone and followed the directions.

***

Field Museum, Chicago

Peter Barnes introduced Kruger to the museum's head of security. "Bob, this is Sean Kruger; he's retired bureau."

As Kruger shook Haskins' hand, the retired detective tilted his head. "I remember you. Spring of 1997, the Chicago PD requested a profiler, and they sent you."

"They did."

"You were the first person from the FBI I liked. What can I help you with, Sean?"

Kruger preceded to explain his role in the investigation. He then said, "Can you walk me through what you think happened the night of the robbery?"

"Sure." The three men were standing in the warehouse and receiving section of the building. Haskins pointed to a door to the left of the loading dock bays. "This is the door we believe they used to gain access."

Kruger studied the entrance and the interior of the museum's small warehouse area. He looked at the door and allowed his gaze to shift toward the staircase on the opposite wall. He pointed. "Where do those stairs lead?"

"Those are the emergency escape stairs. They access all floors."

As Haskins spoke, Kruger walked toward the stairwell. When he reached where the steps began, he turned and pointed toward the open space between where they stood and the entrance door. "Is this space always empty like it is now?"

"No, generally, we have crates and display cases staged

here."

"So, if someone entered in the dark, there could be obstacles between the door and the stairwell."

"Yes. As a rule, when we change exhibits, this area gets cluttered."

"How often is it like we see today?"

"Around holidays. The curator doesn't like to change exhibits before key dates where we experience high visitor traffic."

With a nod, Kruger started up the stairs. "July 4th is in three weeks."

"Yes."

"So, for Easter, the warehouse space would have been empty."

"Correct."

"And you were closed on Easter?"

"Yes." The retired detective displayed a slight smile. "Do you think they had inside help?"

"I'm leaning that way."

"I've mentioned that to the curator several times. But she doesn't see how it would be possible. She trusts everybody on the staff."

Stopping on the second-floor landing, Kruger looked at Barnes. "What do you think, Peter?"

"Only way it could have happened would be with inside help."

Turning to Haskins, Kruger asked, "How long has the curator been here?"

"Longer than me. She was hired in 2010."

"I'd like to talk to her."

Haskins shot a quick glance at his wristwatch. "Uh, probably need to wait a half hour or so."

Placing his hand on the door leading to the third floor, Kruger turned his attention back to Haskins. "She's not here, yet?"

"No, she's here. But she hasn't had time for her second

cup of coffee. She's not a very pleasant person to encounter if she hasn't had her coffee."

Shaking his head slightly, the retired FBI agent said, "Fine."

***

"It's nice to meet you, Ms. Ross." Kruger offered his business card as the woman stared at him with narrowed eyes.

"I don't understand why the insurance company is still dragging their feet on settling the claim. Walter Wagenaar, the CEO of Goldmax, calls me on a daily basis threatening to sue the museum if it isn't. You need to tell him the museum had nothing to do with the theft."

Folding his arms, Kruger let the curator vent her frustrations at him. He chose to remain silent while she spoke.

"We have a state-of-the-art security system and an IT team better than any similar facility in the country. I'd put their skills up against anyone."

Kruger said, "Yet, someone still managed to hack your system, unlock doors, erase security videos, and make off with one hundred and fifty million dollars' worth of diamond jewelry."

Sitting behind her desk, she suddenly stood and shook a finger at him. "Allegedly."

"Ms. Ross, there is no alleged theft. The diamonds were stolen and replaced with fakes. That's a fact. The only alleged aspect of this is who did it. My job is to determine who might have done so. Once I discover exactly how the robbery was accomplished, then the insurance company can assess their legal liabilities."

"What if the diamonds were fake when they arrived?"

Raising an eyebrow, Kruger said, "Are you telling me no one examined the diamonds before they were put on display?"

The woman stared at Kruger and hesitated. "No, I didn't say that. But you're telling me I have to put up with Wagenaar until it is determined how they were stolen?"

"I'm not telling you anything. I am merely informing you that until my investigation is completed, the insurance company will not be settling any claims."

She folded her arms. "I wanted to avoid this, but apparently, our attorneys will need to get involved."

"Ms. Ross, I am not a lawyer. You and your board of directors will need to make that decision."

The glare Kruger received almost made him laugh, but he kept a neutral expression.

She sat again, shuffled a few files, and then returned her attention to Kruger. "How long before you conclude your investigation?"

"At this time, I can't say."

She waved her hand in a dismissive manner and picked up a folder. Haskins touched Kruger's elbow and used his head to motion toward the door.

When they were outside her office, Kruger asked, "Is she always that charming?"

"She's actually calm today."

"Nerves?"

With a shrug, Haskins said, "Personality."

CHAPTER 5

Johannesburg, South Africa

At six foot two, with coal-black hair and streaks of silver at the temple, and an athletic build, Hunter Holden commanded attention in whatever setting he found himself. Sometimes the attention was congenial, but more times than not, adversarial.

As the principal partner of the private equity firm Transnational Financial, his prowess in acquiring businesses through leveraged buyouts sent fear into the hearts of CEOs and company owners.

Goldmax Industries, his current target, suffered from an unexpected loss of one hundred and fifty million dollars in assets. Assets used as collateral for debt accumulated during the acquisition of a specific company during the past year.

Holden sat on a leather sofa in the office of Goldmax CEO Walter Wagenaar. He watched as the head of the mining company paced nervously in front of him. "I must say, Walter, your situation worsens as the days pass."

Wagenaar stopped walking and glared at his uninvited guest. "Your constant reminders are not helpful, Hunter."

"I am merely pointing out the loss of the diamond collection could have grave consequences if your investors grow impatient. You did, after all, use it to buy the Australian company that mines and processes lithium. Which was a wise decision at the time. With the increased interest in producing electrical vehicles, the need for lithium batteries will continue to rise. A wise investment indeed."

"You rarely compliment people, Hunter. What's your point?"

Holden stood and walked to the window behind Wagenaar's desk. "My point is, if your investors call in their loan due to the loss of collateral, you would be forced to declare bankruptcy or sell." He turned to stare at the South African businessman. "Unless you sell the company to Transnational Financial."

"We've had this discussion before. The company is not for sale. The diamonds are covered by insurance. There is no need for the loan to be called in."

"But the insurance company has not paid the claim yet, Walter. Your investors are concerned there's a problem."

"How do you know my investors are concerned?"

Holden shrugged.

"Because you are keeping them informed, correct?"

"They believe my acquiring Goldmax will protect their investment."

"I have been assured the insurance company is investigating the incident and, once this is completed, the claim will be settled. Like I said, no need to call in the loan."

"Investors can be fickle at times. Particularly when they see a possible loss of their money. If I buy Goldmax, their investments will double."

Wagenaar glared at Holden. "You son of a bitch. You paid someone to steal my diamonds, didn't you?"

With a shake of his head, Holden gave the Goldmax CEO a smile. "Walter, you are being melodramatic. Of course, I didn't pay anyone to steal your diamonds. Now, agree to my terms. I will buy you out, and all of your problems go away."

"The only problem I have right now is you attempting to steal my company."

"I see why you can't make it as a businessman. You're too emotional. It's just a company. Which you have run into the ground with your obsession with diamonds."

Wagenaar marched to his desk and picked up the handset on his phone. "Send security to my office. My guest is leaving." He hung up, turned, pointed toward the office door, and screamed, "Get out!"

With a dismissive sneer, Hunter Holden casually strolled to the door. He turned just as he opened it. "You will sell to me, Walter."

***

The Gulfstream G650ER streaked above the steppes of northern Africa, the first leg of its roughly ten-thousand-mile journey from Johannesburg to Minneapolis with a midway stop for fuel and an overnight planned for Barcelona. Halfway through this first leg of the trip, Holden listened to a conference call held by a venture capitalist. The call included discussion of possible financial backing by Transnational Financial for two high-tech start-up companies.

When any question came his way, Holden would answer. Otherwise, he did not participate in the call.

Jack Mitchell, the call organizer finally said in exasperation, "Are you even listening to our conversation, Hunter?"

"Not really. The ideas you are proposing are half baked at best. If I wasn't on an airplane with nothing else to do, I would have hung up a long time ago."

"Honestly, Hunter, you are not…"

"Listen, Jack, my answer is no. Get back to me when you have solid market research." Holden ended the call and looked up as the flight attendant approached his chair near the back of the plane.

"Can I get you anything, Mr. Holden?"

"How long until we touch down in Barcelona?"

"About an hour."

"Good. We'll spend the night there and fly on to Minneapolis in the morning."

"Very good." She started toward the front.

"Have you ever spent the evening on Las Ramblas, Ms. Evans?"

She turned back to him. "I've never been to Barcelona."

A small smile came to his face. "Then I will escort you. It's one of my favorite spots in the city."

"That sounds wonderful."

"Could you close the door to my office? I have an important call to make."

"Yes, Mr. Holden."

After she left, he dialed a number he chose not to record in his contact file. The call was answered on the third ring.

A gruff voice said, "I wondered when you would call."

"Give me an update on the project."

The individual hesitated. "Are you on a cell phone?"

"Yes."

"Okay. I'll be brief. Items have been distributed across several contractors. I have been assured all were modified to meet our distribution goals."

"How much revenue?"

"Seventy-five cents on the dollar valuation."

"Good. Can they be traced?"

"Not in their current condition."

"Excellent. We can discuss this in more detail when I arrive tomorrow."

"I'll make myself available."

***

Chicago

Following his interview with Margaret Ross, Kruger returned to his rental car. Just as he inserted his key in the ignition, his cell phone vibrated. Checking the caller ID, he answered. "Find anything interesting?"

JR said, "Let me put it this way, Walter Wagenaar is up to his eyebrows in debt. He used his diamond jewelry collection as collateral to buy a lithium mining company in Australia."

"Lots of businessmen do that, JR. The collection is covered by insurance, so he should be fine once the claim is settled."

"In a normal situation, I would agree with you. But the lithium mining operation just signed a contract to supply lithium to Tesla and Ford for their new EV battery plants. The stock value of the mining company is exploding."

"Good timing on Wagenaar's part."

"Yes, but the theft of the diamonds is a problem. There's a private equity company sniffing around and telling the holder of Wagenaar's note the diamonds weren't real in the first place. The PE company bought the note from the creditors."

Kruger remained silent for a few moments. "Which means, if the diamonds are not found or the insurance company declares fraud, the PE company will own the lithium mining operation."

"Bingo."

"What's the name of the PE company?"

"Transnational Financial. The general partner is a guy named Hunter Holden."

"Never heard of him. Have you?"

"Not until I started digging into his company."

"I've heard that tone before, JR. What about him?"

"He makes Abel Plymel look like a choirboy."

"Abel Plymel was a sleeper agent planted in the United

States during the Cold War to disrupt our financial markets. When the Berlin Wall fell and his handler died of a heart attack, he disappeared into the maze of Wall Street, believing no one in Russia knew about him. He amassed a fortune as a merger and acquisition specialist."

"I lived it, Sean, I know all about him."

"So why is Hunter Holden so bad?"

"He has a reputation as a scorched-earth operator. He likes to find companies experiencing financial distress and depressed stock value. He then buys all the stock and takes it private. Afterward, he fires the management team and replaces them with his own people. Workers are displaced, and those who are left have to put in fifty-to-sixty hours a week without additional compensations."

"JR, that sounds like most private equity operators."

"Yes, but Holden goes a bit further. He has a team of auditors who swoop in and examine the books. The results of those audits are then made public. Once this information is released, those former managers are then investigated by their country's regulatory agencies. If charges are filed, those executives are fired and their careers tarnished."

"That seems a bit harsh."

"Once the investigation finishes, nine out of ten times, the charges are dismissed. But by then, the damage is done. Those individuals disappear from the lofty ranks of top management."

Kruger did not respond right away. Finally, he said, "I'll be home tomorrow afternoon. I would like to spend a little more time going over what you've found on Hunter Holden."

"You got it. Let me know when you're available."

CHAPTER 6

Chicago

Wednesday morning found Kruger back at the Field Museum walking the path he suspected the intruders took on their way to the third floor. Bob Haskins followed a few feet behind, keeping silent as the retired FBI agent climbed the steps. On the third-floor landing, Kruger opened the door to the exhibition area.

A new exposition occupied the center of the room where the Goldmax diamonds had been displayed. Kruger turned to Haskins. "Where are the showcases that housed the Goldmax diamonds, Bob?"

"Basement storage."

"Can I see them?"

"Sure. We'll have to take the elevator."

Five minutes later, Kruger felt a note of frustration on finding all the cases pushed together against a wall. "I take it the police department finished their investigation and released them?"

"A month ago. Sorry."

"Not your fault." He paused for a moment. "Which case

had the misaligned necklace?"

Haskins pointed to a large unit on the left side of the room. "That one. I made sure it was not bunched up with the others."

Placing his hand on Haskins' shoulder, Kruger nodded. "Good man. You're still a detective at heart."

A smile crossed the security man's lips.

Kruger spent the next ten minutes looking over the unit. Finally, he sighed. "I'm not seeing any signs of forced entry."

"Nope. I didn't see any, and neither did the Chicago PD."

Crossing his arms, Kruger leaned on the case and looked straight at Haskins. "What does that tell you?"

"They had the combinations to the keypads."

"Exactly. I don't suppose there were any fingerprints."

"Nope."

"Didn't think so." He paused for a moment. "Bob, what else does that suggest to you?"

"Uh, I hate to say this, but I think they had help from inside the museum."

"That's the CPD's conclusion, also. Who knows the procedures and codes?"

"Myself, Ms. Ross, and her assistant."

"Who's the assistant?"

"A young grad student from Loyola."

"Is he here today?"

"He's a she, but yes she is." Haskins motioned Kruger to follow him.

***

Roberta Kirby stared at Kruger, her brown eyes wide, lips quivering. Bob Haskins said in a gentle voice, "Robbie, it's okay. He just wants to ask you a few questions."

"I honestly don't know anything, Bob." The tremor in her voiced emphasized her nervousness.

Kruger clasped his hands together and leaned forward in the chair across from the assistant. "I'm not here to accuse anyone, Robbie. I am just trying to find out what happened over the Easter weekend. Can I ask you a few questions?" She nodded.

"Thank you. Can you think of anything unusual that might have occurred prior to the robbery?"

She shook her head. "I remember April as a boring month, actually. We didn't have new exhibits scheduled until the summer, and the ones we did have remained unchanged since the Christmas holidays."

"So I am clear on it, what are your duties, Robbie?"

"I'm Ms. Ross' assistant. If she's out, I handle everything. Even if she is here, I handle all the problems, which Ms. Ross doesn't like to do. In fact, she has mentioned several times she feels her expertise should be better compensated."

Raising an eyebrow, Kruger asked, "She doesn't like to handle problems?"

"No, she'll tell anyone who asks, she's not here to solve problems, she's here to make the museum better."

Shooting a glance at Haskins, the security chief shrugged. "Robbie's correct, Ms. Ross doesn't keep that fact a secret."

"What kind of problems do you solve, Robbie?"

"Day-to-day issues. I trace shipments, make sure exhibits being shipped to another location are properly packed and picked up, plus, I schedule all the new exhibits."

"What does Ms. Ross do?"

The young woman hesitated and then looked up at Haskins. He nodded once. She returned her attention to Kruger. "She's the public face of the facility."

"What does that mean?"

"She's in charge of PR for the museum."

"How often is she out of the office?"

"Two or three times a week. She attends fundraising events and meets with our benefactor and patron groups on a regular basis."

Kruger sat back and placed his elbows on the chair arm. He made a steeple with his hands and tapped his lips. "You say this happens every week?"

The young woman nodded.

Looking up at the security chief, Kruger asked, "Is the benefactor-and-patron group list public information?"

"No, but I can get you a copy."

"Thank you." He turned back to Roberta. "Do you remember Ms. Ross' schedule the week prior to the robbery?"

"No, sorry." A short-lived smile appeared on her lips. "Wait a minute. I remember she wasn't here very much. Let me check her schedule." She turned to her computer and clicked on a few icons, read what was on the screen, and turned back toward Kruger. "She had appointments every day that week."

"Is this unusual?"

"Very. She's always in the office at least two days a week working the phone."

"But not that week?"

"No."

"Do you know if she has a boyfriend or significant other?"

The young intern looked at the floor for a moment and then back at the retired FBI agent. "Ms. Ross doesn't like men, Mr. Kruger. If she has a partner, she doesn't talk about them. I don't think she does."

"Ah." Kruger stood. "You've been very helpful, Robbie. Thank you for your time." He looked at Haskins and nodded his head for the security chief to follow him. When they were out of the main offices, he turned and asked, "Could I see the donor-and-patron list?"

"Sure. You suspect something, don't you?"

"Just trying to look at all possibilities."

"Let's go to my office. I can access the information on my computer."

***

Looking over the museum's list of patrons, Kruger's attention settled on a name on the third page. He asked, "Bob, can you access, Margaret Ross' schedule from here?"

"I can. Why, is something wrong?"

"Don't know yet."

"What dates do you want to look at?"

"Can we look at her appointments from the first of the year to the break-in?"

When Haskins displayed the calendars on the computer monitor, Kruger saw what he suspected but kept quiet. "Thanks."

"What are you looking for, Sean? Maybe I can help."

"Bob, I would appreciate it if you don't discuss our meeting with anyone."

"Roberta will mention it to Margaret, I'm sure."

"That might not be a good career decision for her. Please ask her to keep our meeting confidential."

"Can you tell me what you suspect?"

"Eventually, but not right now."

***

Sitting in his rental car outside the museum, Kruger called JR. When the call was answered, Kruger said, "Feel like hacking a bank account?"

"Haven't done that for a while, I might be rusty."

"Doubt it."

With a chuckle, JR asked, "Who and why?"

"I've got a couple of coincidences I need you to check on."

"You don't like coincidences."

"Exactly."

"Want to explain?"

"The curator of the Field Museum is a woman named Margaret Ross. She is the public face of the museum and meets with all the patrons and contributors. A new patron of the museum is Transnational Financial."

"Uh-oh."

"Yeah. She's met with the company nine times since the first of the year. No names, but the initials HH appear by each appointment."

"I see where this is going."

"Kinda thought you would. I need you to see if Ms. Ross has made any large deposits or major purchases recently."

"I don't suppose you know her social security number, do you?"

"No, but I am sure you can find it in the personnel records of the museum."

"Man, you were far more subtle about this type of activity when you were with the FBI."

"Refreshing, isn't it."

"At least I don't have to guess as often. Where are you going to be?"

"I'm going back to my hotel and make some phone calls."

"I'll get back to you when I know more."

***

That Evening

After an hour phone call with Stephanie, Kruger checked for any missed calls and saw none. Just as he sat the phone on the nightstand, it vibrated.

"Kruger."

"I have to say, when you have a hunch, it's usually correct."

"What'd you find, JR?"

"No huge cash deposits or a new Audi in her driveway."

"But…"

"She is now the proud owner of five hundred thousand shares of Goldmax Industries. They were bought when the stock was at five dollars a share. They jumped to fifty-four dollars after they announced the contracts with Tesla and Ford. Analysts are speculating the stock will climb to eighty bucks a share this summer."

"Where did she get two and a half million to buy the shares in the first place?"

"Her own money and a margin through her brokerage firm. She started buying the stock in September and increased her holding through most of the fall. All before the company announced their acquisition of the Australian lithium mining company."

"Did she purchase other companies' stock?"

"Nope. Just Goldmax."

"Sounds like insider trading."

"More than a little."

"Hang on a second, I want to check something." The call went silent as Kruger looked over some notes. "Goldmax closed the deal on the mining company just after the first of the year. The diamond display was already at the Field Museum."

"Looks like this was well planned, Sean."

"Extremely. And since she used her own money and her margin account to buy the stock, no one can accuse Transnational Financial of bribing her. There is no way to officially connect the dots."

"Unless you are a certain retired FBI agent."

"Well, thanks for the compliment, but it was just basic police work."

"Which no one else thought to do. Now what?"

"I think I need to visit with a certain Chicago PD detective tomorrow morning. Then I'll be headed home."

"You're not going to hang around for the arrest?"

"Nah. I'd rather spend tomorrow night in my own bed."

CHAPTER 7

Minneapolis

"Mr. Holden, Margaret Ross on line one. She said it was urgent she speak with you."

The CEO of Transnational Financial frowned as he contemplated not taking the call. After several moments, he reached for the handset of his desk phone and picked it up. "Margaret, how nice of you to call."

"Cut the crap, Hunter. There's an insurance investigator poking around and asking questions no one is supposed to be asking."

"What kind of investigator?"

"He's ex-FBI."

"Did he give you a name?"

"I believe the name is Shane Gruber, or something similar."

"You're not sure."

"It took me by surprise, and I stopped listening."

Holden closed his eyes and pinched the bridge of his nose with his free hand. "Margaret, it is standard procedure for insurance companies to hire an investigator for large settlements. I'm sure everything is going to plan. Don't worry about it."

"How can I not worry about it?"

"You acquired the stock using the method we suggested. Plus, you used your own money to purchase it. There is no way they can trace it back."

"Still, it makes me nervous."

"Take a few days off and don't talk to the investigator."

"I have no plans to do so."

"Good, I have a meeting in a few minutes, I need to get off the phone."

He heard a sigh and then an exaggerated, "Fine." The call ended, and Holden replaced the handset. After tapping his index finger on his lips, he picked it up again and dialed three numbers.

"Yes."

"Come to my office, our plan is starting to bear fruit."

***

Thursday a.m.

Peter Barnes folded his arms as he listened to Kruger.

"While I realize the evidence is a little circumstantial, it does point a finger at Margaret Ross being the inside source for the computer breach. She would also have the authorization to allow someone access to the diamond display to take the pictures needed for the copies."

"I'm struggling with motive, Sean."

"As did I, at first. But if you think about it for a moment, it makes sense."

"Convince me."

"What is the salary of a museum curator?"

"I have no idea."

"Neither did I, until I checked. The average is around seventy-nine thousand a year. Not a bad salary, especially in

Chicago, but you're not going to get rich doing it."

"Okay."

"She has to deal with high-income individuals who are the financial backbone of the museum. From my experience, she possesses the type of personality that could become envious of these individuals fairly quickly. If the stock she owns in Goldmax reaches eighty dollars a share or higher, she is positioned to make close to forty million dollars in profit."

"Capital gains will grab a chunk of that."

"Yes, but there would still be eight figures remaining. There is another reason I think she would do it. Her assistant mentioned Ms. Ross feels undercompensated. My guess would be she is looking for an exit plan."

"And?"

"She would be susceptible to making a deal with one of those benefactors who might want access to the museum."

"And you think it's Transnational Financial?"

Kruger nodded. "The very company who now owns the controlling interest in a financially strapped Goldmax."

Barnes remained quiet for a few moments. "You sold me. Can you give me all of this in writing?"

"I can do better. I can send it to you electronically."

"It will take a few days to get a subpoena prepared to examine her financial records. You gonna wait around for the arrest?"

Kruger shook his head. "Nah. I'll let you have the fun. I'm going home today."

***

Chicago Pre-Dawn Friday

After a restless night, Margaret Ross fell into REM sleep around 4 a.m. Even then, her dreams reflected the turmoil she felt about her part in the disappearance of the Goldmax diamond display. Her trendy loft apartment near the Chicago loop took a hefty portion of her monthly salary, but it allowed her to mingle with high-income residents of the downtown region.

At exactly 4:22 a.m., a gloved hand clamped over her mouth, and her eyes sprang open.

"Do I have your attention, Margaret?"

She stared wide-eyed at the face above her and nodded once. The combined stench of cigarettes and whiskey assaulted her.

"I need to ask you a few questions. Are you going to scream if I take my hand away?"

With difficulty, she moved her head horizontally twice.

"Good. If you scream, I won't be responsible for the consequences." The man straightened, removed his hand from her mouth, and waited. She remained quiet. "Good girl."

"What do you want?"

"It's not what I want. It's what I've been instructed to do." He paused for a brief moment. His eyes locked on her. "How many people know you bought Goldmax stock?"

"It's nobody's business. I've told no one."

"Good. Make sure you don't."

She had started to relax when his arm rose with a swift motion, a small gun in the outstretched hand. Margaret Ross did not have time to register the danger she was in before her world went black.

***

Peter Barnes put paper booties on over his shoes before entering the loft apartment. The sun streaming through the tall windows on the east side of the room contrasted with the somber and muffled conversations between the crime scene technicians dusting for fingerprints.

A young patrolman Barnes did not know escorted him to

the bedroom. The open door revealed two nude bodies lying in a king-size bed, their pillows soaked in blood.

"Beverly, want to give me a quick rundown of what I am looking at?"

A middle-aged, heavyset woman, turned from taking pictures to give him a half smile. "Thought you were the detective, Pete."

"Funny, very funny. Any estimates about time of death?"

She nodded. "The current state of rigor mortis tells me at least six hours, but probably more. I'd say sometime between three and six a.m. I can tell you more after we get them to the morgue."

"I know the woman is Margaret Ross. Who's the guy?"

"We're not sure, yet. We think the motive was robbery. We can't find a purse for the woman or a wallet for the man."

Barnes peered at the woman and saw the small bullet hole in the center of her forehead. He looked at the man with a similar wound above his right eye. "Looks like a twenty-two. What do you think, Beverly?"

"I'd have to agree. But I'll give you an official statement after I get them to the lab."

"Anything else I should know?"

"Not a single piece of electronic equipment can be found. All of the drawers were rifled. There's a large gap in a desk drawer where files appear to be missing."

"Hmmm."

"Kind of what I thought. A little strange."

"I need to know who the guy is. Has anyone contacted the Field Museum?"

Looking over her glasses, Beverly stared at the detective. "Now, how would I know? The only reason we knew her name was the building manager. He's the one who called it in."

"Where is he?"

"Front room being interviewed by a patrolman."

Leaving the bedroom, Barnes observed an elderly man

talking to a uniformed cop. He walked over to where they stood and said, "Excuse me. Are you the building manager?" The balding man narrowed his eyes. "Yeah. Who are you?"

"Detective Barnes. What's your name?"

"Eric Perez."

"I'm told you're the one who called this in."

"Yes."

"Mind telling me how you knew?"

"As I was telling this police officer, I got a call this morning about ten. The woman sounded strained and said she needed help. She told me the unit number and then hung up. When I got here, the front door was open. I peeked in and saw the place trashed. I called out but didn't get an answer. That's when I decided to call the police."

"You didn't go in?"

"Hell no. I've been doing this for a couple of decades. When I see an apartment trashed like this one, I call the cops."

"Do you know who lives here?"

"Yeah, Margaret Ross."

"Does she have a husband?"

The man laughed. "You didn't know her, did you?"

"No."

"I've never seen her with a man. Seen her with a few women, but never a man."

"Got it. Thank you."

Barnes walked back into the bedroom. "Beverly, we need to find out who this guy is, and we need to know now."

***

Friday Afternoon

After checking caller ID, Kruger raised an eyebrow and pressed the accept icon. "Kruger."

"Sean, it's Peter Barnes."

"Didn't expect to hear from you this soon."

"I've got a puzzle, and it may concern the Field Museum diamond theft."

"What is it?"

"Margaret Ross was murdered last night in her condo." Sitting straighter in his office chair, Kruger pressed the phone closer to his ear. "Murdered. How?"

"Single 22 caliber hollow point to the forehead."

"Shit."

"It gets worse."

"I'm listening."

"There was a man in bed next to her with a similar wound above his right eye."

"Boyfriend?"

"Margaret Ross was gay. No boyfriend. The dead guy in the bed was her stockbroker."

Neither man spoke for a few seconds then Kruger asked, "Was it made to look like murder-suicide?"

"No. From the condition of the condo, whoever did it wanted us to think it was a simple robbery gone bad. Only one problem."

"What's that?"

"The guy had some serious drugs in him. He was barely alive when he was attacked. If he hadn't been shot in the head, the ME says he would have been dead within an hour or so anyway."

"Have you told Bob Haskins this?"

"Yeah. He confirmed the Ross woman was gay, and he also ID'd the stockbroker."

"Shit."

"You think someone is tying up loose ends?"

"I think someone is trying to prevent us from looking too closely at Margaret Ross as the insider." He paused. "Mind if I pay a visit next week?"

"I was hoping you might be available. Didn't you

mention you had a computer expert on your staff?"

"Well, he's more on retainer."

"Bring him. Bob Haskins doesn't trust the IT staff any longer. He wants someone else to see if they can recover any missing files."

"JR excels at finding deleted files."

"Looking forward to meeting him."

CHAPTER 8

Southwest Missouri
Monday

Kruger leaned against the doorframe leading to JR's home office. "I'm going back to Chicago tomorrow, and you need to go with me."

"Why?"

"I need you to dig into the museum's computer. I think the answers to a lot of my questions are hidden on its hard drive."

JR Diminski pursed his lips. "I'd need permission from management."

"You already have it. Bob Haskins, head of security for the museum, wants an audit of the security systems. He's of the opinion there might be deleted files that could tell us what happened Easter morning."

"I'm not flying commercial."

"Not necessary. The company jet is at our disposal."

Raising his eyebrows, JR smiled. "Why didn't you say so before we started this conversation?" He paused for a moment. "Exactly, what is the security guy looking for?"

"He's like me. He suspects information still exists that might provide us with electronic breadcrumbs leading to who and what happened the night of the break-in. So far, the museum's IT team can't find anything. You, on the other hand, probably can."

"I appreciate your confidence in me, but, until I see the system, I'll reserve any comments."

"Fair enough. I'll pick you up at six in the morning. We'll be in Chicago by eight."

***

Tuesday
Chicago

After shaking Haskins' hand, Kruger said, "Bob, this is JR Diminski. He's the individual I told you about."

With a nod, the museum's security chief shook the computer expert's hand. "Our IT department is pretty good, but they can't seem to find any signs of someone hacking into the system."

"It's possible for a hacker to get in and out without leaving a trace. But in almost twenty-five years of experience, I've only seen a handful of individuals successfully do it."

Kruger said, "JR won't say it himself, but he is one of those individuals."

"What do you need from me, Mr. Diminski?"

"First, call me JR. Second, I will need a terminal connected directly to the server, no Wi-Fi."

"We can do that."

"One more question. Is the security system connected to the main computer?"

"Yes."

"Even better."

Leaving JR by himself at the terminal, Kruger and

Haskins went to his office to wait.

"How long do you think it will take him, Sean?"

"Depends. Couple of hours to a couple of days. I've seen him find something in five minutes, but, normally, it takes longer."

Haskins nodded. "Have you spoken with Peter Barnes lately?"

"No, not since last Friday. Any new developments?"

"Unfortunately, it gets worse. The stockbroker she used to buy the Goldmax stock was the man killed beside her. The police found handwritten notes in a file marked Goldmax in his office desk. The notes were in his handwriting and appeared to be from a phone call or meeting he attended. Whoever he met with suggested he start buying small blocks of Goldmax stock. This all occurred last August, before they merged with the Australian mining company. He then sold those blocks to clients, one of whom was Margaret Ross. She bought half of them, mostly on margin. Apparently, he had over a million shares in inventory built up."

"Do you know who gave him the suggestion?"

Haskins shook his head. "That information died with him."

"Someone is covering their tracks pretty efficiently."

"So it would appear, Sean."

Kruger drummed his fingers on the conference table where they sat. "Did any of the security cameras capture images of the intruders that Sunday morning?"

"None of the museum cameras did."

"What about the surrounding businesses?"

"That would have been done by CPD."

"What's around here?"

"Restaurants, retail, and a lot of professional offices."

With a frown, Kruger remained quiet for a few moments. "Damn, most of those types of businesses only hold their security videos for thirty days or so. Unless..." He locked eyes with Haskins. "Any banks around here?"

"Yes, a couple of them. Why?"

"They have to hold their security camera footage for at least six months to comply with banking regulations."

"Didn't know that."

At that moment, JR stuck his head into Haskins' office. "Found something. Want to take a look?"

***

Haskins and Kruger looked over JR's shoulder as he explained what they were seeing on the computer monitor.

"Computers have an internal timestamp that keeps everything organized and gives technicians a source of reference should something go wrong. Without getting into the weeds with the technical jargon, it acts like an air traffic controller and keeps computer programs from crashing into each other."

Kruger smiled. "Go on, JR."

"From the hours of 3 a.m. to 6 a.m., the air traffic controller of the museum's security system went on a three-hour coffee break. Someone tried to do a patch job on it but failed miserably."

"Why didn't the IT department see this?" Haskins now stood with his hands on his hips.

"I can't answer that. I don't know their skill sets or training. But it should have been obvious to even a mid-level computer analyst."

The museum's security chief's face grew crimson, and he stormed out of the room. JR looked up at Kruger. "Did I touch a nerve?"

Having watched Haskins leave the room, Kruger returned his attention to the computer monitor. "I think you just discovered there could be more than one person from the museum involved with this incident."

"Wonderful."

***

By 1 p.m., Detective Peter Barnes with the Chicago PD arrived at the Field Museum and interviewed the IT staff. One individual confessed to being complicit with the computer breach.

Barnes sat across from the IT expert. "Ronny, we need to know exactly what you were told and by who."

"Like I told you before, Ms. Ross demanded certain files be deleted. I thought the request a bit strange, but she was the boss. Then I learned the diamonds were missing. I tried to cover up what I had done, but apparently didn't do a very good job."

"No, you didn't. How much were you paid?"

"I didn't get paid. She told me it was part of my job."

Looking at Kruger, who sat at the end of the table, the detective said, "You buying any of this, Agent Kruger?"

With a sad smile, Kruger shook his head. "No. If I were you, Detective Barnes, I'd read the man his rights."

The tech, whose full name was Ronald Stanford, looked at both Barnes and Kruger with wide eyes. He then stammered. "No—no, don't. I'm telling you the truth. She threatened my job if I told anyone. She didn't pay me a thing."

Kruger said, "Why you, Ronnie?"

"I was new and still a probationary employee."

Barnes looked at Haskins. "Is that correct?"

The museum security chief nodded.

Barnes continued. "So, when Margaret Ross asked for the access code, you gave it to her?"

"Yes, sir."

JR walked into the room and handed a piece of paper to Kruger. After glancing at it, he passed it to Barnes. He scanned the sheet, stood, and walked toward the office door. As he passed Haskins, he offered the page to the security chief.

Less than a minute later, Barnes returned with two uniformed police officers. "Gentlemen, please read Mr. Stanford his rights and place him under arrest."

When the now-under-arrest rookie computer technician for the Field Museum had been escorted out of the room, Barnes took his glasses off and pinched his nose. "How much would the stock be worth now, JR?"

"A thousand shares are worth about eighty thousand at today's price."

He nodded. "Could you tell if he paid for it?"

"He didn't. The account was set up by Margaret Ross, and she's the one who transferred the stock into Stanford's name."

Haskins held an open manila file in his hand and skimmed the contents. "Margaret is also the individual who recruited Stanford to join the museum."

Standing, Kruger went to where Haskins stood and took the file. After a few moments, he said, "JR, when you found the information about Stanford, could you find any connection between him and Transnational Financial?"

"No, and I looked."

"What about Ross and Transnational?"

"That's where it gets murky. Her contact reports filed about her meetings with patrons and contributors indicate she met with representatives of the company on nine occasions from the fall of last year to the week before the break-in. Hunter Holden's name is not in her records."

"Does it say who she met with?"

"No, just that it was a representative."

Haskins said, "Which is a breach of museum protocol when someone from the staff meets with a contributor off-site."

With a nod, Kruger said, "You want to introduce JR and myself to the banks in the area? We might get lucky with some security videos."

"Sean?"

"Yeah, JR?"

"Uh, there's a chance the stolen diamonds might have been fake as well."

Kruger's expression did not change. Barnes and Haskins frowned. The CPD detective asked, "Then why the charade of a theft?"

Clearing his throat, Kruger gave both men a slight smile. "An idea I've been playing with from the beginning. On one of my earlier trips, I asked Ms. Ross if anyone confirmed the diamonds were real. She assured me she had examined them and they were genuine. No one else was allowed to inspect them."

Haskins nodded slightly. "I remember when we got them, I wanted to have an independent appraiser check them, but she overruled me."

"Then why the break-in, Sean? It doesn't make sense."

The ex-FBI agent said, "Sure it does, Peter. What better way to cover up the fact they were fake in the first place? Steal the fakes and make sure there were no witnesses. All we need is proof a burglary actually occurred." He paused. "Let's go talk to a few of the banks."

CHAPTER 9

Chicago

By late afternoon, having checked with three banks, their search for a security camera file with a possible image of one of the bank thieves bore fruit.

With the presence and insistence of Chicago Police Department Detective Peter Barnes, the unenthusiastic bank branch manager acquiesced and allowed JR to examine the bank's security camera files from the hours of midnight to 6 a.m. Easter morning.

Barnes and Kruger stood over his shoulder as they watched the minutes fast-forward from midnight. At 2:44 a.m., the trio watched as a ten-year-old Toyota Camry parked at the corner of Michigan Avenue and East 14th Street.

Kruger said, "Stop there, JR."

"You got it."

"Back the tape up and see if we get a shot of the front license plate."

After JR rewound the recording, he slowed the forward motion. As the car came into frame, the camera recorded the absence of a front plate.

The former FBI agent folded his arms. "How about that. Let's see what happens next." The car's position and the location of streetlights kept the individual behind the wheel in a shadow. Five minutes passed before the front driver's door opened. A man dressed completely in black emerged. He turned and opened the left passenger door and extracted what appeared to be a heavy black backpack. The driver then positioned it on his back, locked the doors on the Camry, and jogged toward the east and the Field Museum.

Leaning closer, Kruger asked, "Can you back this up and zoom in on the face when he opens the back door?"

"Sure." Stopping the video as the driver faced the back door, JR zoomed in on the figure. "There you go, Sean. The guy's got a balaclava covering his face."

Kruger put his half-readers on and studied the picture. "Bingo, that's one of them."

Barnes frowned. "What do you mean, one of them?"

"Had to be at least two men. Three would be too many, and one would take too long. My guess is two, and they arrived in separate cars. Plus, they parked in separate locations."

JR scanned over the next hour and fifty minutes at twice the normal speed. Nothing moved or approached the parked Toyota. Finally, from the right side of the screen, a figure emerged out of the dark and approached the car. Just before the man opened the driver's side back door, he lifted his balaclava and shook his hair.

The detective asked, "Can you stop the tape and zoom in?"

"Sure."

Barnes leaned over and studied the image. With a chuckle, he straightened. "I know that guy. He used to be a regular guest at the Cook County Jail, but I haven't seen him for a while."

"How long?"

Looking at Kruger, Barnes shook his head. "Can't

remember, but I know it's been at least a year, maybe more. Let me check with the jail." The detective pulled his cell phone out and left the small space where Kruger and JR remained.

"Why don't you let the video continue, JR. We might get a glimpse of the license plate."

As the video progressed, the camera caught a glimpse of the back end as the car pulled away. JR stopped it. "No plate, just like the front."

"Back up the video, JR. There is some kind of frame on the area where the back plate should be."

As the images reversed, JR zoomed in and centered on the frame. "It's going to be fuzzy."

"That's okay. I know what it is."

Looking up at Kruger, JR smiled. "Want to tell me? Or is it a secret?"

"It's a promo license plate holder. I can't make out the name on this one, but they're common."

"You think the car was stolen from a used car lot?"

"It's a strong possibility. Steal the car and have it back before anyone knows it's missing."

Barnes returned to the room. "The guy's name is Dugan, and there isn't a record of him being arrested for eighteen months. We've got patrol cars on the way to his last known residence."

"My guess is he won't be there."

"I would agree, Sean. But we have to try."

"We found something." Kruger pointed at the monitor. "What does that look like?"

"A license plate frame."

With a slight smile, Kruger said, "If you are going to remove the plates from a car, wouldn't you also discard the promo frame?"

"Yeah, I would think so."

"JR, zoom in on the sticker on the car's trunk. I bet that will tell us exactly which lot we need to visit."

***

Three patrol cars, a detective's car, and a rented Ford Mustang pulled into the Lakeview Auto Smart used car lot. Barnes, accompanied by the uniformed officers, disappeared into the office building while Kruger and JR looked around the lot on the slim chance the Toyota Camry might still be there.

JR touched Kruger on the arm. "Second row, last car on the left."

Directing his attention to the car, Kruger nodded. "Maybe we got lucky."

"What are the odds?"

As they walked toward the location, Kruger said, "Fifty-fifty. I'm not counting on it. Gray Toyota Camrys are a dime a dozen. Particularly with rental agencies."

When they arrived at the car, Kruger used his cell phone to take a picture of the rear bumper and the trunk. "Looks the same."

"As you said, the lot might have more than one."

Barnes walked up and said, "He bought four identical cars at an auction four months ago. This is the last one."

Folding his arms, Kruger said, "That will make it more difficult to determine if this is the car we saw in the security video."

With a wide smile, Barnes said, "This one's been off the lot for about two months. The owner had it at a body shop after discovering a huge dent on the driver's side door. They never knew where the dent came from because it wasn't there when they took possession after the auction. My guess is, we might have gotten lucky."

Looking at the detective, Kruger asked, "Did you tell him you needed to impound the car?"

"Yeah. He wasn't too happy about it."

"Peter, JR and I will spend the night and meet you in the

morning. I want to see if we can tie the car to the museum heist."

"Meet me at the impound center in the morning." He gave Kruger a card. "There's the address. I'll be there at nine. We should be able to determine something by noon."

***

At precisely nine, Kruger followed Barnes into the garage area of the impound center. JR had stayed at the hotel in an attempt to find a digital trail of the illusive Gerald Dugan.

Kruger asked Barnes, as they watched the gray Toyota being examined by a crime lab technician, "Did the owner tell you when they took this car off the lot?"

"The Monday after Easter. Bodyshop told me they only opened the driver's side door."

"With the car coming from a rental agency, you're going to get a variety of DNA samples out of it." Kruger paused for a moment. "If you have Dugan's DNA on file, any hits you get from inside the car could be compared to his sample. That would, at least, prove he was in the car."

Barnes nodded thoughtfully. "Hadn't thought of that. CPD started collecting DNA samples a long time ago. We should have his, since he was a frequent guest of the city."

"What about known associates?"

The detective handed Kruger a sheet of paper. "I pulled this list before I came over here."

After scanning the sheet, he handed it back to Barnes. "Looks like Dugan was kind of a loner."

"Yeah. I've asked a couple of other detectives to check on the whereabouts of the guys on this list."

The two men fell into silence as they watched the methodical examination of the car. Kruger's cell phone vibrated at ten minutes before ten. "Did you find something, JR?"

"Yeah. Are you with Barnes?"

"Yes."

"Let me talk to him."

Kruger handed the phone to Barnes. "It's JR. He has a question."

"This is Barnes."

"Detective, how hard would it be for you to get cell phone records for Gerald Dugan?"

"Not too, why?"

"From what I can see, he vanished off the face of the earth Easter morning. If you can get his complete records, we can follow his GPS locations. It might give us a clue to where he might have been at the time."

CHAPTER 10

Minneapolis

Two events occurred on September 26, 1969, one major and the other only important to two individuals. The first event, the album *Abbey Road*, the last album recorded by the legendary band the Beatles, was released. The second event was the birth of Hunter Holden, solitary child of Rebecca and Richard Holden.

Richard, a salesman for The Minnetonka Corporation, and his wife celebrated the birth of their son by buying a small cottage in Minneapolis not far from the airport. When Hunter reached the age of eighteen, two events cemented the future course of his life.

The owner of The Minnetonka Corporation sold their liquid soap brand to Colgate-Palmolive. That same day, his father, then a vice-president of sales for Minnetonka's soap division, was informed that he would not be hired by the larger corporation and thus was out of a high-paying job. While his severance settlement left the family relatively well off, Richard Hunter, an astute businessman and investor, decided his windfall needed to be invested in the stock market.

Known as Black Monday, the stock market crashed on October 19, 1987. The stocks owned by the elder Holden lost the vast majority of their value during this event. With the contraction of the global economy and the loss of his investment, Richard Holden panicked. Instead of waiting for the recovery, he chose to end his life. His body was found in a rented storage unit where he parked his car, closed the garage-sized door with the motor running, and left his wife and son to fend for themselves.

Rebecca reacted to this event by finding solace in dry martinis, which she consumed constantly during her waking moments after Richard's death.

Vowing not to repeat the mistakes he perceived his father to have made, Hunter enrolled in the University of Minnesota Twin City business school. There, he perfected his already dark, uncaring personality. His mother died two years later from alcohol poisoning. Hunter, having not seen her during those two years, refused to attend the funeral.

By the age of twenty-five, he had an MBA, his first million dollars, and was well on his way toward the second. His company, Transnational Financial LLC, sprang forth two years later in 1996.

Over the subsequent decades, Hunter Holden demanded and received loyalty from individuals he considered key associates. This mandatory loyalty was encouraged by six-figure salaries and promised seven-figure bonuses.

On this particular Tuesday afternoon, he sat at his office desk poring over financial statements for a company he would soon take public and exit ownership of. This particular transaction would net Transnational Financial a profit on the initial investment of over one hundred million dollars.

A knock on his door brought his attention away from the data on his computer screen.

"Have you got a few minutes, Hunter?"

The individual at the door, Dean Melton, a longtime associate and unscrupulous business partner, exhibited a sly smile.

"Go ahead."

"The IT guy at the Field Museum was arrested earlier this afternoon."

"How does that affect us?"

"It shouldn't, but I thought you needed to know."

"Dean, if the plan was executed properly, the only individual he should have communicated with would have been Ross."

"That's what she told me, although, we need to have legal prepare a statement negating any accusations that could come our way."

"Make it so."

"Got it."

Melton had turned to leave, when Holden said, "Wait a moment."

"Yes, sir?"

"How did the police uncover the IT guy?"

"Not sure. The Chicago PD basically swept the whole affair under the rug until the museum's insurance carrier brought in an investigator."

Holden remained silent as his assistant stood in the doorway. Finally, he said, "Well, did you bother to inquire who this investigator might be?"

"Not yet."

"Don't you think that would be good information to have right now?"

The man standing at the door shrugged. "I've never heard of an insurance investigator being that good. They're usually old washed-up police detectives."

With his lips pressed together, Holden considered his response. Thinking better of what he wanted to say, he replied, "Very well. Just find out."

Melton left as Holden tapped a pen on his desk. "Do I

have to think for everyone around here?" He stood, walked to his office door, and closed it. Returning to his desk, he extracted a cell phone from a drawer in the credenza behind him. The call was answered on the second ring.

"Yeah?"

"Are you still in Chicago?"

"Maybe, what'd ya need?"

"They've uncovered the IT guy."

"He doesn't know shit."

Holden said, "I realize that, but we can't take a chance. Make it look like a suicide."

"That shouldn't be too hard."

"Why do you say that?"

"Think about it for a few minutes. The guy has his nose glued to a computer most of the time."

"Find one of your bail bondsman buddies and get him out. Then he can be so despondent, he takes his own life."

***

Ronny Stanford stared at the man who picked him up after being released on bail. "Why are you helping me?"

"You wanna go back to jail?"

"No. But I don't know you."

"You don't need to, kid. I'm getting paid to help you."

"By whom?"

"Does it matter?"

"It could. I would like to know why someone I've never met wants to help me."

"Relax. I'll take you to your place and then you can contact your lawyer."

"I don't know one."

"When we get to your apartment, I can give you a few names."

"Thank you."

***

Patrol officer Brenda Garcia knocked on apartment Five C and waited for a response. When none came, she repeated the process. After four attempts, she spoke into her shoulder microphone. "Wellness check, this location, unsuccessful. Send backup."

"Acknowledged, Car 33. Detective enroute. Wait for the man."

"Roger."

Twenty minutes later, escorted by the building manager, Detective Barnes, Officer Garcia, and another patrolman entered the apartment of Ronny Stanford. Once inside, Barnes called the crime lab.

While he waited for them to arrive, he dialed the number for Kruger's cell phone.

"Kruger."

"You still in Chicago?"

"Heading toward the airport, why?"

"Ronny Stanford, the museum's IT guy."

"Yeah?"

"I'm at his apartment. He got bailed out and immediately went home. Now we find him in bed, dead, with a needle sticking out of his arm."

"Did he have a history of drug use?"

"He's never been arrested for it, if that's what you mean."

"Kind of convenient. Who bailed him out?"

"Don't know at the moment, but I'm checking on it."

Kruger remained silent for a few moments. "Pete, someone is tying up loose ends before we even realize they're loose."

"I would agree."

"Can you send a copy of Dugan's cell phone records to JR when you get them?"

"Sure."

"I don't want to step on your investigation. However, I

believe we can assist you and provide information you might not be in a position to obtain."

"I can live with that. Let me know where to send the phone records."

***

In The Skies Above the Midwest

JR looked over at Kruger sitting next to him on KKG's leased corporate jet. "You've been quiet ever since we took off."

"Thinking."

"That's dangerous. About?"

"The diamonds at the Field Museum."

"You having second thoughts about what you'll recommend to the insurance company?"

"No. Everything we've learned, so far, points toward a cover-up. Anyone who could actually confirm they weren't real has conveniently died or disappeared."

"Oh, boy. Here's where you say you don't believe in coincidences."

Kruger gave his friend a slight grin. "You know me too well. I don't."

"Sean, you're not with the FBI any longer. You're an experienced investigator who will be making a recommendation to an insurance company. That's what you were hired to do."

"I know. But I'm finding it hard to let go. First, Margaret Ross said she examined the diamonds herself, not an independent appraiser. Second, we learn she bought stock in Goldmax six months before the diamonds arrived at her museum. Third, Transnational Financial, a company in Minneapolis, became a patron of a museum in Chicago. And, finally, Ms. Ross, who was gay, was found dead in bed with her stockbroker, who just happened to be loaded with a fatal dose of fentanyl."

"If the real diamonds weren't at the museum, where are they?"

"Don't know. Maybe they never existed in the first place."

"Surely, someone would have appraised them prior to their being considered as collateral for a loan."

Kruger fixed his attention on his friend for a moment. "I didn't think of that. But you're right. They would have been." He grew quiet for a moment. "JR, when I inform the insurance company there's a strong possibility the diamonds were fake in the first place, they will reject the claim, and KKG will earn a ton of money. I'm not sure we've earned it yet."

"You need to start thinking like a businessman. Sometimes you make a good profit without a lot of work. Other times, you lose money on projects where you've worked your butt off. I've experienced both."

Taking a deep breath, Kruger leaned back and slowly let it out. "I know. Sandy and Jimmie tell me the same thing." He stared out the window at the landscape passing beneath the plane then suddenly leaned forward and turned his attention to JR. "What did you say about thinking like a businessman?"

"All I was saying was you need to think more like..."

"No, the profit part."

"I was simply reminding you that sometimes you can make a lot of money without a lot of expense or effort."

"That, my friend, is exactly what has happened in Chicago."

"Not following you, Sean."

"Someone else is manipulating the events. Who stands to gain if the insurance company declares fraud and rejects the settlement?"

"I don't think anyone would gain."

"Not necessarily. Goldmax would suddenly have

financial issues. The diamond collection was collateral for their acquisition of the Australian lithium mining company. If they lost the collateral, whoever loaned Goldmax the money would demand repayment."

"Where are you going with this?"

"Bear with me. I'm getting there. Here comes Transnational Financial as the knight in shining armor. They buy the note and take over Goldmax. However, before all this transpired, they've become a new patron for the museum and been having regular meetings with Ross. What if they are the ones who hatched the inside job with her? She bribes a rookie IT guy to do all the dirty work of letting the crooks in on Easter morning to make it look like someone stole the real diamonds. That way, no one would suspect the original diamonds were fake as well."

"Whew, that's a stretch even for you, Sean. Where'd this come from?"

"Think about it for a second. Transnational Financial sets up the heist and somehow gets Ross to do their bidding. Everything is blamed on Ross. The insurance carrier claims fraud and doesn't cover the loss of the diamonds. Which leads Goldmax to declare bankruptcy, leading to Transnational Financial taking over the company at a fraction of the cost it would have had to shell out. I'd make a bet one of the burglars was told to leave a necklace askew."

"How much have you had to drink?"

"Three cups of coffee."

JR leaned back in his chair. "When do you think I'll get the cell phone records for Gerald Dugan?"

"You probably have them now. You can check when we land."

He looked at Kruger. "Apparently, I've been around you too long. Your theory is actually making a little sense. If I find something goofy in those records, I'll…"

"You'll what?"

"I might actually believe the convoluted story you just

told me."

"Trust me, JR. I'm not sure I believe it, either. But why kill Ross and her stockbroker? Why did the IT guy conveniently overdose? The only way the pieces of this puzzle come together is if the theft was used to draw attention to the fake diamonds."

"You suspect Hunter Holden, don't you?"

"You said it yourself. He makes Abel Plymel look like a choirboy."

"Who has the real diamonds, Sean?"

"If I were a betting man, I'd say Holden."

CHAPTER 11

Southwest Missouri

With the plane serviced and parked in the hanger portion of KKG's building and JR on his way home, Kruger searched the Internet for information on Transnational Financial. In the middle of the afternoon, he sat back in his office chair and stared at the picture on the monitor. He picked up his cell phone and called JR.

The computer expert answered on the third ring. "I was just about to call you."

"What'd you find out?"

"Apparently, Dugan never turned his phone off. He can be tracked with the GPS function on his phone every second of each day for the past eighteen months, until Easter morning."

"Did it show him at the museum?"

"Yes."

"Where was he when the signal stopped on Easter?"

"Middle of Lake Michigan."

Kruger remained quiet as this information took hold. Finally, he said, "That would make sense."

"I agree. Dead men do not expose conspiracies." He paused. "Have you found anything else about Hunter Holden?"

"He doesn't have a presence on social media. Nothing on Facebook or Twitter."

"That you could identify."

"No. I've learned a few things from you. He's just not there."

"What about professional sites like LinkedIn?"

"Nothing."

"Want me to take over?"

"You're going to have to. The only information I can find comes from places like CNBC or the *Wall Street Journal*. They don't paint a very flattering picture of him. Other than that, I'm stuck."

"Okay. You want to call Barnes about Dugan?"

"Yeah, I'll take care of it."

"Talk to you later."

The call ended, and Kruger found the detective's cell phone number and made the call.

"Detective Barnes."

"It's Kruger."

"I hope you have better news than I do."

"That will depend on your point of view. JR traced Dugan's last location to the middle of Lake Michigan. The GPS function on his cell phone disappeared there on Easter morning."

"Ahh, geez."

"What's your bad news?"

"A witness showed up claiming Ronny Stanford used drugs all the time."

"How convenient."

"Kind of what I thought. An autopsy on the body revealed no evidence of needle tracks or effects of long-term drug use."

"Who was the witness?"

"Some homeless guy who hangs around the neighborhood close to Stanford's apartment. He told us the guy was always trying to sell him drugs."

"Is he credible?"

"Enough so, a good defense attorney could poke holes in a prosecutor's argument."

"Where's that leave you, Peter?"

"Back where we were when I first met you. Nowhere. Without any additional evidence, I need to jump back on my case backlog. This one's going on the back burner."

"I've been there. Want me to keep digging?"

"Don't make it a hobby, but if you have time, yeah."

"I'll get back to you if we find anything important."

"I appreciate it, Sean."

The call ended, and Kruger stared at the picture of Hunter Holden still open on his computer monitor. The picture, taken by a photographer with the *Minneapolis Star Tribune*, showed a tall athletic man dressed in an expensive-looking suit, sans tie, leaving a Hennepin County courthouse. The caption under the picture described how the richest man in Minnesota had just donated a large tract of land to the county for the construction of an event center. Other articles from the *Wall Street Journal* described a ruthless predator who gobbled up distressed businesses and profited on their demise.

Kruger read the article accompanying the picture and said to the image, "I've met your type before, Holden. But those individuals usually commit their crimes with a gun. It's time to expose you for who you really are."

***

The Next Morning

Jimmie Gibbs leaned against the doorframe of Kruger's office at the KKG headquarters sipping coffee. "I just got off the phone with Nathan Tucker. Nice guy."

"He is. Is this the first time you've talked to him?"

"Yes. He called to compliment you on the quick resolution of the Goldmax diamond heist. After the report you sent him last night, they decided to declare fraud by Goldmax. No claim will be paid."

"I hope they're still going to pay us."

"I reminded him of that. He told me to have someone send them an invoice. Which I did."

Kruger's eyebrow shot up. "You're kidding. The full amount?"

"Every penny. Plus, he asked if they could put us on retainer for future investigations."

"I am assuming you said yes."

"I was born at night, but it wasn't last night. Of course, I told him yes. Do you realize that's the largest contract we've ever collected on?"

"No, I didn't. Sandy and I rely on you to keep the books, Jimmie. I hate accounting. Put it in our operating fund. I might need to return to Chicago a few more times."

Jimmie pushed away from the doorframe and smiled. "Kind of thought you might."

***

Hunter Holden leaned back in his chair as he listened to the whining of Goldmax CEO Walter Wagenaar.

"Hunter, you cannot do this. It is unethical and certainly illegal."

"Walter, what may be illegal is you trying to claim fake diamonds as real. Like I told you last week, your situation is untenable. The insurance company has declared fraud and refuses to pay your claim. Your lenders contacted me, and I offered them a solution this morning."

"You had no right to talk to them, Hunter."

"As I was saying, I offered them a solution, and they

agreed. As of noon, my time, 7 p.m. there in Johannesburg, Transnational Financial holds the note on your debt. There is language within the contract stating if the lender declares the borrower financially insecure, which you are, Transnational Financial, now classified as the lender, can call in the note. Which we will, as of noon my time."

"Holden, you can't just call and demand the note be repaid."

"Read the fine print. I can, and I am."

"You know how leveraged we are."

"Yes, and since you have been negligent with your cash flow, your liquidity is in jeopardy. You have but one way to keep from declaring bankruptcy, Walter."

"What's that?"

"Sell your company to Transnational Financial. Or face having to liquidate, which regulators will insist you do."

The phone call went silent as Walter Wagenaar contemplated his response.

"Take your time, Walter. You have thirty-five minutes until it is noon here. After that, you'll have to face the consequences of not selling to me while your company still has value."

"Who would run Goldmax if I sell?"

"We would want a seasoned and knowledgeable manager."

"Make that person me, and I will agree to your terms."

"A wise decision, Walter. I will have the contract emailed. Sign it and have it returned to me by seven your time."

"I want myself named CEO of Goldmax in the document."

"Of course."

The call ended, and Holden replaced the handset in its cradle on the desk phone. He looked up at Dean Melton. "He agreed. Make sure the restructure plan and name change for Goldmax is buried in the fine print. Add a clause about

Wagenaar being named CEO of Goldmax but only in its current structure."

Melton smiled. "When do you want it emailed?"

"Fifteen till. He won't have time to read it by the deadline."

Standing, Transnational Financial's second-in-command moved toward Holden's office door. After he opened it, he turned. "What happens when his attorneys find the restructuring clause?"

With a shrug, Holden turned his attention to another file on his desk. "It will be too late."

***

Kruger parked his gunmetal-gray Mustang GT in a vacant parking slot just west of Glass Hall on the Missouri State University campus. He sent a text message and, three minutes later, Stephanie Kruger slipped into the passenger seat next to her husband.

"This is a treat. You never take me to lunch."

"For everything there is a first time." He backed the car up and accelerated out of the lot. "We got back earlier than planned this morning, and I thought it would be nice to have lunch with you. When's your next class?"

"You don't know my schedule yet, Mr. Kruger?"

"Yes, I know your schedule, I just wanted to see if you did."

"You've forgotten, haven't you?" She gave him a mischievous grin.

"It might have slipped my mind."

"My last class of the day is at two. We have an hour and a half before I have to be back."

The Mustang's 5-liter V8 growled as he shifted to second and punched the accelerator. "I know a perfect place where we can talk."

Forty minutes later, after the husband and wife had

finished their sandwiches and caught up on the activities of their two kids, Kruger asked, "Do you know if Dr. Kinslow is still with the university?"

"I think so, why?"

"Last I knew, he was on the verge of retiring. I need to have a conversation with him."

"About?"

"He's written extensively about the psychology of CEOs and business leaders. I wanted to bounce a few questions off of him."

"You know him. Why don't you call him?"

"When we last spoke, he was extremely pissed I was leaving the faculty. He wanted me to take over his research. Something I really did not want to do."

"That was a few years ago. I'm sure he's over it by now."

"Doubtful. He can be, uh—difficult at times."

"Sean, you of all people can handle difficult individuals."

"Yes, but he took it personally." He gave her a sly smile. "I was hoping with your charm and good looks, he would agree to meet with me if you asked him."

Returning the smile, she placed her hand on his arm. "My good looks are reserved for you, Mr. Kruger, and only you."

"Then use your charm."

She shook her head and chuckled. "That, I can do. But you'll have to pick up the kids from school."

"I would love to."

***

At ten minutes before the hour of four in the afternoon, Stephanie Kruger knocked on the office doorframe of Max Kinslow, PhD. The man looked up and smiled. "May I help you?"

"Yes, Dr. Kinslow. I'm Stephanie Kruger, from the School of Business. May I have a few minutes of your time?"

The elderly gentleman stood and smiled. "Yes, yes,

please come in." He walked around his desk and offered his hand. "I've seen you around campus. You're married to Dr. Sean Kruger, aren't you?"

"Yes, he speaks of you often."

"How is he?"

"He's retired from the FBI and working as a fraud investigator for a defense contractor."

"Good for him. He always had a sharp mind." He gave her a sad smile. "I miss our heated discussions when he was on the faculty here."

She paused before asking her question. "Professor, Sean was wondering if you would consult with him on a project?"

The man's eyes lit up, and he stood straighter. "Sean Kruger would like me to consult with him? Oh, my." He blinked a few times, and Stephanie saw moisture pool in the corner of his left eye. "I'd be honored. Can you tell me a little bit about the project?"

"Yes, he is investigating a company whose CEO may be, as he called him, a high-functioning psychopath."

The smile on the older man's face only intensified. "Oh my, yes. That would be most interesting."

CHAPTER 12

Southwest Missouri

Maxwell Kinslow, PhD, tenured professor, former department head, and multi-published author greeted Sean Kruger with an energetic handshake and a smile.

"Sean, it is so good to see you. Please, sit." The elderly man motioned toward one of the chairs at a small round conference table in his office. He sat across from Kruger.

"Thanks for meeting with me, Professor."

"Please, just Max. We're old friends."

"Very well, Max. I was hesitant to ask you, considering the last time we spoke."

"Words said in haste. I was so disappointed to see you leave the department. I knew I would miss our discussions. And I have."

"So have I. Teaching isn't in my DNA. I tried it two times. Actually, three if you count the years after I earned my doctorate. It bored me to tears."

"Teaching isn't for everyone, my friend. Everyone on the faculty has commented about missing your input during our meetings." He paused, took a deep breath, and continued.

"Your wife told me you have a puzzling dilemma." Kruger leaned forward, placing his arms on the table and clasping his hands. "I'm seeking your perspective. I reread a number of your published papers on the dynamics of corporate leadership last night."

Kinslow nodded.

"One of them summarized your research into why men who border on having psychopathic tendencies often rise to the top of the corporate food chain."

Another nod from the professor.

Continuing, Kruger said, "What happens when those individuals are actual psychopaths?"

"Many CEOs have an exaggerated ego and can be cunning and manipulative. Their charm can be very attractive to co-workers and other executives within the organization. They usually rise quickly to the top. But most do not exhibit criminal tendencies, parasitic lifestyles, or poor behavioral controls. If they did, they would not be in a position of leadership. I don't see how a fully diagnosed psychopath could reach the level of CEO. We both know only 1 percent of the general population have been found to be truly psychopathic. Whereas 25 to 30 percent of prison populations are diagnosed as such."

"In a normal situation, I would agree with you, Max. Your statistics match my experience as well."

"I hear a *however* in your voice, Sean."

"There is. I have run across several during my FBI career. One went so far as to hire someone to hunt down and kill another person."

"Did they succeed?"

With a smile, Kruger shook his head. "No."

"I take it you stopped it."

"I had help." He paused for a few moments. "During your research, did you ever run across a corporate executive who displayed a total lack of empathy to the point you felt they could become a danger to anyone who worked with them?"

The professor's stare lasted longer than Kruger expected, and his eyebrows rose. "You have?"

A nod from the ex-FBI agent.

Kinslow stood and walked to a shelving unit crammed with books and bound manuscripts. He ran his finger along one of the shelves and pulled out a looseleaf notebook. He opened the binder and scanned the top page. Satisfied, he returned to his seat.

As he pushed the object across the table, he said, "Five years ago, I did a series of interviews with students recruited from within the business school graduate program here on campus. One young man in particular concerned me. After the interview, I used his answers to measure his responses on Dr. Robert Hare's Psychopathic Checklist. He scored a solid thirty-six out of forty on the test."

"I'm familiar with Dr. Hare's assessments. Anyone who scores more than thirty should be considered a psychopath."

"Yes, I know. I brought my conclusions to the attention of his advisor. She surprisingly agreed with me."

"This didn't have a good ending, did it, Max?"

"No, I'm afraid it didn't."

"What happened?"

After taking a deep breath, Kinslow continued. "She took her concerns and my interview notes to the head of the department. The young man was then summoned to the department head's office. The confrontation left both faculty members in the hospital and the young man under arrest."

"Max, it would have happened sooner or later."

"I know, but I still blame myself."

"Has that incident affected your research?"

"Not really. But it has mainly caused me to conclude true psychopaths probably won't make it to the top of a corporation. There will be a trigger somewhere that will set them off."

"I respectfully have to disagree with you, Professor."

Kinslow raised an eyebrow.

"You see, Max, sometimes these guys start their own companies."

***

Kruger left the meeting with Dr. Kinslow an hour later. When he arrived at home, JR stood next to the mailbox at his house across the street. After parking his Mustang in the garage, Kruger walked to his own mailbox as JR stepped over to Kruger's driveway.

"How'd the meeting go with the professor?"

"Fine. He's agreed to consult with me on the Transnational Financial issue. He has more experience with corporate executives than I do."

"The other shoe dropped today. Or, I should say last night."

With a frown, Kruger tilted his head. "What happened?"

"Transnational purchased the outstanding debt of Goldmax and took control of it as of midnight Greenwich Mean Time last night."

Remaining silent, Kruger let his friend continue.

"According to Bloomberg, where I initially saw it, the deal was inked ten minutes before a margin call on Goldmax. Transnational took control and immediately changed the name and the corporate structure. The CEO of Goldmax is screaming bloody murder and threatening a breach of trust lawsuit against Transnational and Hunter Holden."

"Huh."

"I just happened to find a copy of the contract and downloaded it."

"Imagine that."

"Want to read it?"

"Eventually, but give me the 50,000-foot level view first."

"There was a clause in the contract, which appeared to have been added at the last minute. It stated that if Goldmax kept its current structure, the Goldmax CEO Walter Wagenaar would keep his position and management status within the company."

"Let me guess, there was a superseding clause buried within the contract negating that."

"Exactly. Wagenaar was informed of the changes and fired thirty minutes after the contract went into effect."

"That makes sense. Transnational acquires Goldmax at a discount, the stock price will soar, Hunter Holden makes a tidy profit, and he now owns a lithium mining company. Pretty slick."

"You think that's the way he planned it?"

"I don't think, I know it is."

"Does he have the diamonds, too?"

"Probably. But he would have to sell them on the open market to get any value. He wouldn't net that much."

"I'm not following you."

"As a rule, if you steal diamond jewelry, you have to fence it. Which means, the diamonds are detached from the settings and sold as loose diamonds. Normally, at a discount."

"So, they really weren't meant to be a profit center?"

"Nope. Goldmax was the prize. The stock price will soar. What he gets out of the diamonds might cover his expenses for the operation."

"So, what are you going to do?"

"All I have to do is prove it."

"Need help?"

"Yes, I do. First, I need to know more about Hunter Holden."

"In what way?"

"I'd like to start with interviewing him, but I don't think he will allow that to happen. However, if I could find a few former employees who'd be willing to talk, I could use those to start building a profile on him."

"Let me see what I can find."

CHAPTER 13

Kansas City, MO

Wilder Zane, a man in his early fifties who appeared ten years older, eyed Kruger with a perplexed demeanor. He did not offer his hand as the retired FBI agent sat across from him at a Starbucks on Stateline Road near a Walmart Supercenter.

"I only agreed to meet with you as long as my name is kept anonymous."

"I understand, Wilder. May I call you Wilder?"

The man shrugged. "Do what you want. Why are you asking questions about Hunter Holden?"

"As I told you on the phone, I'm a retired FBI agent. I was hired by an insurance company to look into possible fraud committed by Transnational Financial."

The man chuckled. "You won't have to turn over too many rocks to find fraud, Mr. Kruger."

"Please, just Sean."

The man studied Kruger for a moment and then nodded. "The company itself is a fraud. It is more of a play toy for Holden."

"What do you mean?"

Zane took a sip of his coffee. "How much do you know about Hunter Holden?"

"Not a lot, that's why I'm meeting with individuals like yourself."

"None of us will want our names used."

"So I've heard. How many are there?"

"About a dozen. We all joined Transnational Financial with one goal in mind. To make as much money as possible as fast as we could."

"Did you?"

Zane nodded. "In the first year I worked there, according to my contract, I should have earned over fifty million dollars. Most of it in performance bonuses. The amount I was actually paid, well, it was a whole lot less."

"What about the second year?"

"There wasn't one. When Holden discovered how much my bonus would be, he had one of his henchmen plant a small amount of cocaine in my office desk. The police found it, and I was led out of the building in handcuffs. My attorney, bless her heart, convinced a judge to dismiss the charges, but the damage was done. I haven't been able to find a job in the financial markets since."

"What's your background, Wilder?"

"MBA in international finance."

"Did the others in this group of a dozen or so ex-employees have a similar experience?"

"Some did. Others lasted three or four years before they were shown the door and sued for breach of contract. We all left without receiving the compensation we were promised."

"Why not sue Transnational?"

"One of us did. The day before the trial, he died in an automobile accident. A drunk driver T-boned his car in an intersection. No one else has the desire to sue now."

Kruger remained silent and sipped his coffee.

Zane continued. "So, you see, Sean, although we all made

the mistake of going to work for Hunter Holden, we aren't foolish enough to fight him. Bad for your health."

"Thus, the reason no one wants their name associated with my investigation?"

"Exactly, if it ever got back to Holden we were telling tales, we'd disappear or be found dead in an alley somewhere."

"You have my word. Your name will not be used."

"Good. What else do you want to know?"

"Why did all of you accept a position with Transnational in the first place?"

"Hunter Holden is a smooth talker and can charm the pants off anyone. Particularly women. He's very confident in himself and makes you feel warm and fuzzy about his financial prowess. He will also make sure you are aware of how much money he has made. A topic he talks about incessantly. For some reason, that trait is attractive to some females, and he is never without beautiful women hanging around him."

"Did you ever know him to break the law in his business transactions?"

"A better question would be, when did he not break the law?"

"Wilder, you're not painting a picture of a successful businessman, you're describing a mafia boss."

"I never thought of it that way, but you're right. That's exactly what he acts like."

"Any idea why he's never been indicted for his business practices?"

A shake of the man's head became Kruger's answer.

"How much of his business is transacted inside the United States?"

"Very little. I and three others were on the Pacific Rim desk. Most of my transactions occurred in Japan and northeast up to the Bering Sea. In fact, he seldom does any acquisition deals within the States. He always grumbled about too many regulations."

"I'm surprised the Japanese didn't see through him."

"Money flashed in the face of a businessman has the same effect in Japan as it does in the rest of the world."

"Would you say Hunter Holden doesn't care who he hurts in a business transaction?"

"He relishes hurting people. It arouses him."

Kruger raised an eyebrow.

"I mean that literally."

After considering the implications of what Zane revealed, Kruger took another track. "Does he have a second-in-command or an assistant?"

"Dean Melton. Cut from the same cloth. Arrogant, looks down his nose at others and emboldens the boss every chance he gets."

"How long has he been there?"

"Don't know for sure. I heard a rumor Holden and Melton went to school together."

"Where?"

"Holden has a diploma on his office wall from the University of Minnesota Twin Cities. He holds an MBA from there. I don't know much about Melton. I found him offensive and avoided contact with him as much as possible."

Kruger spent another hour talking to Zane but failed to discover anything else helpful.

***

When the Mustang passed Clinton, MO heading south, Kruger called JR. The call was answered on the first ring, something the computer hacker seldom did.

"Where are you?"

"Couple of miles south of Clinton, why?"

"Contractor wants me to do a walk-through of the new building. I really need you to be there."

"Why?"

"Well…"

"I'm an hour and a half away. Will that work?"

"I'm sure it will, I'll let him know. What'd you find out in KC?"

"A new name we need information on: Dean Melton. He's Hunter Holden's partner in crime. Apparently, they may have gone to the same college, University of Minnesota Twin Cities."

"I'll start there. Anything else?"

"According to Wilder Zane, Hunter doesn't like doing business in the US. He feels there are too many regulations."

"Isn't that interesting."

"Kind of what I thought. I'll meet you at your building."

***

The contractor handed a hard hat to both Kruger and JR. "Sorry, guys. OSHA says we have to wear these inside a construction project."

JR shrugged and put his on. "I wanted Sean here so he can review the improvements you and I discussed."

Kruger put his hat on and said, "Lead the way."

The outside of the building retained the same appearance as before the explosion that leveled it ten months prior. A two-story buff brick structure, with no signage identifying the company, stood in front of the trio. The double glass doors leading to the interior seemed identical to the originals. Gary said, "As you know, there aren't any brands of glass that can claim to be bullet proof. Bullet resistant, yes, but not proof. The closest available is a glass-clad polycarbonate. In other words, it is multiple layers of a clear polycarbonate sandwiched between multiple panes of security glass. We've used the strongest on the market on all exterior doors and windows."

Kruger nodded. "It should also improve JR's insurance

rating."

"It has for other buildings where we've installed it." Gary opened one of the front doors. "We also added a security vestibule just inside. Anyone who does not belong in the building will have to be granted access by the receptionist. Otherwise, they're stuck inside. They can't get in the building, and the front doors lock automatically, preventing them from leaving. HD security cameras are installed and, if the receptionist isn't at their desk, JR can admit visitors from his office."

JR mumbled, "I hate that."

With a chuckle, Kruger said, "Sorry, JR. It would have prevented Al-Qaedi from gaining entry and planting the bomb." Al-Qaedi being the Iranian terrorist who planted the bomb and detonated it in an attempt to kill one of JR's clients.

The three men walked toward the stairs. Before entering the stairwell, Kruger asked, "Gary, could a similar glass box be installed here?"

"Sure. We can build it the same as the vestibule. Floor-to-ceiling bullet-resistant glass. It'll be expensive."

"How much?"

The contractor pulled out his cell phone and opened the calculator app. After he paced off the area, he crunched the numbers. Finally, he said, "Depending on the brand of glass, in the neighborhood of ten thousand, probably more."

With a frown, JR stared at his friend. "Sean, I'm spending a fortune on these building upgrades as it is. I don't see..."

"KKG will be paying for it."

With a frown, JR folded his arms. "Care to explain why?"

"Not at the moment."

Taking the hint, JR nodded. "Okay, Gary, revise the plans and make the staircase entry bullet resistant."

"You got it, JR."

The three men ascended to the second floor. When they emerged, the cubicle-farm area offered a totally different arrangement than pre-explosion. Gary said, "Here is the biggest improvement we've made. Note, the glass extends from the top of the cubicle wall to the ceiling. Each unit can be sealed off. The solid walls are hardened steel panels and bullet-resistant glass up to a 50-caliber weapon. The glass is the same material we used in the entry. If someone is in their cubicle, and there's an intruder, they can slide the door shut and duck behind the steel walls."

Kruger said, "Are there fewer cubicles?"

"Yes, per JR's instructions, we've reduced the number by half."

Standing with his hands on his hips, JR pointed toward the room. "I only need twenty or so analysts here at any given time from now on."

The contractor motioned for them to follow him. "One more improvement is the conference room. Not only is it soundproof, the glass is the most robust bullet-resistant laminated product we could source. Per Sean's instructions, we added an exit from the room that will lead to a fire door on the first floor. The stairs leading down are concealed on the first floor by a hardened steel wall."

"Where's the entrance to the stairs in the room?" Kruger surveyed the area as he asked the question.

Gary walked to a switch on an inside wall and flipped it. They heard a click and a panel in the floor popped open. "There." He walked over to the panel and lifted it. "The panel weighs about two hundred pounds. So, we added a counter-balance mechanism to allow it to be easily opened."

"What about the door on the outside?"

"Invisible to anyone looking at the wall."

"Good."

"I was looking over your specs on security cameras, JR. I'll have to hire a subcontractor for that part of the project."

JR smiled. "I've been thinking about that, Gary. I forgot I asked one of my clients to upgrade my security cameras. I saw his system about a year ago, and it was far superior to mine. Let me ask him first."

CHAPTER 14

Southwest Missouri

The client JR referred to stood in front of the buff brick building, his arms folded and his lips pursed. "Yeah, JR, I'd be happy to set up your security camera system. Besides, I owe you."

"I would appreciate you doing it, Michael, but you don't owe me anything."

"Yeah, I do. It was kind of my fault Al-Qaedi thought he needed to place a bomb in your building." Michael Wolfe, a retired Marine sniper, former CIA black-ops agent and now a new father, smiled. "At least, let me do it as a favor."

JR nodded. "That I can do."

Wolfe returned his attention to the building. "You'll need at least five HD cameras on the front and the same on the back, maybe seven. If we place them correctly, you will achieve a 360-degree view of the building's surroundings."

"I've got a few upgrades inside. Want to take a look?"

"Sure, let's go."

Kruger followed the two men as they entered the still-under-construction structure. A plan coalesced as he stared at the glass vestibule and the other enhanced-security measures. After following Wolfe and JR up the stairs, he interrupted their conversation. "Michael, you're fluent in German and Hebrew, right?"

"Yes, and a couple of Middle Eastern languages as well. Why?"

"Just thinking. You two go on with the tour."

The trio moved through the cubicle farm until they reached the conference room where JR pointed to a spot on the floor. "Sean insisted we have an escape route should we have another intruder while people are in the building."

After JR showed him the trapdoor and stairs leading down, Wolfe turned to Kruger. "Clever. Good idea, Sean."

A nod was his response.

Wolfe continued. "What about anyone on the first floor?"

"Similar, there is a door leading into the hidden staircase and the exit door."

"I'm impressed. With the addition of security cameras, this will be a sanctuary."

"Thanks, Michael. Most of these ideas were his." He pointed to Kruger.

Turning to look at the retired FBI agent, Wolfe asked, "How's the private defense contractor business going?"

"Good." He paused. "JR, how hard would it be to produce fake records of a company operating in, oh let's say, Europe?"

JR's eyes narrowed. "I've seen that look before, Sean. You have an idea."

"I do. How hard would it be?"

"Depends on the type of company."

"I'm not that far along with the idea yet." He turned to Wolfe. "Are you a good actor?"

Wolfe slowly displayed a smile. "Depends what've you got in mind?"

"Since your son was born, how busy are you?"

"You have kids. You tell me."

"You're busy."

"At times."

"Not sure how much we would need you, but would you be available to impersonate a CEO of a floundering company so I can catch a psychopath?"

Wolfe folded his arms and laughed. "JR has told me about your exploits. Probably. I spent a few years posing as an international business consultant. I can talk the talk."

With a chuckle, Kruger said, "I remember the first time we met at your place down in Howell County. You told me you were a consultant. I didn't believe you."

Without commenting, Wolfe asked, "What's your plan?"

Kruger told both Wolfe and JR.

Listening in silence, the retired marine sniper nodded occasionally. When Kruger finished summarizing his idea, Wolfe said, "Make it an Israeli company, and I can help JR set it up."

"Not following you, Michael."

"I have friends in low places over there. Besides, my wife is still a citizen."

Kruger smiled at JR. "What do you think?"

"I'm starting to like this idea."

***

Two Days Later

Kruger sipped coffee as he listened to JR summarize his findings on Dean Melton. "Man, you sure know how to uncover assholes." The two men were sitting on the back deck of Kruger's house. Stephanie and the kids were at work and school.

"Tell me about him."

"Where Hunter Holden is charming and sophisticated, Melton is more like a blunt instrument. If he didn't have Transnational's CEO keeping one of the most expensive lawyers in the country on retainer, Melton would have been locked up a long time ago and the keys thrown away."

"How so?"

"Wilder Zane told you he thought they went to a university together, right?"

"He just assumed they did, he wasn't sure."

"Well, they didn't. They actually went to high school together in Minneapolis. Melton's school records should be required reading for new parents on how not to raise a child. I was able to obtain his juvenile records from the Hennepin County Sheriff's Department. They describe the young teenager as an undisciplined bully. He's charged with numerous accounts of assault and suspected of raping a fifteen-year-old girl."

"Suspected?"

"Yeah, the charges were dropped when the girl's parents moved to another state and never pursued the matter."

"Did you determine the reason they did?"

JR nodded. "The father was transferred."

"Then, nothing Hunter Holden did."

"Not that I could determine. Just good luck for Melton."

"Since Holden and Melton didn't go to college together, how did they meet up again?"

"I'm getting there. Melton reached the age of eighteen and, all of a sudden, his crime spree ended."

"Did he graduate from high school?"

"Barely. He graduated 229th out of 230 students with a GPA of 1.3."

"Hard to get into college with a grade point average that low."

"He didn't go to a college. At least not one I could find. He joined the military."

Kruger nodded. "Because his juvenile records were sealed."

"Yes, and he scored an eighty-three on the Armed Services Vocational Aptitude Battery test."

"So, he was a smart kid, he just didn't apply himself."

"That's what one of his high school counselors wrote when he enlisted. He became an MP."

Raising an eyebrow, Kruger said, "Let me guess. He excelled at it."

"Rose to the rank of staff sergeant E-6 and would have risen higher if Holden had not snatched him away and brought him into the fold of Transnational Financial. According to the information I could find, he was originally hired as head of security."

"What's his title now?"

JR gave his friend a sly smile. "Senior Vice President in Charge of Corporate Integrity."

"Lot of words. What are his duties?"

"From what I could find on social media, he's the guy Holden uses to keep the minions in line."

"Figures. Any run-ins with the law since leaving the army?"

"Assault charges, but they are always dismissed after the corporate lawyer gets involved and the plaintiff withdraws their complaint."

Kruger took a sip of his now-cold coffee. "So, Melton is basically a corporate enforcer."

"Kind of how it looks to me."

"Huh." Staring out over his shaded backyard, Kruger drummed his fingers on the table where they sat. "Any progress on setting up a company in Israel?"

"A lot. Michael called me before I came over here, and he thinks we can use a struggling Israeli metallurgy company on the verge of declaring bankruptcy."

With a slight tilt of his head, Kruger said, "That sounds perfect. How much to buy them out?"

"Their shares are about to be delisted on the Tel Aviv Stock Exchange. Michael said he thought if you offered a penny a share, you could buy all the outstanding ones."

"What about the employees?"

"According to Michael, there aren't any. Only the owner, and he's in bad health. You'd basically be buying an existing company with a history. That would be much better than me trying to set up a fake company that only exists on the Internet."

"That was one of the questions I didn't know how to get around."

"Well, this solves the problem."

"How many outstanding shares are there?"

"Ten million."

"So, I could use one hundred thousand dollars from the fifteen million we were paid by the insurance company and buy a defunct foreign business and stop a psychopath."

"Yeah, that pretty much sums up what you could do."

"Seems like a fair trade. Can you set up the purchase if I get you the money?"

"What are Sandy and Jimmie going to say when you start spending company money?"

"I've already had the discussion with them. They're on board as long as I use them in the scam."

"All right, time for me to get busy and buy ourselves an Israeli company."

CHAPTER 15

Minneapolis

Dean Melton walked into Holden's office unannounced. He smiled as he approached the CEO's desk.

Looking up from the computer on his desk, Holden said, "I do hope this is important."

"Important and good news."

Closing the lid on the laptop, Holden folded his arms. "Tell me."

"The museum IT guy, what was his name?"

"Ronny Stanford."

"Yeah, that's the guy. Well, as you know, he met with an unfortunate accident and is no longer of our concern."

"Yes, I'm aware of the matter."

"The Chicago detective in charge of the case has gone back to working other cases, and the insurance investigator left Chicago. The museum heist is now officially a cold case."

Hunter Holden leaned back in his chair and kept his arms folded. "Good. What else?"

"That's all. I thought you'd like to know the status."

"Where'd the info come from?"

"Article in the *Chicago Tribune*, somewhere on page nine."

With another nod, Holden opened the laptop and started reviewing the information on the screen. "You may go, Dean."

"Yes, sir."

When Melton closed the door, Holden kept his eyes on the screen, but a smile gradually came to his lips.

***

Omaha, Nebraska
Offices of Tucker, Neal and Spencer

Kruger followed Nathan Tucker through the halls of a large office building. They passed a large open area with numerous cubicles occupied by women and men with headsets and typing at computer terminals.

After a long walk, Tucker escorted him into a large corner office with two walls of floor-to-ceiling windows, a massive conference table, and a modern glass and metal desk. The top of the desktop held a computer terminal, keyboard, and numerous files neatly stacked on the left edge. Motioning to the conference table, Tucker said, "Can I get you anything, Sean? Coffee?"

"No, thank you. I don't plan on taking too much of your time."

"Nonsense. What do you have for me today?"

"A proposal."

Tucker raised an eyebrow. "Interesting."

"How have you classified the case of the stolen diamonds from the Field Museum?"

"At this point, thanks to your investigation, we have classified it as fraud. Without a certified appraisal of the diamonds before they left South Africa and another when they arrived in Chicago, we are inclined to believe the real diamonds were stolen before being shipped. Which would be outside the terms of our coverage. We offered Goldmax an opportunity to dispute our findings. However, since the company changed ownership, they terminated our coverage and have not responded to any of our communications. They may seek litigation. We just don't know. As a rule, that kind of litigation is lengthy and expensive. They may find it financially unwise to pursue the matter. Why do you ask?"

"If the diamonds were recovered, who would own them?"

"In our experience, stolen diamonds are seldom recovered. After this amount of time, I would guarantee they have been recut and are hopelessly untraceable."

A grin appeared on Kruger's lips. "If you discovered who stole them, what then?"

"We would provide the evidence to the FBI and let them do the investigation. Do you have a lead?"

"No, but I have a person of interest I need to flush out."

Standing, Tucker went to a coffee service and said, "You sure you don't want coffee?"

"Positive, thank you."

As he poured a cup, he remained quiet until he, once again, sat across from Kruger. "You have piqued my interest, Sean. Please, explain."

"Has Tucker, Neal and Spencer dealt with Transnational Financial before?"

"I would have to consult company records." He stood and went to his desk. After typing on the computer for a few moments, he paused and read whatever was on the monitor. "Apparently, we have. We had to settle a claim with them two years ago for over twenty million dollars. Why?"

"Just curious."

"Is this Transnational Financial a suspect in this case?"

"No, but they were instrumental in taking Goldmax private after the theft of the diamonds."

"I see. So, you suspect them?"

"Let's just say I have reservations about the timing and circumstances surrounding Transnational's takeover of Goldmax."

"What does all this have to do with Tucker, Neal and Spencer?"

"Your company has paid out, if you count the fifteen you paid KKG, a total of thirty-five million dollars so far because of them, is that correct?"

Keeping his attention on the computer screen, Tucker frowned. "Here is another five million paid out four years ago. In the short time I've been looking, there are references to several additional claims they appear to be involved in."

"What if those claims were fraudulent as well?"

Tucker grew quiet. "We would need to do an audit on each incident. If we find proof the claims were deceitful, I would have to turn it over to the FBI."

"How would you like to recuperate those fees and put Transnational out of business for good, Nathan?"

"What would we need to do?"

Kruger told him.

***

The flight back to Springfield Branson National Airport from Omaha took less than two hours, and Kruger arrived at his home office before Stephanie and the kids arrived home from school. Satisfied with the day's accomplishments, Kruger walked across the street and rang JR's doorbell.

When the front door opened, JR greeted him with, "Did they agree?"

"Yes."

Opening the storm door, JR let Kruger in. "Let's go sit on the deck, and you can tell me all about it."

When both men were settled in chairs, Kruger said, "We now have a partner. Nathan Tucker is in agreement and will work with us as we reconstruct the Israeli company. Did you figure out a name for it?"

"Yeah, Kaphar Sourcing, LTD."

"What does Kaphar mean?"

"It's an ancient Hebrew word. Michael's wife, Nadia, suggested it. It basically means *atonement* or *to right a wrong*."

"I like it."

"I kinda thought you would." He paused. "What's next?"

"Did you buy the stock?"

A nod came from JR.

"We will need to file paperwork naming the CEO and the board of directors with the Tel Aviv Stock Exchange, correct?"

"Already working on it."

"Then all we have to do is make some noise and draw Hunter Holden's attention to this new international company."

"What if he doesn't go for it?"

"We're going to make it so attractive, there's no way he'll be able to resist."

***

"So how are you going to do this, Mr. Kruger?" Stephanie handed her husband a plate, which he promptly placed in the dishwasher.

"I'm still working on it."

"You have all the wheels in motion and nowhere to steer the car. I don't get it."

"That's not exactly true. The metaphor should be, I have all the actors hired. I just have to find the right play for them to perform."

She chuckled. "Same thing." Handing him another plate, she wiped her hands with a towel and said, "Sean, you're not with the FBI anymore. Why are you trying to hold this Hunter Holden personally responsible? You have no authority to do so."

"That is not exactly correct. We are under contract with the insurance company to pursue the matter. While it doesn't give me the authority to arrest anyone, it does give me a legitimate reason to be involved. When we find positive proof, I can give the information to Tucker, Neal and Spencer, and they can hand it over to whatever authority they deem appropriate. Nathan Tucker promised he would contact the FBI when we find proof."

She folded her arms. "So, you're going to have Nathan Tucker turn it over to the FBI?"

"Ryan Clark, to be exact."

"He's the director."

"My point exactly. He still owes me."

"What if he won't take the case?"

"Someway, somehow, I am going to prove Hunter Holden was involved with the Field Museum heist."

"Sean, that is a lofty goal. How the heck are you going to do it? Invite him to a party and get him drunk?"

He started to say something but suddenly stopped. A grin slowly came to his lips.

She said, "What?"

"You said it yourself. Invite him to a party. It's perfect."

***

"JR, how hard would it be for you to find Hunter Holden's itinerary for the next month or so?"

"Depends on what you're looking for."

"I'm looking for an event where he is in a public setting and out of his comfort zone in Minneapolis. In fact, I would prefer it be out of Minnesota."

"If he has them scheduled on his Outlook calendar, then it shouldn't be too difficult. Are you looking for something specific?"

"I don't want to limit your search."

"He's a busy individual. Why don't you just tell me what you're looking for so I don't waste time looking for when he gets a haircut."

With a chuckle, Kruger said, "No, I don't want to know when he gets a haircut. But I have to assume Holden goes to trade shows on a regular basis. It's the best way to survey a lot of different companies and get leads on those most vulnerable to an easy takeover."

"You could have just asked for those type of meetings."

"Yes, I could have. But you might find a different event that would work better."

"I won't limit my search."

"How hard do you think it will be to hack into their server?"

"I've already got a back door. Does that answer your question?"

Kruger chuckled. "I should have known. See what you can find. Let me know in the morning."

"Consider it done."

***

As a rule, JR did not work past 6 p.m. when attending to business in his home office, but tonight he made an exception. After Kruger's request, he spent the next six hours secluded in front of his laptop at his desk. At 1:12 a.m., his search revealed an opportunity for his friend to spring his trap on Hunter Holden.

The psychopathic venture capitalist planned to attend an international trade show in Toronto, Canada four weeks hence. Without thinking about the lateness of the hour, he dialed Kruger's cell phone.

A raspy voice croaked, "JR, do you have any idea what time it is?"

"No clue. But I did find an event I think will work for your project."

Kruger, now fully awake, replied in his normal voice, "That fast?"

"Third weekend of next month. Holden is scheduled to attend an international trade show featuring companies specializing in sustainable mining activities."

"Can you tell if they are still taking vendors?"

"As a matter of fact, they are. All I have to do to register Kaphar Sourcing is to hit enter. I have all the info already plugged in."

A response from the retired FBI agent did not come immediately.

JR asked, "Yes, or no?"

"Thinking."

"Take your time."

"Yeah, do it."

"Done."

"Get some sleep, JR."

CHAPTER 16

Southwest Missouri

Kruger introduced his new coconspirator to Knoll. "Sandy, this is Michael Wolfe. He will be portraying our fake CEO. I think you'll like his background. Retired Marine sniper, fluent in Hebrew, German, and several of the Middle-Eastern languages, plus he has a degree in international business from Georgetown."

Benedict "Sandy" Knoll, a retired special forces major and now one of the owners of KKG, could best be described as a large man with bulging biceps. They stretched the sleeves of an untucked black polo shirt that hung over faded blue jeans. He kept his dark-blond hair cut short, allowing the streaks of gray to blend in above his ears. His handsome, weathered face was permanently tanned from too many tours of duty in Iraq and Afghanistan. He assessed the man before him. This morning, his normal mirrored Ray-Ban sunglasses were replaced with a pair of bifocals. As the two men shook hands, he tilted his head slightly. "Marine, uh?"

"Yes." Wolfe paused for a moment. "You look like you've seen a few deployments."

"A few."

"Army Special Forces?"

Knoll nodded and pointed to Gibbs. "Guess that means I'm outnumbered. Jimmie there is a retired Navy SEAL, and I was just a simple Green Beret."

A smile graced Wolfe's lips as he looked at the slender man. Jimmie Gibbs' swimmer physique provided a sharp contrast to Knoll's bulk. Swimming was a passion for Gibbs, and he still held several SEAL Team records for endurance and distance. After retiring from the Navy, the native Southern Californian wandered around the country for a while and finally settled in Southwest Missouri. Today, he wore his usual casual wardrobe: cargo shorts, linen shirt, and sandals. Blue eyes rounded out his handsome features. The retired Navy SEAL was now married with a one-year-old son.

"Which team?"

"Three."

"Gentlemen, I'm going to enjoy working with you." Wolfe faced Kruger. "JR said you have a plan."

"The beginnings of one." Kruger pointed to the coffee machine on a bench in KKG's conference room in their building on the business side of the Springfield Branson National Airport. "Grab a cup, and I'll go over what I have so far. Suggestions are more than welcome."

As Wolfe poured his coffee, JR breezed into the room with an open laptop in his hands. "Sorry I'm late."

"No problem, JR. I just introduced Michael." Kruger looked at each man sitting at the round table. "The plan isn't finalized. The purpose of this meeting is to put our heads together and refine it."

Everyone at the table nodded.

"I'll start with the timeline. We lucked out. Hunter Holden is booked to be at the annual Prospectors and Developers Association of Canada, referred to as PDAC, scheduled for Toronto in four weeks. This is a gathering of banking executives, investors, geologists, mining company CEOs, and vendors. From what JR told me, there will be over twenty thousand attendees from one hundred and thirty countries. And Kaphar Sourcing will be making an appearance." Nodding his head at Wolfe, Kruger continued. "Michael will pose as the CEO. His main job is to make contact with Holden. JR is creating a website for Kaphar portraying it as a reorganized and up-and-coming mining company."

Wolfe asked, "How are we going to get around the fact that everyone at this convention will be seasoned mining and geological professionals and will have never heard of Kaphar?"

"That's one of the shortcomings of the plan right now."

Wolfe frowned.

Jimmie Gibbs spoke for the first time. "Why not find a few defunct mining companies and figure out how to make it look like they joined together to rebrand themselves as Kaphar Sourcing?"

The room suddenly grew quiet. The only sound came from JR typing on his keyboard. He looked up and gave everyone a grin. "Jimmie's suggestion is perfect. In just a few seconds, I've found three companies we could use. I'm sure I can find more."

Knoll spoke next. "How much seed money do we need to get this thing started?"

"None." All eyes fell on Kruger. "Tucker, Neal and Spencer are on board to provide whatever financial needs we might require. While I was in Nathan Tucker's office yesterday, he discovered his company had dealt with Hunter Holden before. And not in a good way. In fact, he is having an audit conducted to see how many claims Transnational Financial might be involved in. He suspects, if there are others, they could be fraudulent as well. I told him if the plan worked, they might be able to recover at least some of the millions of dollars they have paid out to Transnational over the past decade."

Gibbs' eyebrows rose. "Millions?"

"Yes, Jimmie, at least forty million. Tucker seems to think it could be more. That's the total he found during the brief time I spent in his office."

Wolfe asked, "How big is Transnational?"

JR looked up from his computer. "Since it's a private company, Transnational doesn't publish financial data, but Forbes ranks Holden in the top 500 richest men in the world."

"Forty million dollars is a drop in the bucket for someone like him."

Kruger nodded. "Correct, Michael. That's why we're going to expose him for what he really is."

"And what's that?"

"A psychopathic criminal who has lied, cheated, and ordered the deaths of individuals for the sake of making a profit."

Knoll drummed his fingers on the conference table. "Sean, then why the charade of Kaphar Sourcing? Why not prove he's a killer and leave it at that?"

"I originally thought that would be the way we had to play it. But his casual disregard for all the individuals involved in the diamond heist caused me to change my mind. He needs to lose the profit as well."

JR chuckled. "Are you now the judge and jury, Sean?"

"Maybe, but unless we stop him, who will?"

"What if he comes after you?"

With a smile, Kruger pointed at Wolfe and then Gibbs. "I've got two of the best snipers ever produced by the US military on my side."

Wolfe folded his arms and leaned back. "How will he know you are involved?"

"I plan on telling him."

With a hearty chuckle, Wolfe continued. "JR told me your plan would be bold. I didn't know it would also be suicidal.

Are you going to tell him before or after we take his money?"

"Definitely afterward. It will be far more effective that way. The only thing I will regret is not being able to slap the cuffs on him."

***

By midmorning, the five men determined they had a workable plan. During this time, JR finished getting the new company paperwork and history solidified. He then explained the structure of the new company.

"The website for Kaphar Sourcing is ready to go online. Just tell me when, and I can hit the publish button."

Kruger looked around the room, and everyone nodded. "Do it."

"Done."

"Now, tell us what Holden will see when he looks at it."

"I am positioning the company through the website as a newly organized innovator in autonomous mining operations. This solves two issues we need to be concerned with. The first is employees. We can hide the fact we don't have many with this approach. The second one is the potential for growth in the future. This will give us a strategic advantage over other mining companies and build the case for Holden to invest."

Wolfe nodded. "That's good, JR. In my experience, private equity firms are more interested in the potential for growth versus current revenues."

Before speaking, Kruger looked at each man around the table. "I would prefer those of us who will be interacting with Holden on a face-to-face basis to have an alternate identity." Kruger paused for a second. "How do you all feel about it?"

Gibbs shrugged. "Either way, I don't care. I'm not scared of him."

Knoll said, "Neither am I. But I do see the benefit of

having alternate IDs."

"Already handled, gentlemen." JR turned his laptop around and showed them the company website where it pointed out the leadership team. "Michael, you are classified as the CEO. Your alternate ego is Michael Lyon."

"I already have IDs in that name."

"I know. That's why I chose it."

With a slight grin, Wolfe nodded.

"Jimmie, you and Sandy are identified on the website as chief geologists. Sandy's name will be Benedict Hill and yours is James Welch."

Knoll rolled his eyes. "You're kidding me. Hill?"

JR shrugged. "Yeah, what's bigger than a knoll? A hill."

With a smile, Kruger said, "JR will have all the appropriate legends prepared on the assumption Holden will have someone do a background check."

Sandy focused his attention on Kruger. "What about you, Sean?"

"I will be posing as Michael's assistant at the trade show. I want to be able to observe Holden up close without suspicion. The more I can glean from their interaction, the better I can anticipate his actions over the course of this operation."

Wolfe said, "We have to anticipate Holden will have us all checked out."

"I'm anticipating that, Michael." JR typed on his laptop. "In fact, I will be disappointed if he doesn't." He turned the laptop around again. "Each one of you will have a profile on the website, and every detail can be independently verified."

"JR, tell them about our bank account." Kruger smiled as he said it.

"If Holden has someone look into the company, he will find it financially stable. With the help of Tucker, Neal and Spencer, we have a mirror image financial structure. In reality, the only assets existing for the company is the stock, but if Holden runs a check on Kaphar, he'll see a financially sound company."

Wolfe added, "If we can get him interested in pursuing a takeover bid, we can inflate our asking price."

Tapping his finger on his lips, Kruger said, "How much do you think we can get out of him?"

"If we do this right, we could get him to throw a half-billion or more at us."

Kruger's eyebrows shot up. "A half-billion dollars?"

"If not more."

"If he goes for it, where does the money go?" This from Gibbs.

JR smiled. "For their part in this charade, Tucker, Neal and Spencer will get all the money they paid out in claims to Transnational over the years. Sean wants to use the rest of it to reimburse as many of Hunter Holden's victims as we can find."

Everyone around the table nodded in agreement.

CHAPTER 17

Toronto, Canada
Four Weeks Later

The Metro Toronto Convention Centre, on the shores of Lake Ontario, occupies two buildings. The north building contains three exhibit halls while the south building offers an additional four larger ones. The total size of the facility amounts to 442,000 square feet, which equals a little over 41,000 square meters.

Every year, the Prospectors & Developers Association of Canada (PDAC), established in 1932 to represent the interests of the Canadian mineral exploration and development industry, meets in Toronto at the Metro Convention Centre. The event will regularly attract up to 25,000 attendees from more than 130 countries.

Into this unique environment, Kruger and JR navigated the first day of the trade show by visiting the exhibition floor. As they toured the many vendors, JR spoke softly to his friend. "Do you understand any of this, Sean?"

"Not really. But I'm starting to get the gist of what the convention's all about. It appears a perfect setting for what we intend to do." He stopped walking and pointed toward a vendor to their left. "For example, that company is openly requesting appointments with investors and, from what I read in the exhibitor guide, there are several private equity companies who have their own booths."

"So, we have competition for Holden's attention."

"Of course, we do. But we aren't going to play fair. Michael said he was checking to determine where Hunter Holden's hotel room is located."

"Holden's at the Ritz-Carlton just north of the convention center."

"He knows that. He's attempting to get a room on the same floor."

JR chuckled. "He could have asked me. That would have been easier."

"You know him better than I do."

"Not really. I've helped him a few times, but he likes to do things his own way."

"Kind of what I gathered from talking with him." He paused as they continued their tour of the exhibits. "I spoke to Joseph about him."

"And?"

"He told me to trust him explicitly."

"I remember he told me the same thing several years ago."

***

Wolfe studied the hallway through the security peephole in his hotel room door. He waited for a certain individual to walk past on his way to the bank of elevator doors in the center of the building. His room, obtained with the help of his wife, Nadia, an up-and-coming computer hacker, was across the hall and closer to the elevators than Holden's. This allowed him to strategically wait for the man to pass his room and then fall into step behind him.

When this specific individual walked past, Wolfe opened his door, let it shut, and fell into step several paces behind his target. Arriving at the elevator bank, they stood next to each other and waited for one of the doors to open. Neither man acknowledged the existence of the other. Both stared at the doors. When one on their left opened, Holden quickly walked into the empty space and pressed a floor button. Wolfe followed, saw which button had been pressed, and just nodded. Still, no words were exchanged.

Both wore expensive suits, Wolfe sans a tie, Holden with a black-and-gold Armani tie which accented his dark-gray Armani suit. The man stood four inches taller than Wolfe's five-foot-ten frame. Slender like Wolfe, he exhibited zero interest in talking to the ex-Marine sniper now posing as a business executive.

When the elevator door opened on the ground floor, the two men were assaulted with the din of multiple conversations emitted by the crowd milling about in the hotel lobby. Allowing Holden to step out first, Wolfe followed close behind. If the opportunity arose, he would instigate the next phase of their plan.

The line for the hotel shuttle bus appeared long and time consuming. Holden glanced at his watch and looked around for another method of transportation.

Wolfe stepped up and said, "I have a car waiting. Would you like a ride?"

Their target looked over Wolfe with a questioning eye. "Depends, where you're going?"

"PDAC, and you?"

"Same. How long do we have to wait?"

With a slight grin, Wolfe said, "It's waiting out front. You want a ride or not?"

After a momentary hesitation, Holden nodded. "Yes, thank you."

"Then follow me."

When the two men exited the hotel, several shuttle buses

took up most of the space beneath the portico. Wolfe pointed to a black Mercedes S Class sedan with Jimmie driving. "That's our ride."

Holden nodded and raised an eyebrow. "Nice car."

"Thank you, it's the company's."

After they entered the back seat, Holden examined the interior. He then offered his hand to Wolfe. "Hunter Holden with Transnational Financial."

Wolfe shook the offered hand. "Michael Lyon, Kaphar Sourcing."

As Jimmie pulled the luxury sedan away from the curb, Holden continued. "What may I ask is Kaphar Sourcing, Mr. Lyon?"

"We are a forward-looking mining company introducing and utilizing automated mining techniques. Most of our systems are revolutionary, utilizing state-of-the-art technology."

"You have your introductory statement down pat."

Wolfe nodded. "Not memorized. It's what we do." He paused for a moment. "What is Transnational Financial?"

"We are an investor group, seeking to help aggressive, forward-looking companies reach their full potential."

"I see. What are your criteria for this type of help, Mr. Holden?"

"A thorough examination of the company's assets and potential for growth."

Handing Holden a business card, Wolfe smiled. "Maybe we should schedule a meeting. We are looking for investors for the next phase of our expansion. Check out our website and see if you are interested. If you are, have your people set up a meeting."

As the Mercedes pulled up to the entrance at the Metro Toronto Convention Centre, Holden slipped the card into his shirt pocket. "I'll do that, Mr. Lyon. Thank you for the ride." He opened his passenger door and slipped out of the luxury sedan.

As he watched the man disappear into the crowd, Wolfe said, "Think he bought it, Jimmie?"

"I did. I was ready to give you a check."

With a chuckle, Wolfe exited the car and followed Holden into the convention center.

***

From a corner of the lobby leading to the vendors' exhibits, Kruger watched Hunter Holden cross the room toward a door where credentials were checked. He moved closer to the door as Wolfe appeared next to him. Kruger asked, "Did it work?"

"He has my business card. If we don't hear from him by this evening, we'll try again tomorrow. But in my opinion, he'll have someone get in touch with us."

"Think I should follow him around?"

"That's up to you. He'll recognize me."

Taking a step toward the door, Kruger smiled. "I'll keep you posted."

After his credentials were cleared, he entered the hall and immediately saw Holden talking to two men in similar expensive suits. Keeping his distance, he managed to stay within twenty-five feet of his target.

Over the course of several hours, Holden roamed the convention floor stopping at random booths, spending a few moments conversing with the occupants and then moving on. Curious about the conversations, Kruger followed the man to one of the larger booths and stood behind him as he eavesdropped on the conversation.

Holden said, "I understand your company is looking for additional investors?"

A tall, burly man with a heavy beard and biceps stretching the sleeves of his sport coat crossed his arms. "Aye, laddie. But not from the likes of you. I know your reputation."

The surprised executive narrowed his eyes. "What's that

supposed to mean?"

"Hunter Holden, CEO of Transnational Financial, I've had dealings with you before. I'm surprised you don't recognize me. But I was with a South African diamond company you invested in about a decade ago. Next thing we know, you own the majority of the stock and fire all of us." The big man leaned over and poked a finger toward Holden's face. "Get the fuck out of my booth before I throw you out."

"You haven't heard my proposal."

"Nay, and I don't want to hear your lies." He leaned even closer. "Now, get out."

Not backing down, Holden stood his ground. He glanced at the bigger man's name badge and said, "Look— McGregor, I'm sure the situation was not as bad as you remember. I treat all of my clients with respect."

Kruger could see the face of the bearded man grow crimson. Knowing what might come next, the retired FBI agent interrupted. "Excuse me, gentlemen. I couldn't help but overhear your disagreement."

Holden looked at Kruger with a frown, turned, and quickly walked away.

The big Scotsman turned to Kruger. "Thanks, I was about to do something I would have later regretted. Although, at the time, it would have felt justified."

"What'd he do?"

"He's a thieving predator. Stay clear of him, laddie."

"Thanks for the advice. I will." Kruger turned and followed Hunter into the crowd.

CHAPTER 18

Toronto, Canada

Hunter Holden ignored those around him as he walked rapidly toward the exhibition hall exit. The encounter with the Scotsman had unnerved him. Not recognizing the man until too late, his lack of paying attention could have resulted in an unfortunate incident. Once clear of the crowded-and-noisy vendor section, he walked to the patio area next to the circle drive. He folded his arms and stared out toward Lake Ontario to the southeast.

His thoughts were interrupted a few moments later. The man who defused the encounter with the Scotsman stood next to him.

"Sorry to have interrupted your conversation, but the big guy looked like he might have gotten violent at any second."

Turning to the newcomer, Holden nodded. "Yes, he was rather agitated."

"Are you okay?"

"Yes, thank you." Regaining his dignity, Holden offered his hand. "Hunter Holden. I didn't catch your name."

"Sean Lyon."

Tilting his head, slightly, the CEO of Transnational Financial replied, "Do you have a brother attending the conference?"

"Yes, we are here looking for investors. How do you know my brother?"

"He offered me a ride this morning."

"He's like that. Always trying to solve the world's problems by himself."

"Kind of like you?"

With a slight grin, Kruger shook his head. "He's more altruistic than I am. I just don't like seeing big guys gang up on those of us who aren't as large."

"Are you also involved with Kaphar Sourcing?"

Kruger raised an eyebrow. "He told you about our company?"

"A little. But not enough." He pulled the business card out of his shirt pocket. "He gave me this and a two-sentence mission statement. Would you like to elaborate?"

Glancing at his watch, Kruger smiled. "I would love to, but I have an appointment with an investor in five minutes. If I don't leave now, I'll be late. It was nice to meet you, Mr. Holden." Turning, the ex-FBI agent returned to the exhibition hall.

Holden stared at the business card and then tapped it on his hand. He pulled his cell phone from his suit coat pocket and punched in the number displayed under the name of Michael Lyon.

***

Wolfe checked the cell phone ID. He smiled as he accepted the call. "Michael Lyon."

"Michael, this is Hunter Holden. You were kind enough to offer me a ride this morning."

"Yes, I remember. Are you enjoying the conference?"

"You mentioned this morning you were looking for

investors. Can we meet?"

"I'm on my way to an appointment at the moment. What is your schedule like tomorrow?"

"I have a better idea. Do you and your brother have dinner plans?"

"How do you know…"

"He and I bumped into each other. Now, what about dinner?"

There was silence on the phone for several heartbeats.

"I'm sure we can work something out. Where would you like to meet?"

"The hotel has excellent room service. My hotel suite tonight at, let's say seven."

"I'll make sure we're there."

Kruger walked up just as Wolfe ended the call. "That was Holden. What did you say to him?"

"Not a lot. He and a big Scotsman got into a terse discussion, and I intervened. The guy was bigger than Sandy Knoll. From what I overheard, he had a previous unpleasant encounter with Holden and wanted a pound of flesh."

"Well, it did the trick. We received an invite to dinner with him tonight."

"Where?"

"His hotel suite."

"Excellent. Even better than we hoped."

"Not sure I like it. We'll be in his territory. I would prefer a more neutral location."

"Relax, Michael. We'll have his undivided attention. If we play our cards right, we can hook him tonight."

Wolfe smiled.

***

Dean Melton handed Holden a sheet of paper. "A cursory search for Kaphar Sourcing is encouraging, Hunter."

Skimming the page quickly, the CEO handed it back to

his assistant. "Yes, it is. I'm curious about something. Was it a coincidence about meeting the brothers so suddenly, or did they plan it? Plus, why have we never heard of this company before?"

"My guess would be they're a privately held company. Those generally fly under the radar and don't draw too much attention to themselves."

"Yes, that is true." Holden paused for a moment and rubbed his chin. "Keep digging into their financial strengths and weaknesses. I need some leverage before they arrive for dinner."

"Yes, sir. The concierge is arranging the dinner for tonight."

"Good. I want another update from you thirty minutes before they arrive."

"You'll have it."

Melton turned and walked out of Holden's hotel suite. As soon as the door shut, Holden made a call on his cell phone. A familiar voice answered.

"Yeah."

"I need some information on two individuals, and I need it yesterday."

"It'll cost you."

"With you, it always does." Holden heard a slight chuckle from the phone.

"Give me the names."

"Michael and Sean Lyon, brothers. They own a company called Kaphar Sourcing. Find out what you can. I'm having dinner with them tonight, and I want to know if they're legit."

"I'll see what I can discover."

The call ended and Holden walked to a large window facing the southeast. With his hands behind his back, he gazed out over Lake Ontario, not seeing the water.

***

Kruger stood with his arms folded, and Wolfe lounged on a sofa in his hotel room. JR stood before them with a smile on his face.

"Traffic to the website picked up dramatically today. Multiple hits from here in Toronto and additional ones coming out of Minnesota and Illinois."

With a frown, Kruger asked, "Where in Illinois?"

"Chicago."

With a glance at Wolfe and then back to JR, he continued. "Who's in Chicago?"

Wolfe stood and walked to the small kitchen area of his hotel suite and retrieved a bottle of water. "If I had to guess, probably someone involved with the museum heist. Maybe even the planner."

JR nodded. "That would make sense, but there's no way to confirm it."

Folding his arms, Wolfe continued. "Holden might consider running into both the brothers within a few hours of each other a possible setup?"

Kruger said, "I didn't think of that, but I agree with you, Michael. We might have been too aggressive."

"You guys are being paranoid." JR closed his laptop. "So what if he does. Weirder things than that can happen."

"Yes, they can. But we are dealing with a psychopath. He will have his guard up when we meet with him tonight."

Wolfe said, "Then we can't act too desperate to make a deal. If he discusses it, we'll have to remain neutral to his proposal."

"Maybe we turn down his first offer." Kruger pursed his lips. "We have to play hard to get. If we act like we don't like his proposal, his ego will take over and make him even more determined to strike a deal."

"Why do you think that?"

"Because he's a narcissist. He's incapable of believing anyone would turn him down. Once we do, it becomes a challenge for him to win. And he has to win, regardless of what it takes to do so."

With a smile, Wolfe added, "Who's playing the bad cop?"

"I'll take that role. Besides, I'll enjoy turning him down."

JR pushed his glasses farther up his nose. "Uh, guys, I thought it was the purpose of this exercise to get him to invest?"

"It is, JR. But Michael and I can't be too fast to accept any offer he makes. He's probably already suspicious of us because of the meetings this morning. With his personality, the more we push back, the more he will want to buy the company."

"If you say so, Sean."

The retired FBI agent gave his friend a grin. "Trust me on this, JR."

***

Following the introductions of Kruger and Wolfe as the Lyon brothers to Dean Melton by Holden, he said, "I hope you two don't mind including Dean in our conversation tonight. He is invaluable to me at Transnational."

Wolfe shook the man's hand. "Not at all. We look forward to our discussions."

Kruger, in the guise of Sean Lyon, merely smiled when they were introduced.

Holden motioned toward a man standing behind a portable bar. "Before we have dinner, please help yourself to a refreshment at the bar."

With a nod, Wolfe strolled over and ordered a beer, while Kruger shook his head. "No, thank you." He wandered over to a sofa in the room and sat. He bent over, adjusted his sock, and then leaned back.

The conversation centered around the conference until dinner arrived at 7:30. The four men sat at a table and, after being served, Holden said, "I'm very impressed with what I see concerning Kaphar Sourcing, gentlemen. Tell me more about your vision for the company."

Over the course of the meal, Wolfe covered various scenarios about the future of Kaphar Sourcing. On numerous occasions, he emphasized the company's commitment to automating the processes of mining as much as possible utilizing state-of-the-art technology.

When the dishes were cleared by hotel staff, Holden sipped coffee and asked, "What type of future investments do you perceive necessary to accomplish these goals, Michael?"

"My brother and I have different opinions on this matter. I, personally, would like to see us do an IPO. But Sean believes it's too early for that step."

Turning his attention to Kruger, Holden raised an eyebrow. "IPOs can generate considerable investment revenue. Why are you opposed to it, Sean?"

"I'm not comfortable going public. We risk a hostile takeover. With the business plan we have in place, I believe we can grow without taking the chance."

"How many shares are in the company?"

After taking a sip of his wine, Wolfe said, "Ten million, all owned by a family trust."

"What's the stock's value?"

Kruger folded his arms. "That's proprietary information, Mr. Holden."

"Gentlemen, I would need to know current value to determine how much I might need to invest. I'm afraid we would need to know this information to make an informed decision."

With a stern frown, Kruger looked at his make-believe brother. "Michael, I'm not comfortable discussing this any further without legal counsel present." He stood and left the hotel suite.

Wolfe rose to his feet. "You will have to excuse my brother. He is passionate about the company and concerned someone will move in and take it over. I do not share his concerns, but I must respect them. Thank you for an enlightening evening." He followed Kruger out the door.

CHAPTER 19

Toronto, Canada

Kruger and JR were waiting inside Wolfe's hotel room when the door opened and the ex-CIA operator slipped in.

Wolfe looked at Kruger. "Did you get it planted?"

"Yes, when you were getting a beer, I sat on the sofa. I was able to attach it to the bottom frame on the left side of the couch. JR tells me he heard everything we discussed at dinner."

"Holden looked extremely agitated after you left. He's not used to anyone going against his demands or requests."

"I could tell." He paused and chuckled. "Originally, I assumed he had more control over his actions. But apparently, his level of pathology is deeper than I realized. I saw him tense up and his eyes narrow multiple times. I wonder how far we can push him before he lashes out?"

"We don't want to push too far. Otherwise, he might walk away from the deal."

While Wolfe and Kruger discussed the meeting, JR returned to his laptop to see if the clandestine microphone had collected any additional conversations. Putting a wireless earbud in his ear, he listened to captured discussions in Holden's hotel suite. After five minutes, he said, "Gentlemen, I believe your plan is working. Holden sounds extremely pissed and continues to bark orders on the phone for his team to do a deep dive on Kaphar Sourcing."

"What will they find, JR?" Wolfe's question made JR smile.

"Everything they are looking for. As long as no one travels to Israel, we should be okay."

Wolfe frowned. "What's supposed to be in Israel?"

"Kaphar Sourcing World Headquarters."

With a chuckle, Wolfe said, "If we learn they are sending someone to check, leave that to me."

"Let's not leave anything to chance, Michael." Kruger paused for a moment. "There's a chance they could hire someone to find the headquarters and we'd never know about it."

Wolfe contemplated Kruger for a few moments and retreated to a bedroom with his cell phone in hand.

Looking over at his friend, Kruger continued. "This is where it gets complicated, JR. These guys are pros and know what to look for when evaluating a company. If our plan is to work, we need everything to be perfect out on the web."

"I know."

"Did Michael help you with it?"

A nod. "If I didn't know his background as an ex-Marine and working for the CIA, you would think he's a business exec with a serious case of OCD."

"Then, all we can do is wait."

**

The sound of a cell phone vibrating woke Kruger before dawn. Glancing at his nightstand, he grabbed the object and accepted the call. "Kruger."

"He took the bait."

"What do you mean, Michael?"

"Holden sent an email late last night requesting a meeting. Just me and him. He emphasized you were not invited."

"Interesting. Have you answered yet?"

"No. Waiting for a more appropriate hour."

Looking at the clock on his phone, Kruger saw that it was just past five thirty. "How do you want to play it?"

"I accept and listen."

"Agreed."

"Someone visited the world headquarters for Kaphar Sourcing early this morning Israeli time."

"What'd they find?"

"The offices of Kaphar Sourcing, courtesy of a friend of mine who works for the Mossad."

Kruger laughed out loud. "Well played, Michael."

Ending the call, Kruger swung his legs over to sit on the side of the bed. He checked emails and found one from one of his contacts at the FBI, Charlie Craft, now the Executive Assistant Director for Science and Technology Branch. He read the email twice, smiled, and called JR's cell phone.

"Do you know how early it is, Sean?"

"Yeah, payback for all those times you called me in the middle of the night."

"Touché. What happened?"

"Email from Charlie Craft."

"And?"

"Apparently, Hunter Holden did something last night that set off alarm bells in Washington. I asked Charlie to monitor the man's emails and let me know if anything strange popped up."

"Uh-oh, what happened?"

"Before we got here, I gave Charlie the name I would be using. Apparently, Holden is hiring someone to put me under surveillance."

"That's not good."

"No, it's not. Holden doesn't want me to leave Toronto alive."

The phone call went silent as JR digested the revelation from his friend. "Can Charlie have Holden arrested?"

"Due to the surveillance being illegal, probably not. But it does give us an edge. We know about it."

"Any word on how?"

"No, but it's supposed to look like an accident."

"Time to bring in Sandy and Jimmie, Sean."

"Yeah, I would have to agree. Michael is having a meeting with Holden sometime today. I wasn't invited."

"Does he need someone to go with him?"

"I think Michael can take care of himself."

"Yeah, I would agree."

***

The meeting with Hunter Holden occurred a few minutes after 10 a.m. in the hotel coffee shop. Wolfe arrived alone to find Holden and Dean Melton waiting for him. When he sat across from the Transnational CEO, the congeniality of the previous night's meeting no longer existed.

Holden was very blunt with his opening statement. "I want to buy your brother out."

Wolfe's mouth twitched. "Why?"

"Kaphar Sourcing has a brilliant and profitable future but not with someone afraid to look at new opportunities."

Crossing his arms, Wolfe narrowed his eyes. "Our stock is held in trust, and both he and I would have to agree to the sale."

"I would assume there is a TOD clause within the trust."

"Is that a threat, Mr. Holden?"

"A business proposition. I would suggest you inform your brother that unless he agrees to sell his shares, the clause might be invoked."

Wolfe narrowed his eyes. "Is this how you conduct

business?"

"When I want something like Kaphar Sourcing, it is."

"How much are you offering for our shares?"

"Ten million shares, ten dollars a share."

Closing his eyes, Wolfe chuckled. "Par value is twenty. You'll have to do better than ten for me to even contemplate your offer."

"Your brother will be dead."

"Then you'll never get the stock."

"Thirty dollars a share."

Wolfe stood. "I can tell you one thing. We've been offered five hundred million for the company and turned it down without even thinking about it. When you decide to make an intelligent offer, contact me." He leaned forward and placed his hands on the table. "Let me explain something. If anything happens to my brother, and I mean anything, I've been in the mining business for a long time. There are a lot of individuals out there of questionable integrity who owe me. Think about it, Holden. Do you want to take that chance?" He turned and walked out of the coffee shop. As soon as his back was to the billionaire, a brief smile appeared on his face.

***

Hunter Holden remained silent, his face a deep crimson, as he took the elevator to the floor of his hotel. Dean Melton stood next to him, knowing anything he might say would be detrimental to his future employment by Transnational Financial.

When they entered the luxury suite, Holden exploded. "Who in the hell does this Lyon family think they are? They're simple miners, and they're threatening me." He paced in the center of the living area, breathing hard. He paused and stared hard at Melton. "Don't you have anything to say?"

"It would only piss you off more than you already are."

"Dammit, Dean, say something."

"You did threaten Lyon first. It's unlike you to be so irrational around someone you are trying to convince to sell their company."

"The brother pissed me off last night."

"So, you threaten to kill him in front of his brother. Some people aren't intimidated by those types of theatrics, Hunter."

Holden's ragged breathing slowed. As he walked toward the window in the suite, it became more regular. He stood in front of it, his hands behind his back, and remained quiet for an extended period.

Finally, he turned. "Have our attorney draw up a contract for seven hundred and fifty million to buy Kaphar Sourcing. Deliver it personally to Michael Lyon. I'm flying back to Minneapolis this afternoon. If they balk at the price, offer them nine hundred million but no more. We can cover that with cash reserves."

"You sure?"

"Yes, from what I've been told by our analysts in Minneapolis, the company could be worth two billion in less than five years." He paused. "Make this a simple stock purchase. I want the Kaphar Sourcing, and I want it before they realize what they've done."

Melton nodded and left the hotel suite.

***

Twenty-Four Hours Later

"Mr. Holden apologizes for his antics. He has been under a lot of stress lately."

Wolfe looked at the contract. "This is a simple purchase of stock, not an investment."

"That is correct."

"So, he will not be keeping my brother and I on as management?"

"That is also correct."

"Any reason?"

"He has a stable of extremely talented executives who he feels will be better suited to increase the profitability of the company. Plus, he will be able to provide the inflow of cash for capital expenditures."

"I see. My brother told me his price to sell is nine hundred and fifty million."

"Mr. Holden is offering seven hundred and fifty million."

"No deal. My brother was emphatic. No deal below nine fifty."

Melton pursed his lips. "Let me make a phone call." He stood and left the lobby coffee shop and stood in the lobby with the phone pressed to his ear. Wolfe watched the animated conversation with amusement. The man paced, waved his hands in the air, nodded occasionally, and then straightened. He stared ahead, said something and then ended the call. When he arrived back at the table where they sat, he said, "Nine hundred, no more. Final offer."

Wolfe smiled. "My brother left this morning but gave me power of attorney. Your offer is accepted. Stock will be transferred to Transnational Financial upon the receipt of the purchase price of nine hundred million dollars to an account of our choosing. Correct?"

"Yes."

"Very well. Make the necessary changes in the purchase price and I'll sign."

"Give me an hour to get the contract rewritten, and I will meet you back here at 11 a.m."

***

Wolfe signed two copies of the contract and then handed both back to Melton. "I take it you have a notary available."

"I do." Melton turned to his left and waved a young woman standing outside the coffee shop. She hurried to the table and watched as Holden's assistant signed the document. She stamped the documents and initialed them. Melton then handed one of the copies to Wolfe. "Transfer of funds should be completed by close of business tomorrow."

"As soon as we have notification the funds are in place, stock will be transferred to your attorney."

"Then we have an agreement, Mr. Lyon."

Wolfe accepted the contract from Melton. "Yes, it appears we have."

CHAPTER 20

Minneapolis
One Week Later

Hunter Holden crossed the lobby of the building containing the offices of Transnational Financial toward the bank of elevators in the center of the structure. Once there, he stayed behind three men already waiting for a door to open. The man on the left, large and bulky, the one on the right, slender and athletic. The man in the middle resembled someone the CEO had crossed paths with recently. As soon as Holden stood behind them, all three men turned.

The one in the middle said, "Good morning, Hunter."

The CEO inhaled involuntarily and glared at the man. "What do you want, Lyon? The deal is done."

"I'm very much aware of that. Have you thought to check on the status of the stock on the Tel Aviv Stock Exchange this morning. It was listed last night." The glare Kruger received made him chuckle. "You might want to know the stock is worthless." He paused. "Well, that's not exactly correct. It's worth about a penny a share today, not sure how much it will be worth tomorrow. Maybe nothing."

The owner of Transnational stayed quiet, but his breathing grew rapid and erratic.

"I think your analysts missed something when they examined the books and may have overvalued it in their initial assessment. You might want to have them reevaluate it." With those words, Kruger walked away, followed by Sandy Knoll and Jimmie Gibbs.

Holden watched them retreat across the lobby and out the front door. An elevator arrived and he rushed into the empty car. When it reached his floor, the doors barely opened before he rushed to his office and picked up the phone. His assistant Dean Melton answered. The CEO screamed, "Get in here."

By noon, Hunter Holden understood the investment he spent nine hundred million dollars on could now be valued at only one hundred thousand. Exactly who perpetrated the con now seemed to be in question. The existence of the two Lyon brothers could not be confirmed. Plus, all the financial records and structure of a company called Kaphar Sourcing suddenly did not exist. Even their offices in Tel Aviv were gone. Instead of a busy mining company headquarters, there stood an empty building with a For Lease sign in the window.

Holden's attorney arrived a few minutes past twelve. When he entered the conference room, Holden handed the man a file folder, crossed his arms, and said, "Well?"

The lawyer accepted the file, found a chair, and reviewed the contents. After five minutes of silence, he looked up at the CEO. "You're basically screwed, Hunter."

"What do you mean, screwed?"

"The transaction took place in Canada, and the stock is only listed on the Tel Aviv Stock Exchange. There are no records of the company existing inside the United States. Plus, as this summary indicates, all the paperwork you have for the transaction no longer exists on the Internet for confirmation. Even if you file a lawsuit in both Canada and

Israel, a good defense attorney could make the argument all of your evidence has been manufactured."

"What about the two Lyon brothers?"

"What about them?"

"They need to be prosecuted."

"By whom and for what? The police would have to locate and identify them as suspects before they could be charged with a crime. From what you've presented in this file, they don't exist. Plus, I'm not sure you can prove a crime has been committed, except maybe fraud."

Holden's breathing became rapid as he clenched his fists and glared at his attorney.

"Even if you sue, a case could be made you purchased the stock in haste without confirming the true owner and value of the asset. The stock you claim to have purchased does exist. However, I'm not sure you can prove legal ownership at this point, either. The identity of whom you bought it from is in question." The attorney handed the file back to Holden. "You may have to face the fact you've been conned. A nine hundred-million-dollar mistake on your part." He paused as Holden glared at him. "I know that's not what you want to hear, but it happens to be the truth. Trust me, you probably will never recover the money."

With a growl, Holden said, "Get out. Your services are no longer needed."

With a shrug, the attorney walked out of the conference room, leaving Holden sitting at the head of the table staring at its polished surface. He looked up at Dean Melton who sat to his left at the table. "Find a new lawyer."

Melton stood. "Yes, sir."

***

The flight back to the Springfield Branson National Airport in the company plane gave Kruger time to think. Knoll sat across from him with Jimmie behind the big man.

135

Thirty minutes into the flight, Knoll said, "Any idea how he'll react once he knows the stock is worthless?"

"I'm sure he will contemplate legal action."

"How's that going to work? Nothing occurred in the United States."

"He also doesn't know who to sue. The stock for Kaphar Sourcing was valued at a penny a share when it hit the Tel Aviv Stock Exchange. I'm sure it has no value now because the company doesn't exist." Turning his attention to the outside of the plane, Kruger grew quiet for a few moments. "I don't know how he'll react. My guess is he'll bide his time, try to figure out who we are and then lash out."

Jimmie asked, "How could he discover who you two are? Michael runs under the radar, and you're not in the limelight anymore."

"No, Jimmie, I'm not. But there is always a chance someone will recognize me from some old news video."

"What are the odds?"

"I'd say not too great. But we can't take the chance. We need to prepare as if we know he'll find out. JR is working on it today."

"Where's the money?"

Giving his younger associate a smile, Kruger said, "JR dispersed the original deposit into a dozen accounts and then transferred those deposits four or five times. He told me the money is completely untraceable."

Knoll nodded. "He should know."

"Our original hundred thousand dollars, plus a nice profit, is back in our company account."

"How much profit?"

Kruger smiled. "After taxes, enough for each of us to pay off the mortgages on our homes."

Jimmie gave a low whistle. "Damn, Sean."

"Plus, JR used his share to pay for improved security at his new building."

"Good. What about the insurance company?"

"Tucker, Neal and Spencer have been reimbursed for all the claims they paid out to Transnational over the years, plus interest."

"What about the rest?"

"We offered a share to Michael, but he turned it down. He told JR he didn't need it and to use it elsewhere. So, JR made an anonymous donation to the Chicago Field Museum and set up a trust fund for the murdered stockbroker's kids. The rest was given to a children's hospital in Memphis."

"Sounds like it's doing some good."

"JR was pleased it worked out like it did."

Knoll and Jimmie nodded in agreement.

"Why did Michael turn the money down?" This from Knoll.

Kruger shrugged. "I'm told he doesn't need it, plus he and his wife aren't pretentious."

"What if Holden lashes out at him?"

"JR told me not to worry, his rural place is a fortress. Those were JR's words, not mine. Besides, he and his wife are planning a trip to Israel."

"Convenient." Knoll chuckled. "Maybe you and Stephanie should plan a trip."

With a shake of his head, Kruger said, "No, not my style. Besides, Michael's trip was already scheduled."

"It was?"

"Yes, they delayed the trip to help us. Apparently, there is a Jewish tradition of naming a child after an important relative. I asked Michael about it, and he told me his first wife's uncle, Ben Wasserman, was that individual. They were naming their son after him. He died a couple of years ago trying to help Michael and Nadia."

"Didn't know Michael was Jewish."

"He isn't, Nadia's parents were, but she's nonpracticing. He told me they do follow some of the traditions though."

Knoll turned and gazed out the window. "Huh."

Jimmie said, "You seem to know a lot about him, Sean."

"Not really. He's a quiet man. He told me about their trip and the reason for it the day he agreed to help us. I do, however, respect him and consider him a friend."

Turning to smile at Kruger, Knoll said, "And a good friend to have, I might add. I had a buddy look up his record."

Kruger raised an eyebrow. "Oh?"

"Yeah, he's considered the best sniper ever produced by the Marines. He has the citations to prove it."

"Huh."

Jimmie said, "Sean, getting back to Holden. What do you believe he will do if he finds out who planned our scam?"

"Oh, he'll find out."

Knoll cleared his throat. "Don't tell me you told him."

"No, not yet."

A chuckle came from Jimmie. "Then what?"

"We shut him down. The more I learned about him, the more dangerous I discovered him to be. I may not be an FBI agent any longer, but I still have connections. And one of those connections wants him in a federal prison."

"Why not turn it over to the FBI?"

"They can't touch him because Transnational Financial hasn't committed any crimes inside the US."

"What about Chicago?" Jimmie was now leaning forward in his seat.

"Technically, it was a South African company affected by the museum theft, and they have never filed a complaint with the agency."

"Want to tell us who the individual is that's taking an interest?"

"Sure, none other than the Director Ryan Clark."

PART TWO

Consequences

CHAPTER 21

Southwest Missouri

JR took possession of his newly rebuilt office building, without fanfare, on a quiet Friday afternoon at four thirty. He and Kruger walked through the building without hard hats for the first time since construction started.

"Should we toast this occasion with champagne, JR?"

"Not sure. It feels like rebuilding might be anticlimactic. The company is thriving with our team working remotely. Productivity is up, and I've heard through the grapevine no one is enthusiastic about physically returning to the building."

"So, what does that mean?"

"This facility could be a very expensive meeting location."

Kruger stood in front of the coffee service and folded his arms. "At least you upgraded the coffee machine."

"That was Mia's idea."

"Tell her thank you."

Smiling, JR poured two cups of coffee. He handed one to Kruger. "Let me know if that comes up to your high standards."

After taking a sip, the ex-FBI agent nodded. "I approve."

"My heart is aflutter."

"Seriously, JR, are you going to keep the building?"

"My accountant thinks I should. He said it's a great tax write-off."

"Worth the upkeep?"

With a shrug, JR took a sip of his coffee. "Hey! That is better."

"Told you." Kruger paused and took another sip. "Let me run something past you."

"Sure."

"What if KKG leased out the second floor?"

One of JR's eyebrows rose. "Why?"

"We're outgrowing our space at the airport, and Steph is getting tired of me coming home smelling like jet fuel."

"Isn't it a farther drive for Sandy and Jimmie?"

"I asked them, and they don't mind. Sandy is only in the office a few days a month, and Jimmie told me he and Alexia could drive in together and save gas by only using one car in their Stockton-to-Springfield commute. There's another reason as well. We've decided to lease a second company plane. We bought the building and need to convert it into hangar space."

"Already spending your profits?"

"No, this was in the works before we looked into Hunter Holden. The influx of cash just hastened the execution of the plan."

"What about Alexia and me?"

"Nothing would change there. You are considered a consultant to KKG, as is Alexia. I don't see why you can't keep your current offices located on this floor."

JR pursed his lips as he stared into his coffee cup. "That would solve a myriad of potential issues."

"Such as?"

"I really don't have a clue what to do with the first floor.

Except for a receptionist, there is really no need for the space. If you take over the second floor, I could transfer these cubicles to the first floor and utilize a couple as client meeting rooms."

"Sounds like a win-win for both companies."

"I hope you three don't want your name on the building?"

"Nope. We don't have our name on our current space. We like the anonymity of it. Besides, when we meet with clients, it is always at their offices."

JR offered his hand. "Sounds like a deal."

Kruger shook the offered hand. "Good, I'll tell Sandy and Jimmie."

The two remained quiet as JR busied himself at his cubicle and Kruger sipped coffee and paced off sections of the second-floor area.

After he returned to the coffee service and warmed his cup, he stepped over to JR's office. He leaned on the doorframe and asked, "Were you able to trace the money Holden used to pay for the stock?"

With a nod, JR turned to look up at Kruger. "A bank in Dubai. Why?"

"Was that where all of it originated?"

"No, that bank acted more as a clearinghouse. The funds were provided by five other institutions and then dispersed through the one in Dubai. You're going somewhere with this, aren't you?"

"Thinking."

"The Dubai bank took a substantial fee for dispersing the money."

"How much?"

"About a million."

Kruger gave a slight whistle. "Damn. That much?"

"Yes, which tells me some of the funds might not have been squeaky clean."

"Where else did the money come from?"

"Two of the largest banks in Europe, HSBC Holdings and

BNP Paribas, supplied about two-thirds of the total transaction."

"Could that be used to our advantage?"

"Don't know. I'm not privy to the arrangements he has with those two banks. Plus, another third of the funds came from numerous numbered accounts in Hong Kong and Switzerland."

"Holden's personal accounts?"

JR nodded. "Probably. I couldn't determine the source."

Kruger remained quiet, sipping his coffee. "How many Transnational bank accounts have you identified?"

"All of the ones involved with the stock purchase. Why?"

"Do you still have access to them?"

A smile from JR answered his question.

"How much money does he have left?"

"In total, over a billion."

Staring at his coffee, the ex-FBI agent-turned-fraud-investigator displayed a slight grin. "If you needed to, could you change the access codes on them?"

"Yes, but if you want to leave a message for Holden, it would be better just to transfer the money out and leave a balance of one penny."

With a smile, Kruger studied his friend. "You've done that before."

"I have."

"Is it possible?"

"Not only possible but simple."

"How long would it take?"

"Not that long." JR paused for a heartbeat. "You thinking what I'm thinking?"

"It depends. That's a lot of money."

"Yes, it is. You also have to remember, they just paid nine hundred million dollars for the stock. Not too many companies sit on that much cash."

"Apple does."

JR tilted his head. "Hunter Holden is not Steve Jobs, and

Transnational Financial is not Apple."

"True. Is there any way to tell if the cash you found is the majority of his liquid assets? If they are, denying him access could bring his company to a standstill."

"I only know about the accounts associated with the stock purchase, so no."

Looking up from inspecting his coffee mug, Kruger said, "Let's see what happens when he lacks access to those funds."

***

Dean Melton's morning ritual always included a check of the company's bank accounts in London, Paris, and Hong Kong. As he checked each account, bile rose in the back of his throat. Every account he accessed contained the same balance. The equivalent of one penny. He knew this news would not be well received by the CEO.

He rose and hurried to the boss' office. When he entered, he asked, "Did you close our accounts at HSBC and BNP Paribas?"

Looking up, Holden's expression gave him the answer. "Of course, not. Why would I do that without telling you?"

"As of this morning, each of our accounts in London, Paris, and Hong Kong have exactly one cent as a balance. Where did the money go?"

"How could..." Holden clenched his jaw as the veins in his neck popped out. He pounded on his computer keyboard. The more he typed, the darker crimson his face became. "What the hell? Who did this?"

"It wasn't me."

"I know that. Who would have access besides the two of us?"

"No one should. Do you think Interpol might have seized our assets?"

"Check the numbered accounts. I was told it would be

impossible for anyone to find them and associate them with our company." He stopped and stared at the computer monitor. His breathing becoming shallower and more rapid.

Melton glanced at his watch. "It's midafternoon in London. Let me call our representative over there and see if she can determine what happened."

Taking a quick glance at his second-in-command, Holden nodded.

***

"Ms. Fitzgerald, Transnational's accounts balances have been stolen. Could you check to see who accessed the accounts?"

"Mr. Melton, from what I can see, you were the one who authorized the transfers."

"That's impossible. Maybe it was Hunter Holden."

"No, sir. The authorization pin was yours."

Catching himself before he commented, Melton took a deep breath. "Perhaps there's a bank error. Could you..."

"I'm afraid it is not the bank's error. It clearly shows our security procedures were followed."

"Ms. Fitzgerald, I can assure you, I did not transfer the money."

"I can check one other option. Please provide your account security code."

"Alpha 95342."

There was silence on the call. "Uh, could you repeat that Mr. Melton?"

He did.

The woman did not reply, and he heard the distinct sound of the call being disconnected.

Pressing the redial button on his phone, he heard the same tedious instructions on how to get to a live individual. After five minutes, he had Ms. Fitzgerald on the phone again. "Do not hang up on me, again, Ms. Fitzgerald."

"I'm sorry, sir, but the security pin you gave me is incorrect. I will have to switch you to another department."

Before he could respond, an annoying instrumental rendition of an old pop song could be heard for five seconds and then a new voice. "This is Gerald. How may I help you today?"

"Gerald, this is Dean Melton with Transnational Financial. There seems to be a mistake with our account."

"I'd be happy to help you with that, Mr. Melton. Can you give me the account number?"

Melton gave him the requested information.

"The only problem I see is the balance is below our minimum."

"I'm aware of that, Gerald. That is why I'm calling."

"I'm sorry, sir, but with this low of a balance, these accounts will be closed when they update at midnight. Perhaps you have contacted the wrong bank."

"No, Gerald, I have not contacted the wrong bank." His voice rose an octave. "There was well over one hundred million US dollars in that account."

"I'm sorry, sir, but our records do not indicate this to be the case. Have a nice day."

The call ended, and Holden's assistant stared at the now-silent handset. Referring to his lists of accounts, he called BNP Paribas in Paris. A similar conversation occurred there as well as four more banks. Finally, after ending his call to a private bank in Switzerland, Melton had to accept that Transnational Financial was facing a liquidity issue.

When Melton returned to Holden's office, the CEO looked up. "Well?"

"Five of our larger accounts have a total balance of one penny each."

"That's impossible."

"Well, it may be impossible, but that's what it is."

"Find the gawd-damn money, Dean. Or look for another job."

Narrowing his eyes, Melton growled. "I know where the bodies are buried, Hunter. You sure you want to threaten me?"

Holden sat up straighter. He glared at his assistant for a few moments and then relaxed. "No, I'm not threatening you, Dean. But if we don't find that money, we will default on several notes coming due, which will basically be the end of the road for Transnational."

"I'm very aware of that, Hunter."

"Then find the money."

CHAPTER 22

Minneapolis

By 5 p.m., everyone in the Transnational Financial company knew a long night lay ahead. As the financial meltdown unfolded, all vacations were canceled, travel expenses rejected, pay cuts announced, and a besieged HR department prepared a layoff schedule.

The CEO sequestered himself in his office calling in notes due the company and having little success. After years of taking advantage of the various business leaders who entered into agreements with Holden, none seemed willing to speed up repayment on their outstanding debts just because Transnational needed an influx of cash. In fact, most wished him a quick bankruptcy, laughed, and then disconnected the call.

As night descended over the city of Minneapolis, Holden sent his staff home and sat in his office pouring Jim Beam over ice in a crystal highball glass. His mood darkened at the same pace as the evening sky.

His cell phone chirped. With no intention of answering, he glanced at the caller ID. He pressed the accept icon.

"Understand you've got a problem."

"Where are you?"

"Chicago, same as always."

"How fast can you get to Minneapolis?"

"Depends on how fast you can pay me. Word on the street is, you're a little short on cash."

"Don't trust rumors."

"I can be there in the morning. What've you got?"

"I need you to find someone."

"Who?"

"I'll tell you when you get here."

***

Dalton Hadley arrived at the Transnational Financial building a few minutes before noon the following day. Melton escorted him into Holden's office. When he entered, the CEO growled, "Thought you said you'd be here by morning."

Hadley glanced at his wristwatch. "It is still morning. You gonna tell me what you need, or do I drive back to Chicago?"

Pointing to the chair in front of his desk, Holden said, "Sit."

"Sure. I'm on the clock, by the way."

"Who investigated the museum incident?"

"You mean cops?"

"Who else would I mean?"

"Barnes was the name of the Chicago detective."

"Anyone else?"

"I'm told there was an insurance investigator?"

Holden frowned. "What was his name?"

"How the hell should I know?"

"Find out."

"Since you haven't offered an advance, and I'm not sure you've got the money to pay, I think I'll leave." Hadley stood and walked toward the door.

"Sit down, Dalton." Holden placed an envelope on his desk.

After looking over his shoulder, Hadley returned to the chair. He picked up the packet and thumbed through the contents. "Thought you were broke."

"I have other resources."

"This is a start. It's enough for me to find out who the insurance guy was. Why do you care?"

"He's the starting point. He might not be important, but I need more information about him. Plus, I need to know if the Chicago cop is still snooping around."

"Is that all?"

"No. I want to know who Michael and Sean Lyon are. They were introduced as brothers, but they don't look anything alike."

Hadley rolled his eyes. "I'll need more than just names."

"That's all I have at the moment. Except the name of the company, Kaphar Sourcing."

"I take it you ran into them in Toronto. Am I correct?"

"Yes."

"International travel will cost extra."

"Hadley, it's just north of Buffalo, New York."

"Still international travel. I'm not exactly welcomed in Canada."

"How much?"

"Couple of grand."

"Very well, but I expect results."

Hadley stood. "Always a pleasure doing business with you, Hunter. And by the way, expenses and incidentals are extra."

"Whatever."

***

Chicago
The Next Afternoon

Dalton Hadley opened the text message from a source within the Chicago Police Department. Cultivated years ago, the man, now a detective, still enjoyed receiving cash under the table to help offset what, in his mind, was a puny salary.

The cell phone photo of the top page of Detective Barnes' report, along with the text message from his inside source, gave him a few details about the museum heist but little else. He did notice the name of the museum's head of security. With this information in hand, he drove to the Field Museum.

Shaking the hand of Bob Haskins, Hadley introduced himself as Darren Smith, an advance agent for a traveling Native American antiquity exhibit looking for accommodating museums across the central United States.

"Thanks for talking to me. I apologize for not making an appointment."

"No problem. What can I do for you today, Mr. Smith?"

"We are looking for a venue that would be interested in displaying our exhibition. However, before we approach the curator, we want to make sure the security is state of the art."

Haskins crossed his arms. This was not the way the process worked. The organizers of an exhibition would approach the curator first and, if they were agreeable, then consult with the head of security. Smelling a scam, Haskins nodded thoughtfully. "I see. Do you have an appointment with our curator anytime soon?"

"Yes, day after tomorrow."

Now, Haskins knew it was a hoax. The museum's search to replace Margaret Ross, at this time, did not have any candidates identified. "Good. What do you need to know?"

"I understand there was a break-in over the Easter weekend this year."

"We did have an incident."

"Can you tell me how it was resolved?"

"Chicago police and an insurance investigator."

"Can you give me their names for reference?"

Haskins crossed his arms. "I'm afraid that is proprietary information."

Hadley raised an eyebrow. "I would need to consult with them if we are to consider your museum."

"The incident is still under investigation." Haskins moved his right hand toward the concealed Glock on his right hip. "How did you know about the break-in, Mr. Smith? It was never announced to the general public. In fact, only a few individuals know about it, and I can confirm you are not one of them."

"Well. I've never been treated like this before. I guarantee we will not bring our exhibition to this museum."

"Good. I doubt there is one."

***

Haskins watched as the fake exhibitor hurried out the front entrance of the museum. As the impostor disappeared, the security man pulled his cell phone out of his sport coat pocket and searched for a number in his contact list. Once found, he made the call.

"Kruger."

"Sean, it's Bob Haskins at the Field Museum."

"Hey, Bob. What's up?"

"Had a strange visitor just now."

"Oh?"

"Yeah, asking about the Easter break-in. Funny thing, the museum's never made a public statement concerning the incident. It's still under investigation."

"Huh." Kruger paused for a moment. "Any idea of who he might be?"

"None whatsoever. He did say his name was Darren Smith."

"I'm sure it wasn't."

"Kind of my thoughts also. Have you stirred up any leads on your end?"

Pausing for just a second, Kruger said, "Ever hear of a company called Transnational Financial?"

"As a matter of fact, I have."

"Really. How?"

"I heard they bought out Goldmax, the diamond company who owned the stolen exhibit."

"You would be correct. They did."

"Funny thing, Sean."

"What's that?"

"They dropped the lawsuit against the museum, claiming the diamonds might have been switched prior to arriving here."

"When did this happen, Bob?"

"Two weeks after you reported your findings to the insurance company."

Kruger paused for a few seconds. "Did your visitor mention Transnational Financial?"

"No, but he knew information he shouldn't have. You think this guy's involved with the Transnational company?"

"I would call it a safe bet. Do you think you got a picture of him on any of your security cameras?"

"There's one behind and above where I talked to him. I'm sure we got a good image. Want it sent to you?"

"Yeah, here's the email address."

***

Kruger leaned against the coffee service as JR ran the picture of the supposed Darren Smith through several facial recognition databases.

Looking up from his monitor, JR said, "He's not in the military or FBI databases."

"Did you try the Chicago PD?"

"No. Why, do you have a hunch?"

With a nod, Kruger pulled out his cell phone. Bob Haskins answered. "Did you ID him?"

"Nothing on national databases. Does the Chicago PD have a facial database?"

"Don't know. Have you asked Peter Barnes?"

"He'll ask where I got the picture."

Haskins smiled. "Got it. I'll send it to him. Your secret's safe with me."

The call ended, and Kruger took a sip of the cold coffee in his mug. "JR, do you have access to the Interpol database?"

A nod was his answer.

"Run it through that one."

Fifteen minutes later, they were staring at a mug shot of a Maurice Dubois from a Paris booking file. "What's his story, JR?"

"My French is rusty, but it seems he was arrested on drug and racketeering charges. It also says he left France after his last release from prison. That was ten years ago."

Kruger's cell phone buzzed, and he accepted the call. "Did you learn anything, Bob?"

Haskins said, "He's a known character to the Chicago PD. His real name is Maurice Dubois, but he goes by the name Dalton Hadley."

"What's he known for?"

"Drugs and extorsion, but he hasn't been arrested for over five years. Seems he went straight or he's working for someone."

"Interesting. Did Barnes have any other details?"

"Not a lot, other than he was used by one of the Chicago families as muscle."

"Really? For how long?"

"Off and on for a few years, but he's been off their radar for a while."

"Thanks, we'll take it from here. I appreciate the heads-up, Bob."

"My pleasure."

CHAPTER 23

Toronto, Canada

The agent at the Detroit-Winsor Tunnel examined the passport handed to him by Dalton Hadley. "Business or pleasure, sir?"

"Business."

"Destination?"

"Hamilton."

The agent smiled, stamped the passport, and handed it back to the driver. "Have a nice stay."

Hadley steered the car toward the entry of the mile-long tunnel. Less than two minutes later, he emerged and eventually headed northeast on the 401 for the four-hour drive to Toronto. After engaging the cruise control, Hadley made a call on his cell phone.

"What've you found, Dalton?"

"Thanks for telling me the museum hadn't reported the break-in, Hunter. The guy knew I was a phony the minute I opened my mouth."

"That's on your end, not mine. So, have you made any progress?"

"Tell me where you ran into the brothers you claim don't exist?"

"First encounter was at the Ritz-Carlton north of the Metro Toronto Convention Centre, why?"

"Thought I'd look through some security camera videos."

"Without the help of the police, how do you intend to do that, Dalton?"

"The old-fashioned way: money. I'm going to need access to cash."

Holden remained quiet for a moment. "How much?"

"Whatever it costs, that's how much."

More silence. "Very well. I'll put ten thousand in your account. You still have access to it, don't you?"

"Of course."

"Try not to spend it all, Dalton."

"It will cost what it costs. You want the information or not?"

"Very well. Make sure you get your money's worth."

After the call ended, Hadley chuckled. "You do have money problems, don't you, Holden?"

***

By two in the afternoon, Hadley walked through the Ritz-Carlton lobby on his way to check in. By his count, he found twelve security cameras. Some in plain sight and others well-hidden from the unsuspecting public. After obtaining the key to his room, he approached the concierge. "Excuse me."

"Yes, sir. How may I assist you?"

Looking at the attractive woman, Hadley almost flirted but held back. "Can you tell me what hours the Metro Toronto Convention Centre is open today?"

"Their business office is open until five. Do you need an appointment?"

"Could you make one for me?"

"Of course. Give me your name, room number, and cell

phone. I'll call you as soon as I have one secured. Are you available tomorrow morning?"

"That will work fine." Handing the woman a business card printed prior to his trip to Canada, he said, "Room 1209."

"Very good, sir."

After depositing his travel bag in his room, he returned to the lobby and positioned himself in the lounge with a direct view of the front desk. He sipped a beer and observed who accessed the offices behind the check-in station.

After nursing the beer for forty-five minutes, he identified an individual who appeared to be a disgruntled employee working the front desk. Paying his tab, he left and placed himself in a lobby chair close enough he could eavesdrop on the young man's conversations.

Thirty minutes later, he received confirmation of his assumption. An individual whose name badge proclaimed him to be the front-desk manager exchanged heated words with the employee. The gist of the conversation revolved around the young man's schedule. This included being by himself at the desk after 10 p.m. until the overnight manager arrived at midnight.

Hadley stood and returned to his room with a plan in place for later that evening.

***

At 10:33 p.m., Dalton Hadley introduced himself to the young man, whose name was Jeffrey. "Jeff, I'm trying to determine if two friends of mine stayed here a few weeks ago. Is that possible to find out?"

"Sure." He stepped in front of a computer terminal and asked, "What are their names?"

"Michael and Sean Lyon."

"Let me see. When were they supposed to be here?"

"They attended the Prospectors & Developers

Association of Canada conference."

"Let me see." He typed away and pursed his lips and then typed again. "I'm not seeing anyone by those names being registered. Are you sure they stayed here?"

"No, that was why I needed you to look it up."

"I'm not seeing anyone registered with those names. Sorry."

"No problem. Thanks for looking." He laid a hundred-dollar bill on the counter. "I appreciate you taking the time to check."

"Uh, sir. I appreciate the tip, but that's a little excessive."

"I overheard your conversation with your manager today, thought that might help."

The young man stared at the money and then it disappeared into his pants pocket. "I could look for your friends on our security videos?"

"Really. How would that work if they weren't registered?"

"You'd be surprised how many people register under a false name. Particularly with all the high-dollar guests we get."

"I don't have a picture of them, so how would you recognize them if they were here?"

The young man looked around the lobby and then back at Hadley. "I'm here by myself for another hour and a half. For a couple hundred dollars, I'd let you look."

"I don't know. Wouldn't want you to get in trouble."

"Don't worry about it."

"Okay." Hadley pulled three additional hundred-dollar bills out of his billfold, folded them, and handed them to the clerk. "What about the cameras trained on this desk?"

"Don't worry about them, either. Unless something weird happens, no one ever looks at them. Plus, in twenty days, the videotapes are recycled."

By eleven twenty, Hadley had what he needed. A printed image of Hunter Holden talking to a man who had just offered him a ride.

***

Posing as an attorney looking for a cheating husband, Hadley was granted access to the security videos of the Prospectors & Developers Association of Canada conference. Once introduced to the technician, he explained the real reason for the search.

The guy looked at him with bored eyes and just shrugged. "Makes no difference to me, dude. I can do the whole search if you want."

"How much?"

"Depends on how hard you want me to work?"

"What will a thousand US dollars get me?"

"A damn energetic search."

Dalton Hadley smiled and counted off ten hundred-dollar bills and handed them to the longhaired twenty-something man. By late afternoon, a picture of two men standing together with Holden could be seen on the video monitor.

Hadley turned to the technician. "How much to get an electronic copy of this?"

"Another C-note."

He handed the man a flash drive wrapped in a bill with Benjamin Franklin's portrait. "Can you copy it to this?"

A nod was his response.

The young man placed the drive in a USB slot and copied the video file. He then handed it back to Hadley. "Is that what you needed?"

"It sure is, thanks."

Forty minutes later, he opened his laptop, inserted the flash drive, and watched the video copied from the convention center's security tapes. He selected a clear shot of the two men in question and saved it as a jpeg. He compared the picture to the one he received from the hotel the night before. Satisfied the shorter man was the same in both pictures, he attached the files to an email and sent it to Hunter Holden.

His phone rang five minutes later.

"Who are they, Dalton?"

"Don't know their names yet. Are those the men you knew as Michael and Sean Lyon?"

"Yes."

"Then, my search just got a lot easier."

***

Two days later, Hadley walked into a tavern across the street from Wrigley Field on North Sheffield Avenue under the 'L' track. Even with the time of day being noon and a cloudless sky, the interior remained a dark-and-dreary place. The man he was there to meet sat in a booth near the rear of the pub.

Slipping into the opposite seat, he nodded at his companion. "Had lunch yet, Jerry?"

The man sipped on his beer. "Just got here. You buying?"

"I'm not. But my employer is."

A grin appeared on the man. "Good. I'll get another beer and a brat."

A tall male with an apron tied around his waist walked up to the booth. "Another beer, Jerry?"

"Yeah, and one for my friend here." Jerry looked at the man across the table. "Old Style?"

Hadley nodded, and the waiter returned to the area behind the bar.

"What's on your mind, Dalton?"

A picture of two men slid across the table. "Have you ever seen these two guys?"

Jerry pointed toward the shorter one of the two in the picture. "Never seen him before. The other guy looks familiar."

"How so?"

"Let me think." The old police detective and Hadley's source within the Chicago Police Department stared at the picture and finished off his beer. By the time two new beers arrived at the table, Jerry held the picture in his hand and examined it with glasses halfway down his nose. "I know I've seen this guy before." After taking a sip of his fresh beer, he laid the picture down and smiled. "Now, I remember. He's an FBI agent. Came through here about three or four years ago working on a serial killer case."

Raising an eyebrow, Hadley said, "FBI? You sure?"

Putting his half-readers back in his sport coat pocket, he nodded. "Yeah, I'm sure. Nice guy, worked closely with our boys and didn't have a big ego. You know, most of the Feds who come through here are really proud of themselves. They have a tendency to look down on us detectives who've been on the streets for twenty years or more. This guy didn't."

"Do you remember his name?"

"I don't pay too much attention to Feds as a rule, but I learned a lot from him. His name's Sean Kruger."

Hadley picked up the picture and stared at it. "Hello, Sean Kruger." As he did, his other hand placed an envelope about a quarter-of-an-inch thick in front of his source. Jerry placed a hand over it, and it disappeared from the top of the table.

CHAPTER 24

Southwest Missouri

Kruger glanced at the caller ID on his cell phone and briefly wondered if it might be a spoofed phone number. The words above the phone number simply read Ryan Clark.

"Kruger."

"Sean, it's Ryan." The voice confirmed the caller's true identity. The director of the Federal Bureau of Investigation.

"Hello, Ryan. Is this a catching-up-with-an-old-friend call or a business call?"

"Wish it was the former, but unfortunately, it's the latter. Your name keeps coming up in dispatches from our Chicago Field Office. Anything I need to know about?"

"Huh."

"I take it you don't know what I'm talking about."

"Wouldn't have a clue." He paused for a moment. "Who's bringing my name up?"

"A Chicago police detective named Jerry Stein. He's asking any FBI agent he can find about how to locate you."

"That's interesting. I've worked a few cases in Chicago over the years and met a lot of detectives, but his name doesn't ring a bell."

"Want us to have a chat with him about his sudden curiosity?"

Kruger didn't answer right away. After a long pause, he said, "Not necessary. Just make sure no one tells him where I live."

"That, my friend, is a well-kept secret. I made sure your records were sealed when you had to retire. Probably the only two individuals left who know are Charlie Craft and myself."

"I appreciate it, Ryan."

"Wish I could talk longer, Sean, but I have a meeting that started two minutes ago."

"Thanks for the heads-up."

"My pleasure. If I hear anything else, I'll let you know."

The call ended, and Kruger pursed his lips. Scrolling through his contact list, he found the number he needed and made the call.

"Detective Barnes."

"Peter, it's Sean Kruger."

"Hey, Sean, how you doing?"

"Good. Are you in a position to talk for a moment?"

"Sure, what's up?"

"Got a call from my old agency a few minutes ago. Have you had any contact with FBI agents recently?"

"I try to avoid talking to them. Why?"

"Someone within the CPD is trying to find out where I live."

"Uh—oh."

"Yeah, kind of what I thought."

The detective remained silent for a moment. "Do you think this has to do with your investigation of the museum theft?"

"Only reason I can think of."

"Do you know who's asking?"

"A guy named Jerry Stein."

The silence on the call lasted longer than the previous pause. "Uh—Sean. Let me get back to you on this."

"Is there a problem?"

"Might be. I need to check something."

***

Chicago

Peter Barnes followed Jerry Stein at a discreet distance as the older detective drove north into Old Town. Turning west on Chicago Avenue, he parked on the street in front of a restaurant called Ole Taqueria. Driving past, Barnes watched in his rearview mirror as Stein entered the café. He made a U-turn as soon as possible and parked across the street, a few doors down from the location of Stein's vehicle.

His wait did not last long. Five minutes after Stein entered, another man, well-known to Barnes, walked up to the Mexican restaurant entrance. Dalton Hadley looked both ways before he opened the door and entered.

Not knowing how long this possible rendezvous would last, Barnes pulled out his cell phone, exited his car, walked across the street, and looked inside the establishment. Sure enough, Hadley and Stein were sitting, hunched over a table, having an animated conversation.

With a slight smile, Barnes snapped two pictures of the scene and walked away from the window to see if his pictures were good. The first one, out of focus, he deleted. The second one showed the Chicago Police detective receiving an envelope from the well-known Chicago thug.

Back in his car, he waited for Stein to emerge from the restaurant. When he did, Barnes took another picture of him getting into his car and then more pictures once the other man walked out.

Starting his car, he drove back to his precinct and wrote his report.

***

The Next Day

Jerry Stein entered the conference room and saw his captain, a woman whose professional business suit screamed federal agent, and a man he recognized as a fellow Chicago Police detective. They were all sitting next to each other at a long table opposite where he stood. Internal alarm bells went off the instant he saw them. "Uh, what's up, Captain? You wanted to see me?"

Veteran police Captain George Day pointed to an empty chair across from the three individuals. "Shut the door, sit, and don't say a word unless asked."

The older detective froze and considered bolting out the still-open door but knew the option did not exist for him. He complied with his captain's demand. When he sat, he remained silent.

Day slipped a photograph across the table so Stein could see. "Care to comment, Detective?"

All the muscles in his stomach contracted, and bile rose in his throat. He swallowed hard. "Not sure what you mean, Captain."

Leaning over the table, Day growled, "Look at it carefully, Stein."

"It's me, sitting in a restaurant. So?"

"Who's the guy handing the envelope to you? Or do you want *us* to tell you who he is?"

Stein blinked several times, placed his hands flat on the table, and said, "I want an advocate from the union before I say anything else."

"If you call an advocate, you'll lose your job and your pension. If, on the other hand, you tell us what's going on here, you get to take a month-long vacation starting ten minutes ago. At the end of your vacation, you will retire. But you keep your pension. What will it be?"

After a deep breath, Stein relaxed. "The guy wanted to know where a certain FBI agent lived. I've been trying to find out for him."

"Did you?"

A shake of the older detective's head was the answer.

The captain turned to Barnes. "You believe him?"

"Not sure." Barnes looked over at the woman sitting next to the captain. "What about you, Agent Monroe?"

She asked Stein, "What's the agent's name?"

"Sean Kruger."

"So, you did not determine where he lives?"

The soon-to-be ex-detective shook his head.

Monroe turned to the captain. "Can you place Mr. Stein in protective custody while agents track down Dalton Hadley?"

Turning to Barnes, Captain Day asked, "Do you want to escort him?"

"My pleasure."

***

The woman in the professional business attire turned out to be Teri Monroe, the supervisor of the FBI Laboratory Division based at Quantico. She was also a close friend of Sean Kruger and volunteered for the chance to help her friend by traveling to Chicago.

Currently in a vacant interview room with the door shut, she pressed her cell phone to her ear, talking to Kruger. "I don't think he learned your location, Sean."

"That's good."

"Hell, I don't even know where you live since you left KC."

"Probably best, Teri."

"Are you coming to Chicago?"

"I'm not an FBI agent anymore."

"I'm sure Director Clark would approve you as a consultant."

"No, I'll stay away from the city. The bureau has some great agents there. I don't need to butt in."

"I'll keep you posted on the results."

"Thank you."

***

The underworld grapevine worked overtime in Chicago. At the same time Monroe was speaking to Kruger on a cell phone call, Dalton Hadley caught wind of the arrest of Jerry Stein. He threw a few changes of clothes and toiletries into a duffle bag and headed for his car. Thirty minutes later, he merged onto north I-90 on his way to Minneapolis four hundred miles away.

The FBI would miss him by five minutes when they raided his apartment.

***

Jerry Stein sat in an interrogation room, waiting for someone to let him out. Peter Barnes opened the door, smiled, and plopped down into the chair across from the disgraced detective. He placed a manila folder in front of him and opened it.

"Well, Jerry, I've got bad news for you."

"When can I go?"

Barnes studied the contents of the file. "Remember when the captain said you could start your vacation today and retire at the end of the month?"

"Yes."

"He changed his mind. It seems you have a secret bank account with well over half a million dollars in it."

Stein's brow furrowed, but he remained quiet.

"The captain's question is how'd you get that much

money stashed away on a detective's salary?"

"I inherited it."

Looking at the file again, Barnes raised his eyes and looked over his glasses. "So, you inherited exactly five thousand dollars in cash each month over the course of the last eight years or so."

No response came from the soon-to-be arrested police detective.

"It looks to me like you were being paid a salary by someone for a service. Would that service have been keeping certain not-so-upstanding members of Chicago society up-to-date on the activities of the police?"

Still no response as Stein stared at the tabletop between the two men.

"No comment, Jerry?"

The older man shook his head.

"That's too bad. Looks like you've not only lost your pension, but you've lost your freedom and your nest egg as well." He stood. "Sucks to be you right now."

Barnes turned and walked out of the interrogation room. As soon as he vacated the area, in walked two uniformed police officers. The taller of the two said, "Jerry Stein, you have the right to remain silent..."

CHAPTER 25

Southwest Missouri

With the airport office closed and the remodel of JR's second floor still in progress, Kruger chose to work from his home office. The giant oak tree outside his south-facing window kept the afternoon sun from turning the room into an oven. The tree also served as a source of amusement provided by a family of squirrels constantly quarreling over fallen acorns. In addition, the window offered him a view of the goings-on within the neighborhood.

The ever-present din of landscaping companies mowing neighborhood lawns could be heard in the background as well as the occasional sound of a FedEx or UPS truck driving east or west.

When the sound of a vehicle stopping in front of his house drew his attention, he turned his office chair to glance out the window. Repeating an occurrence from a month ago, Nathan Tucker and Robert Spencer stepped out of a black Ford Explorer and buttoned their suit coats. This time, they did not pause to survey the area but walked straight to the driveway and followed it to Kruger's front door.

He met them there and opened it. "Gentlemen, please come in." Five minutes later, after small talk and preparing a pot of coffee, he sat across from them and asked, "What can I do for you two today?"

Tucker smiled. "We never did get a proper chance to thank you for the work you did on the Chicago Field Museum theft."

"No need."

Spencer added, "Or the recovery of the funds paid out to Transnational Financial."

Kruger shrugged.

"We understand they have fallen on financial hard times. Were you aware of that, Sean?"

"That's too bad."

Tucker suppressed a grin and took a sip of his coffee. "We have heard that several of our competitors have also opened investigations into the claims paid out to Transnational. No word yet on what they plan to do, but lawsuits are in the works."

With a sly smile, Kruger said, "Nathan, you and Robert didn't travel all the way from Omaha to tell me this. What's happened?"

Both men smiled, and Spencer nodded at Tucker. "Nathan, do you want to present it?"

"With pleasure." The man opened a folio he had brought with him and extracted a stack of paper. "This is a contract formalizing the agreement between Tucker, Neal and Spencer, Incorporated and KKG Solutions. The board has authorized us to offer KKG all insurance fraud investigations we need to conduct moving forward. In addition, we will provide your company with an annual stipend to maintain this agreement."

"May I see the contract?"

Accepting the stack of papers and placing his half-readers on his nose, Kruger scanned the pages as Tucker and Spencer sipped coffee. After he finished, he looked up.

"Gentlemen, I don't see a problem. But I will have to let my partners go over it as well. Unfortunately, we are scattered this week. The company is planning a move into a new office facility, and the remodel is not yet complete. Which means, we are all working out of our homes at the moment."

Tucker continued, "We also suggest you have your corporate attorney go over it."

"I will get it to him today. Couldn't this have been handled electronically?"

"Uh, yes. It could have. But we had other reasons for the trip."

Kruger remained quiet and raised his coffee cup to his lips.

"Robert and I plan to spend the rest of the day at Bass Pro Shop, plus we wanted to present you with something." He pulled an envelope from his inside suit coat pocket and placed it on the table in front of Kruger.

With hesitation, the ex-FBI agent picked it up and studied the document. He looked at the two insurance executives. "What is this?"

"Something we want to offer KKG. Go ahead and open it."

Tearing the flap open, Kruger extracted what appeared to be a certificate. He studied it and smiled. "This is an Indemnity Insurance Policy for KKG."

"Yes, first-year premiums are paid in full. Then, on renewal, your rates are guaranteed to be below market. It's our way of saying thank you, Sean."

Kruger stood and offered his hand. "Gentlemen, I am looking forward to working with your company."

***

"So, you thought they were going to give you a check without including Sandy and Jimmie?"

Kruger placed the marinated chicken on the grill as

Stephanie sat in a tall chair at a bistro table on their back deck, a glass of wine in her hand. He nodded. "Yes, I did. I would've given it back to them. The insurance policy for the company was a surprise."

"I thought you guys already had liability insurance."

"We do. But this policy is a hundred times better. Jimmie canceled our current policy this afternoon."

"Sean, do you realize you've made more money in the past year than you did your entire career with the FBI?"

Staring at the chicken on the grill, Kruger shut the lid and turned to his wife. "Yes, I'm aware of it. To be honest with you, I've never been someone obsessed with making money. I did my job and whatever happened, happened. I've lived within my means and gotten used to it."

She nodded. "It's who you are. One of the many things I love about you. Have I ever told you how much happier I am being your wife and a college professor?"

He grinned and folded his arms. "No, you never have."

"Well, I have. Several times."

"Tell me again. I'm getting old and forgetful."

"You're impossible." She grinned. "Just before we met, I was rethinking my life choices. I wasn't happy."

"I know. You told me one time you felt disconnected from your personal and professional life."

"I was. I didn't have a personal life. When I met you, I saw someone who was happy and successful with their career choice. You didn't worry about the next promotion. In fact, since we've been married, you've turned several down because you didn't want to move our family."

He kept his eyes on her as she reminisced.

"I've never had that strength, Sean. I used to jump at every promotion they offered. And guess what?"

"I'm game, what?"

She smiled. "I still wasn't happy." She slipped out of the bistro chair and walked over to him by the grill. After placing her arms around him, she looked up. "Thank you for rescuing me." Her head now rested on his chest. "By the way, the chicken needs to be turned."

***

Kruger studied the layout on the second floor of JR's building. Sandy Knoll and Jimmie Gibbs stood next to him. Sandy asked, "What do you think?"

"I think Stephanie is going to enjoy my not smelling like jet fuel when I get home at night."

"Linda said the same thing. What about you, Jimmie?"

"I like the fact Alexia and I get to spend more time together commuting."

The eastern side of the floor now contained four offices with a conference room between them. With the cubicles moved to the first floor, their workplaces were enclosed offices offering privacy when they spoke to clients on the phone. The new conference room would offer additional private space for meetings with KKG associates or clients.

On the western wall, JR and Alexia now occupied their own private offices. JR, after much discussion, had relented to the need for privacy. The coffee service remained between them. And the soundproof conference room with the hidden stairwell remained as is.

JR came out of his office and poured a cup of coffee. When he was done, he wandered over to where his friends stood. "I still plan to keep my door open."

Kruger chuckled. "Nobody said you couldn't."

"Well, Alexia and I are on your floor."

"It's still your building, JR."

"I've been meaning to talk to you guys about that."

Sandy turned. "Concerning?"

"What if we form an LLC and buy the building from my company? Then we lease it back to ourselves."

Raising an eyebrow, Kruger said, "Who put that idea in your head?"

"My accountant. He said we could gain all kinds of tax advantages from it."

With a chuckle, Kruger said, "You guys figure it out. Accounting gives me a headache."

CHAPTER 26

Minneapolis

"My source in the Chicago Police Department is under arrest. So, I probably need to lie low and be scarce for a while."

Hunter Holden paced, his hands clasped behind his back, as he listened to the thug from Chicago. His concentration centered on the carpet, his face a mask of indifference. After several additional laps, he looked up, his expression an intense glare. "Can anyone connect you with me?"

"Not unless you've leaked it. I sure haven't."

"Good. Make sure it stays that way." He returned to pacing.

A dense fog of silence settled over the room as neither man spoke.

Finally, Holden returned to sitting at his desk. "Can the CPD connect you with Stein?"

A nod from the Chicago fugitive.

"How?"

"Not sure. But I'd make a bet Stein did something stupid. He wasn't the brightest bulb in the chandelier." Hadley paused for a second. "At least I learned the name of one of those men you're looking for."

"You could have mentioned this earlier."

"Yeah, well, I could have, but I didn't."

"Who is he?"

"The one I was able to identify is an ex-FBI agent. His name is Sean Kruger. He's the man you knew as Sean Lyon."

"Where does he live?"

"That's why Stein's under arrest. He probably asked the wrong individuals the wrong questions. Current and ex-FBI agents don't like to advertise where they live. So, if the moron was asking about Kruger's address, the FBI caught wind of it and got involved."

"Who would know his address?"

Hadley shrugged. "Heck if I know."

Holden grew silent. He then drummed his fingers on his desk. "What about this Stein character? How much does he know?"

"More than he should."

"Is that a problem for me?"

"It could be. However, if something were to happen to Stein, well, you know."

"How much?"

"My normal fee."

"Thought you weren't going back to Chicago anytime soon."

"I'm not planning to stay. Just need to tie up a few loose ends."

Holden pursed his lips. "Then where will you go?"

The Chicago thug answered with a shrug.

"Don't go too far. I might need you."

Smiling, Hadley stood. "At the moment, Hunter, you're radioactive. Try not to call until things calm down." With those words, he walked out of the office.

Dean Melton entered just as the CEO's guest exited. "Where's he going?"

"Don't worry about him. We have other issues to address."

"Such as?"

"I know the identity of one of the Lyon brothers. He's an ex-FBI agent whose real name is Sean Kruger."

Standing in front of the desk, Melton crossed his arms. "Then let's have someone pay him a visit?"

"No one seems to know where he lives, and the FBI guards those types of details with great care."

"I thought you maintained connections in Washington."

"I do. I've thought about using one of them, but…"

"It's not like you to be hesitant, Hunter."

"Hesitant isn't the correct word. The proper word is cautious."

"Why?"

"There's a congressman from Minnesota who owes me a favor due to my singlehandedly getting him elected."

"Call him up."

Holden glared at his assistant. "Not so fast. I don't want him burned in an FBI sting just because he's asking around about this Agent Kruger's address. If we use him, he'll need to do it so that nobody knows he's the one inquiring."

"Leave that to me."

***

On the first day in his new office, Kruger spent an hour answering emails and returning phone calls. The previous evening, Stephanie and he arranged his furniture and decorated the room with family pictures and a few mementos from his days with the FBI.

At 9 a.m., his cell phone rang. The caller ID showed a Chicago area code. He accepted the call. "Kruger."

"Sean, it's Peter Barnes."

"Good to hear from you, Peter."

"You got a few minutes?"

"Sure, what's up?"

"The local FBI field office and Chicago PD have a fellow police detective under arrest. He's charged with taking kickbacks to the tune of half-a-million dollars."

"Not the smartest thing to do."

"I would agree. He got caught after being photographed with Dalton Hadley accepting an envelope of cash. Cash he was given to find your address."

Kruger did not respond, so, Barnes continued. "The FBI raided the guy's apartment. They think they missed him by a few minutes. He hasn't been seen since."

"Huh."

"Thought you should know."

"I appreciate it, Peter. Thanks."

"Do you have some way of protecting yourself and your family?"

"Yes, my company has resources I can utilize if necessary."

"That's good to know. We don't think the detective learned where you live. He says he didn't, but we're checking out his story."

"Is he still in jail?"

"Bail hearing is today. He'll probably get released with an ankle bracelet."

"Think he'll run?"

"No. He's dumb but not that dumb. I'll keep you posted."

"Thanks, Peter."

"You take care of yourself."

"I will."

The call ended. Kruger stood and walked the few steps to Jimmie Gibbs' office next to his. The young ex-SEAL looked up from his computer monitor. "What's up?"

"Do we have anybody between assignments?"

"Yeah, a couple of guys who just got back from overseas. Why?"

"I'm hiring them to keep an eye on my house."

One of Gibbs' eyebrows rose. "Mind if I ask why?"

"I think Hunter Holden knows who I am and is trying to find where I live."

Gibbs grabbed a cell phone lying on his desk and started punching numbers.

**

Hadley watched from the parking lot as Jerry Stein walked out of the courthouse. He was accompanied by a younger man the Chicago thug assumed was the ex-detective's lawyer. The two men stopped at the bottom of the steps and faced each other. After an animated conversation, the lawyer handed Stein a business card, turned, and headed toward a parking lot across the street.

Stein stared at the card and then placed it in his pants pocket. He then looked around and pulled out a cell phone. Five minutes later, a Honda Accord pulled up next to where Stein stood and the disgraced policeman stepped into the back seat.

Starting his rental, Hadley prepared to follow.

Thirty minutes later, the Honda stopped in front of a run-down apartment building in a blue-collar section of Chicago. Stein got out and watched the car drive away. He looked up at the building, shook his head, and entered. Hadley saw all of this as he pulled to the curb and waited.

After darkness fell over the city several hours later, Hadley stepped out of his car and walked to the entrance of the apartment building. As he suspected, it was locked. Pretending to be reading something on his cell phone, he waited until someone exited the building. Before the door could close, he rushed to catch it and slipped inside.

The mailbox with Stein's name on it told him the policeman lived on the fourth floor and the unit number. Taking the stairs two at a time, Hadley pulled a Glock 19 from a waistband holster and approached the apartment.

Placing his ear against the entry, he heard the sounds of a TV.

He knocked four times and waited for a response. Watching the peephole, he saw it grow dark and heard, "What do you want, Dalton?"

"Checking up on you, Jerry. I thought you might need some cash."

The sound of dead bolts being thrown came from the other side. When it opened, Stein glared at the Chicago thug. "Since when did you give a shit?"

"You've got me wrong, Jerry. I'm here to help, man."

"Bullshit." Stein stood aside. Hadley entered and looked around. A small duffle bag lay on the couch and a cell phone next to it.

"Going somewhere?"

"Yeah. I can be in Canada before they know I've skipped town."

"Didn't they give you an ankle bracelet?"

The ex-detective nodded. "Haven't been a cop for twenty years without learning a few tricks. Thanks to a pimp I arrested awhile back, I know how to bypass the circuits." Stein turned to grab his duffle bag. "Now that you're here, you can give me a ride."

Having held the Glock behind his back, Hadley raised it and pointed it at the apartment's resident. "Sit down, Jerry."

Turning, Stein glared. "What the hell is this about?"

"I can't let you do that."

"Can't let me do what?"

"Leave town. You know too much."

"I don't know shit. Now, get out of my apartment. I'll find my own ride."

Stein proceeded to do something Hadley never expected. He swung the duffle bag up against the Glock. With Hadley's finger on the trigger, it fired. The bullet grazed Stein on the arm which now held a small Taurus 856 .38 Special Revolver. The ensuing firefight lasted less than five seconds as the detective pulled the trigger on his gun and Hadley fired his.

The results ended up with a dead ex-detective and a Chicago thug with a bullet in his thigh. Cursing at Stein, Hadley rushed out of the apartment and headed toward the stairs, leg bleeding profusely.

The other tenants of the apartment building knew enough not to open their doors to inquire about the happenings on their floor. That way when the police arrived and questioned them, they could honestly say they didn't see anything.

CHAPTER 27

Washington, DC

Congressman Jordon Brooks could always be counted on by cable news networks for a sound bite. He possessed an opinion on everything and seldom used a verbal filter when commenting on the issue of the day. Congenial and well-liked by his colleagues in the House of Representatives, he represented the good citizens of the 5th District of Minnesota, which included the city of Minneapolis, with competence. Greatness, no, but if one of his constituents needed help navigating the bureaucracy of the federal government, he was your guy.

He did possess one flaw. Greed. A flaw that could one day get him in trouble.

This personality defect meant he coveted the attention of successful—translated as rich—individuals. One in particular being Hunter Holden. Jordon Brooks was owned lock, stock, and barrel by the CEO of Transnational Financial.

So, when Holden's right-hand man, Dean Melton, called for an appointment in Brooks' Rayburn House Office

Building, the good congressman chose not to attend a critical budget hearing to meet with Holden's assistant.

The two men shook hands inside the closed confines of Brooks' office. "What can I do for Mr. Holden today, Dean?"

"Hunter sends his compliments for the fine job you do for the 5th District, Jordon."

"I am pleased he's happy."

"Extremely."

After a decade in Washington, Brooks knew there was more to the visit than just being complimented. He remained quiet.

"You are one of the ranking members of the Judiciary Committee, aren't you, Jordon?"

The congressman nodded.

"And you are also the cochairman, correct?"

"Yes."

"How hard would it be for you to get information from the FBI about a retired agent?"

"Depends. What type of information?"

"Hunter needs to know where this agent lives."

"Uh, that's kind of an odd request."

"Yes, it is. But Hunter has a reason for needing to know."

"I would need the reason, Dean."

"Best if you don't know."

"I see."

"How soon can you obtain the information?"

"What's the name of the agent?"

"Sean Kruger."

Brooks' eyes widened when he heard the name. "Uh…"

"It's important, Jordon."

"The FBI guards their HR records very closely. It's off-limits to someone like me. Particularly concerning this specific agent."

Melton tilted his head. "What's so special about him, Jordon?"

"He's a legend within the agency, and it's rumored he's the main reason Ryan Clark is the director."

"Aren't you on the Judiciary Committee?"

"Yes."

"So, you have oversight and the right to know the details within the bureau."

"Only the agency, not the agents."

Melton stood. "I'm sure a man of your stature and intelligence can figure out how to get this information without ruffling feathers. Hunter would be most appreciative if you can do this one favor for him." He paused. "Most appreciative."

***

"Is everything okay, Congressman?"

The question came from his administrative assistant, Claudine Ward. She kept her gaze on him from his office door, which she had opened slightly to check on him.

He blinked several times and realized she was speaking to him. "Yes, Claudine, everything is fine."

"Sorry to bother you, sir. But your wife is on line one."

"She is? Uh, thank you, tell her I'll call her back in five minutes."

His assistant returned to her desk, leaving the office door open. Brooks took several deep breaths, stood, and shut the door before walking to his private restroom to splash water on his face. After drying it, he stared at his reflection. It took him several moments to realize he almost did not recognize the person staring back at him.

Ten years of building a reputation within the House of Representatives and developing a network of donors who kept him ahead of the pack in campaign funding were suddenly in jeopardy. All because Hunter Holden needed a favor. Providing special services for donors never bothered him, mainly because they were usually innocent in nature.

This particular question did not sound innocent. However, turning down a request from the richest man in Minnesota could cost him his seat. His internal debate lasted five minutes before he made a decision.

Time to call his wife back.

***

Congressman Brooks approached his chief of staff, Julie Abbott and asked, "Do you have a few moments, Julie?"

"Sure, Congressman."

"Let's go to my office."

Once they were seated at the small conference table in the corner, he said, "How well do you know the staff of the other members of the Judiciary Committee?"

"Some I know well, others are just acquittances. Why?"

"I need some information, and I don't want the inquiry to come from this office."

"I see. May I ask why, sir?"

"If it is discovered we asked the question, it could be embarrassing for us."

She folded her arms and leaned back in her chair but remained quiet.

"Now, if you don't feel comfortable doing this, I'll..."

"It will depend on the information, sir."

"I need the address of a specific FBI agent. Actually, he's retired."

Her eyes grew to the shape of saucers. "Sir, that information is hard to get and viewed with suspicion."

"I'm aware of that, Ms. Abbott. Like I said, if you don't feel comfortable obtaining it, I'll find another way."

Leaning forward, she lowered her voice. "I didn't say I wouldn't try, but it might help to know the reason."

"One of my constituents would like to send a thank-you card to the agent for his efforts in a kidnapping incident."

"Oh." She sat back in her chair. "I don't suppose it would

hurt. Let me think." After several moments of quiet, she continued, "Anyone on the committee you don't particularly like?"

"Congressman Black is a bit of a shithead."

"Yes, not too many of his staff like him."

"Do you think one of them would do it?"

With a sly grin, she said, "Yes, if you offered her a job, first."

"Make the offer, Julie. But make sure the individual knows it's contingent on getting us the information."

"What's the agent's name?"

"Sean Kruger."

***

Director of the FBI Ryan Clark returned to his office after a meeting with several executive assistants. When he sat behind his desk, he found an urgent message in his email inbox. He opened it, read the contents, and picked up the phone.

His call was answered on the second ring. "Charlie Craft."

"Charlie, it's Clark. When did this occur?"

"This morning around eight."

"Did they get the address?"

"Unfortunately, they did."

A lengthy pause occurred. Finally, Clark said, "I'll handle it from here. Call Sean and let him know."

"Yes, sir."

Ending the call, Clark slammed his fist on his desk. "Damn. I hate congressmen."

Picking up the phone again, he punched in a number he knew by heart. When the call was answered, he said, "It's Clark."

***

Adrian Black, two-term congressman from the state of Arkansas, read the resignation letter from his legislative director and frowned. Looking up, he asked, "Why now, Leslie?"

"Better opportunity with another congressman, sir."

"If it's money, I can get you more."

"It's not the money."

"Then, what is it?"

"We haven't proposed any new legislation during this term. I feel like I'm wasting my time."

"I've been busy raising campaign contributions."

"Yes, sir."

Black looked at the resignation letter again and then up at his departing assistant. "Very well. I would appreciate it if you would recommend someone to replace you."

She handed him a folded piece of paper. "Here are a few names."

At the same moment she handed Black the list, four men entered the office. All wore dark suits, white shirts, and ties. All were tall with professionally styled haircuts, and all wore earpieces connected to an encrypted radio communication network.

The lead agent held up his credentials and said, "Adrian Black, FBI. Please stand and move away from your desk."

One hour later, the FBI agents established Leslie Unger had made the enquiry into the home address of retired FBI agent Sean Kruger. She was led away by two of the agents. After they left, Congressman Adrian Black received a warning about allowing his staff to violate established congressional rules. Particularly the rules about using their position on congressional committees for personal gain.

His only response was a chastised nod of his head.

By noon, Leslie Unger revealed who had asked her to find the address. Two hours later, the same four agents appeared in the office of the Speaker of the House, requesting an emergency meeting with the leader.

Within the next hour, Minnesota congressman Jordon Brooks stood in the Speaker's office, the four FBI agents standing off to the side. During this meeting, he received the news he would be stripped of his committee assignments and would face a censure vote the following afternoon. A vote, the Speaker pledged, he would lose if he did not reveal the reasons for his actions.

"What do you have to say for yourself, Congressman Brooks?" The Speaker's anger evident in the tone of his voice.

"Fulfilling the request of one of my major contributors."

"Who might that be?"

"Hunter Holden, CEO of Transnational Financial, sir."

The four FBI agents looked at each other, and the lead agent quickly exited the office.

CHAPTER 28

Southwest Missouri

On this particular Wednesday morning, only Kruger occupied the newly relocated offices of KKG. Sandy Knoll, currently in Washington, DC, pursued the courting of several higher-ups at the Pentagon while Jimmie Gibbs traveled to California to interview several recently retired SEALs looking for gainful employment.

A knock on his doorframe caused Kruger to turn around.

JR stood there. "Ever thought about facing the door instead of having your back to it?"

"Yes. I've thought about it."

"Well?"

"Dismissed it as an unnecessary interruption. Which is why I have my back to the window in my home office—too many distractions."

"You and I are the only ones on this floor at the moment."

"And yet, here you are."

With a chuckle, JR said, "I think you need to see something on my computer."

Standing, Kruger walked around his desk. "Lead the

way."

As they entered JR's newly enclosed workspace, he pointed to the middle screen on his desk. "That popped up a few minutes ago."

"Popped up from where?"

JR just smiled.

Bending over, Kruger read the email and then removed his half-readers. "So, Hunter Holden sent someone to Washington hoping to find my address."

"I believe that would be a safe assumption."

"He sure went to a lot of trouble to get it."

"Plus getting two congressmen in hot water."

Folding his arms, Kruger stared at the email. "Confirms my original diagnosis of him as a narcissistic psychopath. He doesn't care about anybody but himself."

"What about those guys Jimmie assigned to watch your family?"

Kruger's mouth twitched. "Per our agreement, even I don't know where they are at any given time. But they are keeping Steph and the kids under watchful eyes."

"What about you?"

"Our home address is incorrect within the agency's HR department."

"How'd you manage that?"

"Paul Stumpf took care of it before his cancer diagnosis."

"So, where do those records indicate you live?"

"The address where I grew up. My parents lived there for over thirty years. When Dad retired, they moved to KC to help me with Brian while I traveled for the agency."

"Any way you can be traced from that address?"

"I don't see how. I left for college and visited occasionally until they moved to KC. I've never been back."

"What about USPS mail-forwarding information?"

"Never submitted one. When I was in college, Mom and Dad kept my mail for me."

"So, the FBI has no record of you living in this area?"

"Correct."

Sitting down at his desk, JR's hands flew over the keyboard.

"What are you doing?"

"Checking county real-estate and personal property tax records to make sure the changes I made are still in effect."

"Is that why my tax statements come under Stephanie's name?"

"Yes. Mine come under Mia's name."

Both men were quiet for a few moments. Finally, Kruger asked, "With all the information available on the Internet right now, how in the world can someone make sure they can't be found?"

"It's difficult. I've got us hidden as best as I can. But, if Hunter Holden has access to someone who is good enough, they'll find you."

Kruger folded his arms. "How?"

"Think about it. FedEx, UPS, and the post office know where you live. So does your pharmacy and anyone you do business with. The good thing is, their databases are private compared to the county records which are public."

"Steph and I are not on social media."

"Wise."

"What about the university?"

"It's possible. But their information isn't public, either."

"If Holden has anyone like you working for him, they'll find us."

JR nodded. "Eventually. There are just too many databases out there with your real address identified. I'm curious, how did the insurance guys find you?"

"I asked the same question."

"And?"

"Sandy told them."

JR chuckled.

Kruger folded his arms and tapped his finger on his lips. "Maybe it's time for us to be the hunter, not the other way around."

"What do you have in mind?"

Kruger told him.

***

"One of our associates visited the house at the address Jordon Brooks provided."

Holden looked up at Dean Melton. "Let me guess, no one by that name lived there?"

"The house was torn down several years ago to make way for a condo development."

"So, he's had help from someone within the FBI."

"It would appear so."

"Does anyone with the last name Kruger live in the town?"

"No. It's a small town in the Lake of the Ozarks area."

"What about in the county?"

Melton shook his head.

"Damn. In other words, a dead end."

"For the moment, yes." The assistant paused. "There has to be information out there with his address. Knowing his name will eventually lead us to him. But it will take time. Particularly if he has help."

Holden tilted his head. "What do you mean, help?"

"I don't know. I was thinking out loud."

"No, you're correct. What if he does have help? Who could it be?"

A smile came slowly to Melton's lips. "Remember the guy we used to manipulate the Field Museum's cameras?"

"He's dead, Dean."

"I'm aware of that, but he wasn't the only computer nerd we've used in the past."

"True."

"Why don't you use one of them?" Returning his attention to his desk, Holden continued. "Whoever you use needs to be discreet. Also, expendable."

"Yes, sir."

***

In the small town of Boxy Flats, Iowa, Mollie Lewis lived a quiet life. After fleeing an abusive husband ten years before, at the age of twenty-five, she had relocated to this quiet out-of-the-way community. Hiding in plain sight, she now earned a modest wage working at the mayor's office in the town's city hall. At night, she used her skills with a computer to earn her real income, draining the bank accounts of men who abused their wives or girlfriends.

At first, she gathered names from social media and then made contact with the victims. After she solved the problem for half a dozen grateful women, her reputation grew, and now business came to her. As a rule, she kept 25 percent of the assets she discovered, and the victim kept the rest. These funds were then transferred to an offshore bank account. She figured by the time she hit forty, she could disappear and live comfortably for the rest of her life.

At 10:03 p.m. on a Thursday night, a private message appeared on her monitor. *Interested in making a six-figure bonus?* With a derisive shake of her head, she deleted the message and went on with her current project. The next night, a more personalized message arrived at the exact time as the previous evening's communication. *Hi, Mollie. This is not a scam. We have a job for you if you are interested. Like we told you last night, six figures.*

This time, she did not delete the message but traced it back to a server in Minneapolis. Once she discovered this information, she went a bit further and found who sent the message.

Intrigued with the results of her inquiry, she answered using a proxy server. *Maybe. Need more information.*

She did not receive an answer right away. Finally, at

11:43 p.m., it arrived. *We need the physical address of an individual who seems to be well hidden.*
What is this individual's name, and who is he?
Not until you agree to help us.
Won't agree until told who it is.
Will 100,000 USD help you make a decision?
Mollie Lewis sat back in her office chair and stared at the screen. The sum of money being offered would cut her timeline for retiring by a year. She typed out her response. *No physical meetings. All correspondence via this format. Fee to be 200,000 USD and deposited in an account of my choosing prior to starting search. No negotiating. Take it or leave it.* She paused and reread the note several times. Finally, she hit send.

Her answer did not arrive until early Thursday morning. The search for Sean Kruger began Saturday morning after the sum of 200,000 USD arrived in a makeshift account in the Caymans, a deposit she immediately transferred several times until it was untraceable.

***

JR Diminski heard his cell phone chirp with a preprogrammed sound he knew to mean trouble. He immediately went to his home office and opened the message. After reading it, he dialed Kruger's phone number.

"Good morning, JR."

"Someone's looking for you again."

"Who is it this time?"

"Don't know. Whoever it is, they appear to be good."

"As good as you?"

"No, but they know their way around the Internet and how to make soft inquiries. Plus, they're hiding their location with great skill."

"Should I be worried?"

"Not until I tell you to be."

With a chuckle, Kruger said, "Well, it sounds like I'm in good hands." He paused. "What have they found so far?"

"They found a couple of trip wires I've had set up for years."

"I remember you told me about those. What about Stephanie?"

"Nothing yet. Let me get busy on this. I'll call you later."

"JR?"

"Yeah."

"Find out where they are. Jimmie and I will pay them a visit."

"Got it."

CHAPTER 29

Southwest Missouri

JR frowned when several messages from a tracking routine popped up on his monitor. Whoever the individual he had been playing cat and mouse with might be, they were good. His numerous attempts to backtrack the electronic probes ended in broken connections or misdirected IP addresses. With the frustration and failure of traditional methods, he felt no choice but to fall back on a program written when he was deep into the hacker community. He utilized it for the first time in several years. The results were not immediate. But, several hours after switching to the old program, his search narrowed itself down to one distinct location.

The individual looking for his friend Sean resided in a small town in Iowa. And since the number of computers in this tiny community were relatively few compared to a large metropolitan area, pinpointing the Internet provider did not take long. Once inside their database, he had the address and name of the individual attempting to find Sean Kruger.

With a few keystrokes, he informed the Internet provider the individual's account was past due and shut off their access to the Web. The inquiries into Kruger's whereabouts abruptly ceased.

He then hacked into the Iowa Department of Transportation and retrieved the picture on the individual's driver's license. Holding the printed picture in his hand, he tilted his head. "You look familiar."

Composing an email, he sent it and dialed a number.

"It's Saturday, JR. I'm off."

"I know, Alexia, but I need you to look at a picture I sent in an email."

"Is it a who or a what?"

"A who."

"Just a minute." The call went silent for twenty seconds. "Her name is Anna Cole."

"That's kind of what I thought. The woman in the picture is identified as Mollie Lewis, residence in Boxy Flats, Iowa."

"Well, it might not be Anna. I have not heard anything about her since I moved here from Mexico City."

"Thanks. I wanted confirmation the woman looks like Anna."

"JR, there's more to this than what you're telling me."

"She is doing a thorough job of trying to find Sean's physical address and hide the fact she's looking."

"That sounds like Anna."

"Sure does." He paused. "What are you and Jimmie doing right now?"

"Apparently, we're getting ready to drive to Springfield to meet with you and Sean."

"Isn't that a coincidence? I was going to ask you to do so."

***

The soundproof conference room next to JR's newly enclosed office space remained the only unchanged area on the second floor. Except for the newly installed hidden staircase leading to an exit door, it looked the same as it always had despite being rebuilt after imploding when a bomb detonated inside the building.

Kruger looked at the picture as he sat across from Jimmie and Alexia. "She doesn't look like a hacker."

Alexia smiled. "Did I look like a hacker, Sean?"

Realizing he was thinking out loud, Kruger looked at her. "No, and you still don't. Bad choice of words." He handed the picture to Jimmie. Returning his attention to Alexia, he asked, "How do you and JR know her?"

"She was always in a chat room JR and I sometimes patronized a decade ago. Her skills weren't that good, if I remember correctly. But she openly admitted to who she was and posted her photo numerous times. Something I never did."

"Nor did I," said JR.

Jimmie Gibbs studied the image. "How old was she back then?"

"Twenty-five." This from Alexia.

"She looks older than thirty-five to me."

JR nodded. "If she's in hiding, that can age you rapidly."

Kruger reached for the picture. "What's she doing working for Hunter Holden?"

"She probably doesn't know who she's working for, Sean. This type of work is normally done via back channels. And, it is normally paid up front."

Looking at the picture, Kruger said, "I think I need to have a conversation with her."

Standing, JR nodded. "Me, too. Let's go."

***

About a third of the way between Des Moines and Omaha, Nebraska, south of Interstate 80, lay the sleepy town of Boxy Falls, Iowa. With a population of less than one thousand in the previous census and regular appearance of

U-Hauls, the town now held fewer citizens than stated on the city limits sign.

The KKG private jet landed in Des Moines as dusk faded to night. Kruger, JR, and Jimmie Gibbs drove the final ninety-five miles and parked across from the small bungalow two blocks south of the town square. Lights inside the home were not visible, and the only outside light illuminated the front porch.

Folding his arms over the steering wheel of the rented SUV, Kruger rested his chin. "Towns of this size sometimes have alleys running behind the houses."

Jimmie asked, "How can you tell?"

"No driveways. Access to the garage is normally from the alley."

"Didn't know that."

"I grew up in a town like this."

JR said, "Should we check out the house from behind?"

Glancing at his watch, Kruger nodded. "It's still early. We might see a light in the back half of the house." Placing the transmission in drive, he steered the SUV as they searched for the entrance to the alley.

Three minutes later, they saw a single light on the rear southwest corner of the house. "Apparently, someone is home." Kruger turned to look at JR in the back seat. "Anything?"

He nodded. "I'm getting a strong Wi-Fi signal from the house. She apparently got her account straightened out."

"Can you access her network?"

"Not quickly."

Gibbs said, "I would bet if JR knocks on the front door and she checks to see who it is, she'll make a fast exit out the back. Sean, you and I could wait there."

Putting the SUV in park, Kruger flipped the inside light switch to off and opened his door. "Great idea, Jimmie. Let's go."

***

JR stepped onto the large front porch of the single-story Craftsman home. He pressed the button on the doorbell, heard a chime inside, and waited. Thirty seconds elapsed, and he pressed it again. Still no response. After a third ring, he sensed rather than heard footsteps approach the door. Then a pause occurred, and the steps receded into the interior of the house.

He waited a minute before he pressed it a fourth time. Ten seconds later, the front door opened, and Kruger stood there. "Jimmie was right. She practically ran out the back door. She understands we aren't here to hurt her. But she wants to talk to you."

"She recognized me?"

"Apparently."

"How the hell did she do that?"

"Why don't you ask her."

Once inside, JR followed Kruger toward the back of the house. Anna Cole, now living under the name Mollie Lewis, sat at a small kitchen table. A petite woman, her gray hair gave her the appearance of someone fifteen years older than her thirty-five years. She looked up as JR entered the room.

"You're John Zachara, aren't you?"

Tilting his head, JR appraised the woman. "What name are you using these days, Anna?"

She shook her head. "Not Anna. I can tell you that."

"Is it Mollie Lewis?"

Her eyes widened briefly, but the expression of indifference returned. "Maybe." She paused for a few moments. "How did you find me? Or, more importantly, why did you find me?"

Nodding his head toward Kruger, JR said, "You were trying to locate a friend of mine. Rather clumsily, I might add."

The woman looked at the tall man indicated by JR.

"You're Sean Kruger?"

A nod was her answer.

"Damn. Guess I've lost my touch."

Kruger said, "Why?"

"Why what?"

"Why were you trying to find my address?"

She shrugged.

"Mollie. May I call you Mollie, or do you prefer Anna?"

"Whatever."

"How much were you offered to find me?"

Looking at Kruger then JR and back to Kruger, she smiled. "A bunch."

"Who offered it?"

"Haven't got a clue. The money was deposited, and that's all I needed to know."

Pulling out a chair next to her, Kruger sat and clasped his hands in front of him. "Anna, I'm a retired FBI agent. The man who hired you is trying to kill me. If you hadn't been discovered by JR, and they were successful, you would have been an accessory to murder. Do you know what the punishment is for killing a retired federal agent?"

With wide eyes, she shook her head.

"It's a capital offense."

"I didn't know you were an FBI agent."

"Doesn't matter."

Tears leaked down her cheeks. "I—"

JR said, "How did they contact you, Anna?"

She sniffed. "Encrypted emails."

Leaning forward in his chair, Kruger asked, "So, you know who they are?"

"I didn't say that."

"But you've communicated with them before?"

She shrugged.

Having remained quiet during the first part of the interview, Jimmie asked, "Why did they contact you, Anna?"

She directed her attention to the ex-Navy SEAL. "I'm good at finding people who don't want to be found. Normally, it's husbands or boyfriends who have abused their partners and then disappeared."

Keeping eye contact with her, Kruger said, "A noble cause. Do you know what would have happened to you after you found me?"

"Nothing, I assumed."

"Someone would have showed up at your front door one day, and that would have been the end of your assisting abused women."

"They don't know where I live."

"We found you."

She blinked several times and then put her head in her hands and sobbed.

Kruger gently placed his hand on her shoulder. "Anna, it's okay. We stopped you just in time. No harm done."

She shook her head violently and brushed his hand away. "You don't understand. I found you another way. They know where you live."

CHAPTER 30

Iowa

Anna Cole's statement startled Kruger. He stood and paced. JR sat in the vacated chair. "Anna, tell me how you did it?" Her face grew crimson, and her nostrils flared. "You're the great John Zachara. How did you not think of it." She glared at him and crossed her arms. "You were always condescending in the chat room. I felt you considered yourself above everyone who didn't quite meet your standards."

A frown appeared on JR. "I don't remember it that way, Anna."

"Oh my gawd. You're kidding me. I begged you to explain your techniques, but you ignored my requests."

"Well, I apologize if I hurt your feelings. I tried to stay in the background during those sessions."

She suddenly slammed a fist on the table and stood. "You constantly bragged about your exploits. How dare you say you tried to stay anonymous. I was the invisible one."

Kruger placed his hand on her shoulders and pushed her back onto the seat. He growled, "Sit down."

She glared at him but followed his instructions.

JR contemplated the woman for a few moments. With his voice as calm as possible, he said, "Please tell me how you found Sean."

"It's easy. Since the explosion of social media apps, I've learned how to find people on Facebook, Instagram, or Twitter. His wife is a professor at a university. Her students mention her name all the time in their posts. After a few false starts, I found her. Afterward, I backtracked on those threads until someone mentioned the school's name. Once I discovered where she taught, I hacked into the college HR department. All I needed to know was right there in her personnel file: husband's name and their address."

"When did you find it?"

Her eyes locked onto JR. With an accusatorial smile, she folded her arms. "I'll bet you're the one who got me kicked off the Internet, weren't you?"

JR nodded.

"It makes sense now. I couldn't figure out who did it. Once I got back online, I stopped looking for him and trolled social media for the last name."

With a frown, JR nodded. "You're right. I didn't think of that." He looked up at Jimmie. "Better let your team know."

With a nod, the retired SEAL pulled his cell phone out and left the kitchen.

Kruger stopped pacing. He took a deep breath and then looked at the woman. "How long ago?"

"What do you mean?"

"When did you tell them my address?"

She shrugged. "Couple of hours ago."

On the verge of a growl, Kruger bent over so he could lock eyes with her. "This isn't a game, lady. The people you are dealing with have no qualms about taking the life of anyone who gets in their way. If anything happens to my family, so, help me God, I will make it my mission in life to see you on death row. Is that clear, Anna?"

Standing suddenly, her faced turned crimson, and she pointed a finger at him. "I didn't say anything about your wife, I just gave them the address. Nothing more."

Kruger frowned. "You don't get it, do you?"

"I'm smarter than you think. I didn't tell them about your wife. Just you."

Closing his eyes, Kruger suddenly recognized the personality disorder he was dealing with. He took a deep breath and let it out slowly. "My wife lives there, too, Anna."

Her hand rose to her mouth as she gasped. "I didn't think of that. Everyone I deal with on the Internet is separated. I thought…" She collapsed back into the chair and cradled her head in her hands. "I'm sorry."

"For your sake, I hope it's not too late."

Turning to JR, Kruger said, "See if you can find out who communicated with her."

Looking at the woman, who now sobbed uncontrollably, JR asked, "Do you want to give me access to your computer?"

She stopped crying. Her face grew crimson, and she glared at JR. "Not in a million years."

Turning to Kruger, JR said, "Why don't you call the FBI? It's no use trying to deal with her. I'm sure they would love to have a chat about her recent activities."

After a few moments of hesitation, she told him her access code.

***

Minneapolis

Dean Melton handed the piece of paper to Holden. "The hacker found him."

Scanning the information, the CEO then looked up at his assistant. "Springfield, Missouri?"

"Yeah."

"Where the hell is that?"

"Southwestern part of the state, close to the Arkansas state line."

"That tells me nothing." He paused as he studied the page. "What are you going to do about the hacker? Her past usefulness is unimportant because she's now a liability."

"I don't know. What do you want done?"

"Can they trace her inquiry back to me?"

"Doubtful. But you never know."

"Hmmm…" He paused. "Do you trust her?"

Melton shrugged. "I have no reason to. Why?"

"Dean, I don't need to remind you, she must not be allowed to trace anything back to this organization or me."

"Understood, sir. I'll take care of it."

"See that you do."

Melton left the office. Holden watched the door close as he drummed his fingers on the desk. After pursing his lips, he shut his computer off. Grabbing his suit coat from the back of his chair, he locked the door and hurried toward the parking lot. Once safe in the car, he used the hands-free function to place a phone call.

By eight that evening, Holden sat in a back booth of an out-of-the-way Italian restaurant in St. Paul. Nursing a whiskey tumbler of Maker's Mark, he checked his watch. Hadley was late. An event the CEO could never tolerate.

At five after, his guest hobbled toward the table. When the man sat, Holden scowled. "You're late."

"Tough shit."

"Why are you limping?"

"Because that asshole Jerry Stein shot me."

"I hope you returned the favor."

"Yeah. He didn't walk away from the encounter like I did."

"Good."

Pointing toward Holden's glass, the man from Chicago said, "Order me one of those."

"Order it yourself."

"Aren't we compassionate tonight."

"Whatever. I know where Kruger lives."

Hadley appeared not to hear the news as he flagged down a server. After giving the young woman his order, he turned back to the CEO. "What'd you say?"

Closing his eyes and shaking his head, Holden took a sip of his cocktail. "I said, we know where Kruger lives."

"Good for you."

"Time for you to fulfill your obligation to me."

Leaning over the table, Hadley snarled, "I'm a little laid up right now, Hunter. Or did you fail to notice."

Holden paused, frowned, and took another sip of his drink. "How long?"

"At least a month."

"That's too long."

Hadley's drink arrived, and he took his time with a long sip. Finally, he glared at the man sitting across from him. "It is what it is, Hunter."

"Then you need to find someone to handle your obligations."

"No, Hunter, you need to gain some patience. Kruger's not going anywhere, and I doubt he's aware you know his location."

"You don't know that."

"How would he learn about it? Did someone call him and tell him to be on the lookout, Hunter Holden knows where you are? I doubt it."

"I'm sure you know people who, for the right price, will handle these types of projects."

With a chuckle, Hadley sipped his drink again. "Projects. That's funny, Hunter." He paused. "The answer is yes. I know a few guys. But they're expensive."

"How much?"

"Thought you were in financial hard times."

"The company is. I have plenty of personal money. Are

these individuals good?"

Hadley didn't answer immediately. He sipped his drink and watched the CEO with practiced neutrality. "I'm sure all the associates you laid off at your company will be pleased to know you still have plenty of money."

"My personal finances are nobody's business. Answer my question. Are any of these individuals good?"

"One is."

"Who is he?"

"He's a she."

"A she."

Hunter Holden's personal fixer nodded.

"A woman might actually work better. Tell me about her."

"I don't know a lot other than she used to be an MP in the army. Served in Iraq and Afghanistan. Left the service and went to work for a private military contractor. She specializes in providing protection for high-level government clients. Rumors are she also moonlights providing services for clients who have special needs."

"What does that mean?"

"Use your imagination, Hunter."

"Do you know how to get in touch with her?"

"I might know a guy who can."

"You might know a guy." Holden slowly shook his head. "That sounds like a throwaway line from a movie, Dalton."

The thug from Chicago shrugged.

"Talk to your guy. Find out what she would charge for taking care of our Mr. Kruger."

Standing, Hadley gave Holden a grin. "I get a cut if she agrees."

"We can discuss it after you secure her services."

"When do you want to meet with her?"

"This is your project, Dalton. She is not to know of my involvement."

"Whatever you say, Hunter."

CHAPTER 31

Iowa

"Do you believe anything she's saying, JR?"

Standing next to Kruger, the computer genius folded his arms. "I honestly don't remember much about her. What I do remember is she struck me as a wanna-be hacker. Apparently, at the time, her skills did not impress me."

"How did she know your real name?"

"A question I can't answer. The only name I ever used in those chat rooms was Zardoz."

"Alexia seemed to know more about her. Maybe she needs to get involved?"

"Before we do that, I want to ask her how she knew my name. Want to listen in?"

"Wouldn't miss it."

Returning to the interior of the small house, they found Jimmie leaning on the kitchen cabinet, a watchful eye still on Anna Cole sitting at the kitchen table. Looking at Gibbs, Kruger asked, "Did she say anything while we were outside?"

"Nope, just kept looking out the back door like she was

expecting someone."

Turning his attention to the woman, Kruger said, "Anticipating guests, Anna?"

She narrowed her eyes and glared at the retired FBI agent. "The police know you're here. They will show up and arrest all of you for kidnapping me."

"Kind of hard to be kidnapped when you're still in your own house."

"You know what I mean."

"No, Anna, I don't. How do the police know we're here?"

"I told them."

"When?"

"Just before you broke into my home."

"When did we…" He paused, realizing if she had called the police, they would have showed up a long time ago. "Never mind. JR has a few questions for you."

Taking a seat in the chair next to her at the table, JR said, "Anna, think back to the days when we were in the chat room."

"Not sure if I want to."

"Okay. I'm curious, I never used the name John Zachara online. How did you know it?"

"You used it all the time."

"No, I didn't."

She studied him for a few moments before raising her chin in defiance. "I'm smarter than you think."

"Anna, I never thought of you as stupid. I barely remember you."

Her eyes narrowed. "See? I knew it. You paid zero attention to me. I was just as good as you were back then. Plus, over the years, my skills have improved tenfold."

"You haven't answered my question. How did you know my name?"

She folded her arms and glared at him. "You don't remember, do you?"

"Like I told you, I don't remember you that well from the

chat rooms."

With a slow shake of her head, she gave him a cold stare. "To think I worshipped you. What a waste of my time. I had just gained my dream job right out of college at CWZ Software. I was in my second week when the company was bought out by Abel Plymel. You were one of the owners and should have warned us about what would happen. I lost my job a week later. I've never forgiven you for that."

JR frowned. "Yes, Anna, I was one of the founders, but I chose not to be in management and therefore was not privy to Plymel's plans."

"Liar."

With a roll of his eyes, JR turned to his friend. "Your witness."

Kruger asked, "How long have you worked for Transnational Financial?"

"Who?"

"Hunter Holden."

"Oh, him. I've been helping him for years."

"Really?"

"Yes."

"Are they the ones who hired you to find me?"

"Of course not."

Kruger looked at JR, who frowned.

Motioning JR back outside, the retired FBI agent walked to their vehicle. JR followed. When they were both inside and the doors closed, Kruger turned to his friend. "I thought you said when you accessed her computer, the text messages traced back to Dean Melton."

"They do, Sean." He stared at the back of the house. "She's not playing with a full deck of cards."

"Unfortunately, I'm not sure how firm her grasp of reality is. Do you remember her working for CWZ?"

"No, but I didn't know half our associates. We grew too fast."

"So, that's how she knew your real name."

"Apparently." He paused for a moment. "Can we take advantage of her association with Holden?"

"Not following you, JR."

"Let's taunt Melton, make him think she knows all about him and the organization. They might lash out, and we could be ready."

"Can you take over her persona on the Internet?"

"Yeah, I guess so. Why?"

"I like your idea of making them lash out. I'm tired of being chased by Hunter Holden. It's time to turn the tables on him."

"What about Anna Cole?"

Pulling out his cell phone, Kruger pressed on a name in his contact list and turned to JR while he waited for the call to go through. "We're going to let the FBI put her on ice for the next few weeks."

***

Three black Suburbans arrived just as the first light of dawn appeared in the eastern sky. Two were parked in front of Mollie Lewis' small Craftsman-style home with one positioned in the rear. By mid-morning, a crowd gathered around the small home, whispering among themselves. Their comments centered around the crazy lady who lived there and how horrible it was something like this could happen in Boxy Falls. Nobody in the assembly knew what *this* might be, but it was a horrible event nonetheless.

Men and women agents wearing dark-blue windbreakers with the letters FBI in bold yellow on the back swarmed over the house. Occasionally, one of these agents would carry out a white bank box and place it in the rear of the SUV parked in the back.

The Special Agent in Charge of the FBI field office in West Des Moines stood in the living room listening to a phone call. Kruger stood in front of her with his arms folded and a slight smile.

Special Agent Bridgett Nelson, who had worked with Kruger just before his retirement, finished her conversation and ended the call. "I haven't spoken to Director Clark since you and he discovered Kevin Marks was actually Kreso Markovic in Landers, Wyoming." She smiled. "He still remembers me."

"Probably why you're now a Special Agent in Charge, Agent Nelson."

"He told me to give you my 100 percent cooperation, which I had planned to do anyway."

"Thank you."

"What do we do with Anna Cole?"

"How long can you hide her and keep her under arrest?"

"Director Clark is suggesting we charge her as a domestic terrorist."

"That means you can keep her tied up indefinitely, correct?"

"Not indefinitely, but we can find a judge who will agree to deny her bail. How long do you need her held?"

"My guess would be two weeks, maybe three. Plus, we need to keep her laptop."

"I don't think that will be a problem."

CHAPTER 32

Iowa

By nightfall, the black Suburbans were gone, as was Anna Cole. The crowd around the Craftsman-style home had dispersed, returning to their daily routines. Inside the small house, three men remained.

JR sat at the desk the homeowner used for her computer work. He looked up at Kruger and said, "You won't believe what's here, Sean."

"On her computer?"

"Yes. She was involved with the Field Museum heist."

"You're kidding?"

"Nope. I'll have to study it, but there's a lot here."

Glancing at his wristwatch, the retired FBI agent pursed his lips. "If we leave now, we can be back in Springfield by midnight. You'll need to bring her laptop."

***

Thirty minutes remained in the HA-420 HondaJet's flight from Des Moines to Springfield Branson National Airport.

JR concentrated on Anna Cole's laptop. He sat across from Kruger.

The silent retired FBI agent stared out the window. Finally, he turned to JR. "What is Hunter Holden's largest problem at the moment?"

"Besides you?"

"Yeah."

"Probably money."

"Exactly. What is the biggest problem the FBI has in nailing him?"

"He doesn't commit crimes inside the United States."

"Exactly. What if we tempt him into trying to take over a company inside the US and, when he takes the bait, the FBI will be waiting for him?"

"How are we going to do that?"

Kruger turned to Jimmie who sat in the seat behind JR. "Do you think Alexia would be willing to help us set up Transnational into committing a crime inside the US?"

"I learned a long time ago not to speak for her."

"I'm going to ask Stephanie and her to pose as their former selves who are in the process of starting a new Internet company. We'll position them as former executives seeking investors in a new startup."

"Similar to how we set up the Kaphar Sourcing scam?"

"No, this will be a nonexistent entity. I don't think Holden will fall for a scam like Kaphar again."

"If Stephanie is involved, I'm sure Alexia will, but she'll have to answer for herself."

"There's a possibility of putting them in harm's way. So, we'll need someone who can help protect them as an associate."

"I can do it."

"I thought of you, Jimmie, but you were in on the Kaphar Sourcing scam. Someone might recognize you. It will have to be someone we've not used before."

The three men sat in silence as the pilot started his descent for landing. JR cleared his throat. "What about Michael Wolfe's wife, Nadia?"

Kruger's eyebrows rose.

JR continued. "She used to work for Israel's Mossad and, from what I've learned, can take care of herself."

"Thought they were in Israel."

"Got back last week."

"Huh." He paused and stared out the window again. Finally, as the plane's wheels touched down on the runway, he said, "That might work even better."

***

"What do you mean I will need to become Stephanie Harris again?"

"You still have your old driver's license with your maiden name on it, don't you?"

"Yes, but it's probably expired by now."

The time approached 11:30 p.m. as they prepared for bed. He leaned against his side of the vanity as she washed her face.

"That can be changed."

She stopped, dried with a towel, and studied him for a few moments. "You're serious, aren't you?"

"Yes."

"Sean, I'm not a business person anymore."

"No, but you used to be the president of sales at a very large corporation. You can talk the talk and know your way around a board room."

She tilted her head slightly and studied him. "So, what would I have to do?"

"Be charming and convincing."

With a smile, she said, "Since you put it that way, who do I have to be charming to?"

"The man who wants me dead."

Her eyes widened, and she placed her hands on her hips.

"Then I will need to be as convincing as possible."

"You'll have help."

"Who?"

"Alexia Gibbs and Nadia Wolfe."

"Alexia, I know. I don't believe I've met Nadia."

"You will tomorrow. You and I are meeting with them in JR's conference room at four."

CHAPTER 33

Southwest Missouri

Stephanie Kruger shook the hand of Nadia Wolfe as JR introduced them. The woman's long dark-brown hair streamed around an oval face and highlighted her slightly upturned nose. Emerald-green eyes hinted at an innate intelligence. Stephanie liked her immediately. "It is nice to finally meet you, Nadia. Alexia speaks of you often."

"I'm glad to meet you as well, Stephanie. Alexia and I have become good friends over the past few years. We both speak French, my native language. It helps keep me from feeling homesick."

With a smile, Stephanie said in her far-from-fluent French, "I have not spoken the language for years. There are not too many individuals who speak it around here."

Nadia laughed and replied in the same language. "No, not too many."

Petite in stature, Stephanie had been described by her husband on numerous occasions as strikingly beautiful with naturally curly brown hair. Her pale-blue eyes sparkled as she smiled at the sound of the French language. A smile all who knew her found infectious.

JR left the room to retrieve his laptop and returned, setting it up next to Kruger who took the seat near the door. Alexia was the last to arrive, having spent time in her office before the meeting.

Nadia and Alexia hugged and kissed each other's cheeks. She then hugged Stephanie and sat next to her. Kruger started the meeting.

"Thank you all for coming this afternoon. I want you to consider what I am going to propose very carefully. No one is obligated to join us, and you may not wish to after you hear the details."

Silence filled the room.

"As a preamble, I want to discuss Stephanie's background and what her role will be in this endeavor. When we met, she was the president of US sales with an international greeting card company. She reported to the CEO. This gives her an insight to how big corporations work. She also understands what it takes to start a new business. One of her duties included recruiting new franchise owners to sell the company's cards."

Nadia and Alexia grinned.

Kruger pursed his lips. "You both already knew this, didn't you?"

Alexia said, "Yes, Sean, we did. Nadia and I are on board, otherwise we wouldn't be here. Now, let's hear the plan."

"I want you three to solicit financial backing from Hunter Holden for a new startup."

Nadia nodded, Alexia smiled, and Stephanie said, "What kind of startup, Sean?"

"Internet. Since I am not well versed on those types of businesses, we need input from everyone around the table. I will say, we need it to be unique and one with large profit potential."

"Why?"

"Well, Nadia, our Mr. Hunter Holden needs to feel he will

make a huge profit and has to get involved right now before you take the idea to someone else. We have to appeal to his ego. Plus, he needs cash to assist in getting his company, Transnational Financial, out of debt and back in the good graces of his clients."

"How are we going to build his interest in our company?" Stephanie had already grasped the first hurdle.

"Holden has a lot of contacts across the globe who provide tips on companies. We don't know this for a fact, but I am guessing they are compensated somehow. All we have to do is find one to leak the information about our new company."

Nadia raised her hand. "Let's say we get Holden's attention with this company. Say we get him to agree to invest. How's that going to get the FBI involved?"

"As a rule, Holden seldom invests his own money. The last time he did, he got burned. So, he will be more interested in gathering a group of investors. From what we can tell, his company is under financial stress and needs to recoup some of its losses. We want him to find others to commit money to this new venture. Once he takes ownership of the investment dollars, we will leak information to the SEC the company he's representing doesn't exist. He is then in violation of a number of federal fraud statutes."

"Aren't we as well? Since we will be selling the idea to Holden."

"No, Nadia. We won't leave any evidence behind that the three of you were the ones with the idea. JR will plant evidence on Holden's corporate computer explaining how he was responsible for thinking up the whole scheme. It will also have information on the hard drive outlining how he had the diamonds at the Field Museum in Chicago intercepted, copied, and delivered to the museum. He staged the theft to bankrupt Goldmax."

"Is that evidence faked?" This from Alexia.

Shaking his head, Kruger said, "No. JR found it on Anna

Cole's computer. She was involved in that scam as well."

"Why not just turn that info over to the FBI, Sean?"

"The evidence was obtained illegally. Once his new investors contact the SEC accusing Holden of fraud, all his computers will be confiscated. Once that is done, the FBI will find the evidence about the diamond heist. Since the theft of the diamonds drew national attention, it has a higher profile. I've been assured the investment fraud case will take a back seat while the FBI pursues prosecution on the diamond heist."

Stephanie smiled. "Now, I wonder who would have assured you of something like that?"

Her husband grinned but did not respond.

Alexia clasped her hands in front of her. "Now all we have to do is figure out what kind of company to sell Hunter Holden."

JR looked up from his laptop. "I think I found the perfect concept."

***

Utilizing Anna Cole's computer access to the email account of Dean Melton, JR wrote a program to mine data from Transnational's email server. The program searched emails for key words attributed to investment opportunities. It also sought out contacts within the international financial news media who might have communicated with Holden or Melton.

Over the course of the inquiry, JR found a *Bloomberg* reporter based in Switzerland, who seemed to have successfully leaked information to Melton on numerous occasions resulting in a successful takeover. Her name was Zoe Oppelt. In addition to finding the information, if the deal worked, she received compensation from Transnational Financial. JR used her email address to send a message.

Zoe: *Have information concerning a startup seeking*

financing. Word on street is the concept deserves serious attention.

Ten minutes later, JR received the response.

Melton: *Need more information. Website and business plan.*

Zoe: *Find link to website and SEC document attached to this email. Background on principals: CEO is a veteran of corporate America. Fifteen years with a Fortune 500 company as VP and president of sales. CTO has decade of helping startups with online security and technical consulting. CFO is French with multiple years working for BNP Paribas.*

Melton: *Will get back to you if interested.*

The email string stopped, and JR displayed a slight grin. Once Holden read the fictional business plan and viewed the fake website, the man's greed and narcissism would demand he get involved.

***

Sipping a glass of Maker's Mark, Hunter Holden finished reading the paperwork handed to him by Dean Melton. "Have these three individuals been vetted yet, Dean?"

"We have two staff researchers working on it as we speak."

"I don't want another fiasco like the Kaphar Sourcing deal."

"No, sir. Neither do any of us."

"I'm a little hesitant to get involved because the company would be incorporated in Delaware. We never invest in US companies."

"True, but we haven't found a lot of prospects lately."

"I'm aware of that. What do you think?"

"If everything checks out on the three principals, I think the concept has merits. But I wouldn't do it with your own or Transnational's money."

"That's what I am thinking. Transnational will take a little time to recuperate from the Kaphar incident. Let's get a consortium together and raise the seed money for these ladies. If they check out, we invest. If they don't, we find another investment for our clients. We won't give the money back."

With a nod of his head, Melton turned and walked out of Holden's office. After taking another sip, the CEO searched his contact list for a specific number. After he found it, he pressed the call icon. It was answered on the fourth ring.

"I haven't heard from you in a long time, Hunter. Word on the street is you lost a lot of money a while back."

"Rumors, Gary, just rumors. Don't believe everything you hear."

"Right. Why the call?"

"You have your finger on the pulse of corporate America better than any reporter working for the *Wall Street Journal*."

"Now you're blowing smoke up my ass. Got a story for me?"

"I wondered if you have ever heard of a woman named Stephanie Harris?"

"Name sounds familiar. Why do you ask?"

"Just checking on her background."

"You planning to hire her? Can I quote you on that?"

"You never know. And you can't quote me. Do you know anything about her?"

There was silence on the phone call for a few moments. "Now I remember. She used to be the second-in-command at Hallmark. She was being groomed to take over the company at some point."

"You used past tense."

"Yeah, she left suddenly some years back. Haven't heard anything about her since. Does she have something going on?"

"Maybe. Any idea why she left?"

"No. It's a privately held company. They don't share a lot of information with us members of the press."

"But she did work there."

"I just said that, Hunter. You know something, don't you?"

"Do the names Alexia Montreal or Nadia Picard ring any bells?"

"Can't say they do. Not like the name Stephanie Harris. You've got a lead on a new start-up, don't you, Hunter?"

"Use your imagination, Gary. If something develops, you'll be the first reporter I call."

"Why do I not believe you?"

Holden laughed as he pressed the end-call icon.

CHAPTER 34

Chicago

Lakeside Tavern's clientele ranged from wanna-be bikers to Gen X burnouts. Situated a few blocks from the western shore of Lake Michigan north of the Chicago Loop, the pub featured cheap drinks, cheaper women, and the occasional fistfight.

Dalton Hadley sat with his back to the wall in a corner away from murmured conversations occurring throughout the bar. The beer he nursed sat half empty on the sticky tabletop, growing warmer with each passing second. At twenty-six minutes past the agreed-upon time, his contact entered the pub and made a beeline to the bar area. Once there, he leaned over and said something to the bartender, after which, a beer was poured and placed in front of the man. Leaning against the bar rail, he sipped the beverage and casually surveyed the clientele. When he locked eyes with Hadley, the man straightened and walked nonchalantly toward the table.

When he sat, he said, "You have something for me?"

A white envelope appeared in Hadley's hands, and he

tilted his head. "Depends. Did you get the information I asked for?"

His answer was a nod.

Using his left hand, Hadley pushed the envelope across the table. Picking it up, the man glanced inside, smiled, and said, "She's interested. But it will be expensive."

"Understandable."

"She wants a hundred K up front and another hundred on completion of the job."

Hadley narrowed his eyes. "When can she get it done?"

"She's out of the country right now."

"My client is not a patient individual. They will want to know."

"A week, maybe two."

"A week would be better."

The man shrugged. "She doesn't answer to me."

Tapping a finger on the table, Hadley kept his eyes locked on the visitor. "How does she want to be paid?"

The man handed him a business card. "Wire transfer. When you have it, call this number for the details."

Hadley took the card, stood, and walked out of the tavern.

***

"You normally don't solicit investments, Hunter."

Holden smiled as he addressed the six people attending his virtual meeting. "As a rule, Frank, I don't. But all of you on this call have invested with me in the past and reaped exceedingly high percentage returns when you did. I've decided this particular opportunity has one of the best long-term returns prospects of any new start-up I've seen in a long time. The management team is top notch, and the concept is timely and on point."

"How much are you investing, Hunter?" This came from Gabriel Patel, the top-left image of the seven-member gallery view.

"I've set this opportunity up in one hundred equal shares. Someone can buy all of them, multiple shares, or just one. I am buying ten."

Patel continued. "What are your long-term expectations?"

"I personally believe in five years it will return four times the initial investment."

"Lofty goal, Hunter."

"Yes, Gabriel, it is. I've investigated the CEO's experience. She has a history of accomplishing these types of returns in the past."

"So, we're to take your word?"

Holden smiled at the question. He looked at the bottom-right image, a middle-aged woman with a harsh glare, a harsher tongue, and a mid-level slot on the *Forbes Richest Self-Made Women* list, Alisha Bennet. "Alisha, you don't have to take my word for it. Once you sign a nondisclosure agreement, you are welcome to all the information I have available. Then you can make up your own mind."

She pursed her lips but remained silent.

"I'm not holding a gun to your head, but I want to ensure someone doesn't do an end run around me and keep me out of this opportunity. That's why I need the agreement signed before I share the business plan with any of you."

Everyone nodded except Frank Baxter.

"Sign them and send to Dean as an email attachment. As soon as we have them, I will continue with the briefing."

Baxter folded his arms. "Not so fast, Hunter."

"Do you have a question, Frank?"

"I've got several, and I am not signing a nondisclosure agreement."

"Those are my terms concerning receipt of the business plan and staying on this conference call."

"Are you going to guarantee our initial investments?"

Shaking his head, Holden remained silent for several seconds. "There are no guarantees in this industry, Frank.

You know that."

"In other words, no."

"I didn't say that. If it will help you make a decision, I'll put in our contract that I will buy back your initial investment myself, should you want out."

"You feel that strongly about it?"

"I do."

"Very well. Let's go over the business plan."

***

"How'd the call go, Hunter?"

Holden looked up to see Dean Melton enter his office. "I got all of them except Baxter. He's going to mull it over, so he said. Well, too bad for him. I've sold all the shares. We now have one hundred million in seed money available to us."

Melton nodded. "When do you want to schedule the meeting with Stephanie Harris and her team?"

"In person or virtual?"

"From what they told me, in person. They'll travel here."

"Excellent. When?"

"That's up to you."

"The sooner the better. I don't want Frank Baxter going behind my back. This is the best startup prospect I've seen in years."

"Shall I go ahead and pay our friend at Bloomberg?"

Holden directed his attention to his second-in-command. "Not yet. Let's hold off on making payment for a while."

"You are planning on paying her, right?"

"Haven't decided."

Melton shook his head. "Whatever, Hunter. She's helped us numerous times, and you always paid her."

"We'll see."

His second-in-command clasped his hands behind his back and remained silent.

***

Springfield Branson National Airport

The HA-420 HondaJet sat just outside its home-base hangar on the tarmac. A Phillips 66 fuel truck parked beside it topped off the tanks for the first leg of a flight to Minneapolis. The corporate pilot for KKG Solutions, Stewart Barnett, walked around the plane doing his pre-flight inspection. When the truck pulled away, the pilot walked up the airstairs and prepared the plane for takeoff. An old acquaintance and newly minted jet pilot sat in the copilot's seat. Barnett said, "Glad you got your commercial pilot certification."

Michael Wolfe glanced at Barnett and chuckled. "Why, so you can nap?"

"That's part of it. Sometimes I need a copilot on these excursions."

As he spoke, a gunmetal-gray Range Rover pulled up next to the plane. Three women exited the vehicle and climbed the still-extended airstairs to the cabin.

The first one, Stephanie Kruger, possessed a new ID proclaiming her last name to be Harris. With her hair pulled back and a dark-blue skirt and jacket, she once again projected the image of the boardroom executive she maintained before marrying Sean Kruger.

Alexia Gibbs, also with new identification credentials, followed Stephanie into the cabin. She wore a dark-gray pantsuit with a black blouse. The last to enter the cabin was Nadia Wolfe. Professionally dressed like her companions, she wore a pinstriped navy pantsuit.

Barnett turned to greet his new passengers. "Good morning, ladies. Please prepare for takeoff. We will be flying to the Charles B. Wheeler Airport near downtown Kansas City. After a brief stop, we will then fly to Minneapolis and land at St. Paul Downtown Holman Field. Total flight time will be approximately two hours, and we should have you there in time for your 1 p.m. meeting. I will also be your driver for the trip to the Transnational Financial offices in Minneapolis."

Stephanie smiled at him. "Thank you, Stewart."

"My copilot will follow us in a separate vehicle as an added precaution."

Wolfe turned. Nadia chuckled, and the two other ladies said in unison, "Good."

Barnett grinned at his copilot and said, "Apparently, they like you better than me."

"Nope, they all know I carry a gun."

CHAPTER 35

Minneapolis

With the reduced staff count currently employed at Transnational Financial, Holden did not want his guests to see all the empty offices throughout the building. Taking this into consideration, the first-floor conference room became the designated spot for the meeting scheduled to begin at 1 p.m. A receptionist would be at the lobby desk, and Dean Melton would greet them.

Melton escorted the women to the conference room. "Can I get any of you ladies coffee?"

All three shook their heads.

One o'clock came and went without the appearance of their host. Stephanie glanced at her cell phone and stood at precisely ten minutes after the hour. A discussion between Sean Kruger and the three women prior to their departure for Minneapolis predicted Holden would be late to the meeting.

"Mr. Melton, your boss is ten minutes late. If he is not interested in discussing our proposal, he should have had the courtesy to inform us prior to our taking the time and expense of traveling to Minneapolis."

Raising his hands, palms toward Stephanie, he said, "I agree with you, Ms. Harris. But sometimes pressing matters do necessitate his being late to meetings. I'm sure he will be along shortly."

"His lack of informing us about being detained is also troublesome, Mr. Melton. Is this how he communicates with clients? I'm inclined to cancel the meeting and pursue alternate sources of funding."

Nadia and Alexia stood, ready to follow Stephanie out of the conference room. They could see Melton typing a message, presumably to tell Holden the women were leaving.

Stephanie, Alexia, and Nadia left their spots at the conference table and walked toward the door. It opened just before they reached it.

"My apologies for being tardy. Please, let's all get back to our seats so we can start this meeting immediately."

***

Wolfe sat in the rented SUV in the parking lot of the Transnational Financial building. Before they left for the airport, JR transformed Nadia's cell phone into a microphone to record the meeting. It would pick up every sound in the conference room. Listening to the proceedings served two functions. One, to record it. Second, it would alert Wolfe to any possible danger the women might be subjected to should Holden discover the subterfuge. He had confidence in Nadia's ability to defend them, but Wolfe would be backup, just in case.

He chuckled when the CEO came in late, just like Kruger predicted. But, after the initial pleasantries, Holden's attitude toward the women took a dark turn.

***

"Ms. Harris, has your business proposal been submitted to the SEC for scrutiny?"

"We are in the proposal stage, Mr. Holden. When we get to the prospectus phase, proper procedures will be followed."

"I'm concerned that if my company moves forward with funding your venture and then the SEC determines you have violated certain rules, it puts our investment in jeopardy."

Stephanie smiled. "Mr. Holden, I have been providing financial statements for Fortune 500 corporations for years. When we submit our prospectus to the SEC, it will be properly prepared."

"I can't find what you've been doing for the past few years. After you left Hallmark, where did you go?"

"That is a personal question, Mr. Holden. We are here to discuss a business opportunity."

Holden turned to Nadia. "Ms. Picard. I find no records of your activities in the United States. What is your background?"

"I was born in France. My parents immigrated to Israel when I was young. I worked for the government for a number of years."

"What did you do for the government?"

"My activities helped bolster the economy."

"So, you were in the financial sector?"

"At times."

"What do you mean, at times?"

"My activities were sensitive, I'm afraid that is all I can say."

"Hmmm. How am I to judge your experience if you are not forthcoming, Ms. Picard?"

Nadia just smiled and remained quiet.

He frowned and turned to Alexia. "What about you, Ms. Montreal?"

"My degree is from the University of Barcelona. I have worked in the IT sector both in Madrid and Paris. My role in this venture will be supporting our online business strategy. As we have outlined in our proposal, online activity will comprise 80 percent of our projected revenue."

Holden kept his eyes locked on Alexia. "Yes, so your proposal stated."

Stephanie leaned forward. Her hands clasped in front of her. "Mr. Holden, all of this information was provided to you in our proposal. Why are we rehashing backgrounds when we should be discussing how to move forward?"

Dean Melton interjected. "Ms. Harris. We are aware of your team's credentials. Mr. Holden is merely getting a feel for your potential for success. That's all."

Keeping his glare on Stephanie, Holden did not change his expression. He folded his arms and tilted his head. "I find your lack of experience in online commerce troubling, Ms. Harris. In today's environment, if a company does not have a dominant position on the web, chances of success decline."

"I couldn't agree more with you. That is why Ms. Montreal is on our team. She has more than a decade of Internet commerce experience. My expertise is in gathering corporate partners, which we will need to expand our market and increase revenue."

Melton asked, "Where do you foresee your company in five and ten years?"

"If we execute our business strategy correctly, and I don't see why we would not, I believe we can earn back any initial investment within two years. Within five, we will double it. Within ten years, I expect to have sold the company for a tenfold ROI."

"So, you expect to sell the company within ten years?"

"Yes, Mr. Melton. Doesn't everybody?"

Holden's expression did not change. "What personal funding are you and your team providing?"

"We will be stakeholders, Mr. Holden. The details are in our business proposal."

"Yes, but I want to hear it from you. If I am to supply

funding as well as management assistance, I will need to know more than what is in your proposal."

Stephanie smiled but did not take the bait. "Mr. Holden, if you do not wish to invest in our proposal, that is fine." She shut down her iPad and returned it to the computer bag she utilized.

"Where are you going?" This from Melton.

"Judging by Mr. Holden's attitude, we seem to be wasting his time as well as ours." She stood. "Good day, gentlemen." Nadia and Alexia also stood.

As she turned toward the conference room door, Holden said, "Relax and sit down, Ms. Harris. Transnational Financial will agree to provide you with seed money. I just needed to see how dedicated you were to your proposal."

Turning toward Holden, Stephanie clutched the computer bag to her chest. "I'm not sure we will accept your offer. My team and I do not need a fourth member of management. If you wish to offer funding, you will need to sign an agreement to stay hands-off."

"I never agree to those types of agreements. My business instincts are—"

"Inconsequential, Mr. Holden. This is our project and ours alone. If you wish to invest, we welcome your money. However, if you are looking to buy in, that's a deal killer." She stood still and locked eyes with Holden.

"Where else will you get the money, Ms. Harris?"

"We have multiple avenues open to us. We would prefer funding come from one source, but, if we must, we have several offers on the table from Europe and Asia."

With a nod, Holden said, "Give me a few days. Mr. Melton will be in touch."

"Our decision will be made in two days. If you are interested, please provide a notarized letter of intent prior to Thursday. Hardcopy only." She turned and walked out of the conference room followed by Nadia and Alexia.

When the door closed, Melton turned to his boss. "What

do you think?"

"Better than I anticipated. Prepare the letter and include a contract for them to sign. Make sure you have a provision in it for me to take over should things go south on them."

"But she said—"

"I know what she said, but, with her attitude, she'll be successful. At which point, we will walk in and take over."

***

Sitting in his rental SUV, Wolfe heard the last comment from Holden. Nadia had attached a small transmitter to the bottom of her chair just prior to leaving the conference room. They now had a recording of the meeting and the last comments of Holden. He disconnected the app on his cell phone that had recorded the conversation and the offhand remarks.

He watched the three women enter the SUV driven by Stewart Barnett. After the vehicle left the parking lot, Wolfe waited a few minutes to see if the microphone picked up any further conversation. He heard the door opening and the exit of Melton and Holden.

Putting the vehicle in gear, he followed the SUV back to the airport.

CHAPTER 36

Chicago

Amber Willis ducked into the Lakeside Tavern north of the Chicago Loop. At a few minutes after noon, the place resembled a depressing retirement home. Most of the clientele were older men who sat by themselves and stared at the sweat rings their beer glasses deposited on the table. She leaned against the bar and waited for the bartender to approach. Standing at five foot one, three inches above the minimum for a female to join the military, Amber Willis made up for her small stature with a rock-solid physique honed by training in mixed martial arts. While no one would call her beautiful, she possessed a pleasant face accompanied by an unpleasant attitude. However, when the situation required it, she could be deceptively nice. The meeting she would soon attend did not require her to be pleasant.

The bartender approached and said, "Haven't seen you in a while, Amber."

"Been out of town. Any messages for me?"

The bartender nodded his head toward a table in the back corner. "Dillard's got something. Ask him."

With a frown, she said, "How about a beer. Put it on his tab."

"You got it."

When the beer arrived, she wandered over to the table. Without sitting, she said, "Mac says you got something for me."

"Sit down."

"Well, do you?"

"You're drawing attention to yourself. Sit down."

Lowering herself into the chair opposite the man, Amber took a sip of beer. "I'm sitting. Happy?"

"Thrilled. You want to make a hundred K?"

"Who wouldn't. What's the catch, Dillard?"

"Fifty K up front. Fifty when completed."

"What've I got to do, kill someone?"

The man smiled and sipped his beer.

Shaking her head, Amber said, "Not in Chicago."

"Missouri."

"St. Louis or KC?"

"Springfield."

"Where the fuck is that?"

Rolling his eyes, the man said, "Southwestern part of the state, near Arkansas."

"Still doesn't tell me anything."

"You want the job or not?"

"Who is it?"

"Some guy who pissed off another guy bad enough, he'll pay a hundred K to get rid of him."

Amber chuckled. "You're not a very good salesman, asshole. Unless I'm told who it is, I ain't touching the job."

"Why?"

"I'm not in the mood to kill a cop or a federal agent. That's a good way to get locked up and the key thrown away. Now, if it's just some regular Joe, and nobody'll give a shit, I'll do it."

"I don't know his background, just his name."

"What's that?"

"Sean Kruger."

"Where does he live?"

He gave her the address.

"Let me think about it. Be here tomorrow, same time."

She stood and left the tavern.

***

The apartment Amber Willis reluctantly called home consisted of a living area separated from the kitchen by a breakfast bar, with one bedroom and a cramped bathroom. Situated in an old warehouse renovated in the late 1980s, it desperately needed another round of updating. But the rent was cheap, and it kept her out of the cold Chicago winters.

Using an HP Chromebook, she did a Google search on the name Sean Kruger. Nothing came up except a CNN report about his investigation into the death of Deputy Director of the FBI Alan Seltzer. She vaguely remembered the incident and the media circus following the event. The fact her target was an FBI agent gave her pause. At the same time, she realized this might be an opportunity to find a way out of Chicago. She stared at the somewhat grainy image of the man. Even though he was not her type, she found him to be a handsome man. Tall with a bit of gray at the temples, he appeared to be in good shape for someone his age. A further search on the Internet revealed zero information concerning his personal life. Even when she checked Facebook, nothing could be found.

"Aren't you the mystery man, Sean Kruger."

With her decision made to take the job, she checked the bank account where she kept her money earned from extracurricular jobs. If whoever wanted the man dead wanted it badly enough, they would have to pay for it.

With a plan in place, she packed a duffle bag with what few personal items she owned and fell asleep with the knowledge it might be her last night in the city she had grown to hate.

***

The table in the back corner of the Lakeside Tavern already contained a customer when Dillard entered the bar. A satisfied grin crossed his lips as he sat across from Amber. "I take it you want the job."

"I do, but it will cost a hundred K up front and another hundred when the job's done. My terms are cash, preferably a wire transfer."

"I can't authorize that, Amber."

"Obviously, you have no clue who the guy is they want taken out?"

The man shook his head.

"He's a retired FBI agent. The bureau doesn't take kindly to someone offing one of their own. Whoever does the job is going to have all kinds of shit falling down around them."

Her companion tilted his head. "Then, why do you want the job?"

"It's my ticket out of this hellhole people call a city."

"The client wants it done as soon as possible. When could you start?"

"I'm already packed. Once they transfer the money, I'm out of here."

He blinked several times, grinned, and said, "Let me make a phone call." He stood and walked out of the tavern. She sipped her beer and waited.

Ten minutes later, he returned to his chair. "How long will it take?"

"A week, maybe a few days more."

"You've got a deal. Give me the routing and account number."

"Not so fast." She held up a cell phone. "I want to see the money in the account then I'm gone."

"That will take a few days."

"BS. It can be done by four this afternoon." She handed him a piece of paper with a Bank of America routing and account number. "Have the cash in this account by four."

"Where will you be?"

"Around. Where is none of your business. I'll monitor the bank account with my phone."

"I'll let the client know."

"Those are the words I wanted to hear." She stood as he typed on his cell phone. "Pleasure doing business with you, Dillard."

***

A little after four in the afternoon, Amber Willis' ten-year-old Honda Accord approached the city limits of Litchfield, IL. She stopped at a McDonald's to grab something to eat and check her bank app. She was surprised to see the money already in the account. As she munched on French fries, she realized she was a little intimidated at her balance. Prudence dictated the need to transfer most of it to the account she kept for her planned exit from Chicago. After checking the clock on her phone and a Google search for Bank of America branches in St. Louis, she made a hotel reservation at a Drury Inn in Creve Coeur. The town, on the western outskirts of St. Louis, offered two Bank of America branches within a few miles of the hotel.

Returning to the car, the awareness she possessed enough money to simply vanish struck her. All she needed to do was drive to St. Louis, buy a ticket on some airline, and retire to a small island in the Caribbean. The odds of anyone finding her would be slim. She could then live a life of relative peace. A question arose within her as she drove the Honda out of the McDonald's parking lot. Did she have the nerve to walk out on the contract? She did not know.

The pragmatic side of her brain told her she should.

Nothing good could come from killing an FBI agent. The cynical and greedy side wanted the second payment. Whether she might be smart enough to outwit an FBI agent remained an unanswered question.

CHAPTER 37

Southwest Missouri

Stephanie glanced at her husband as he drove her home from the airport. "Hunter Holden is not a pleasant man."

Kruger smiled. "Hunter Holden is a lot of things, and you are right, pleasant is not one of them. I listened to a recording of your meeting. You handled yourself perfectly."

"Once he started with the attitude, I knew exactly what to do. I've had to deal with men like him in the past and, the only way to shut them up is to return the insolence."

"After you three left the meeting, he told Melton his plans to take over the company after a few years."

She slowly shook her head. "How do individuals like him make it so far up the ladder?"

"First, he doesn't care what people think of him and, second, in his mind, he can do no wrong."

With a Cheshire cat grin, she said, "I finally got to say a few things I've always wanted to say to jerks like him. It felt good."

After a quick glance at her, he said, "I'm questioning my judgement about getting you involved."

"Oh, don't be silly, it was fun."

"Anything to do with Hunter Holden cannot be labeled fun. He's a dangerous psychopath, Steph."

"And you predicted him showing up late to the meeting. How did you know?"

With a shrug, Kruger concentrated on the road. "His behavior is textbook perfect as defined by multiple studies of narcissism and sociopathic tendencies. It was his way of letting the three of you know he was in charge. Unfortunately, I've had to deal with his kind before. The common trait individuals like Holden exhibit when cornered is they become totally unpredictable. And not in a good way."

"Sean."

"Yes."

"Do you think he's going to seek revenge for the Kaphar Sourcing incident?"

"I'm positive he will. JR is monitoring the situation." He paused for a moment. "We need to be constantly aware of who and what surrounds us until he's out of the picture."

"In jail?"

"Preferably, dead."

Stephanie turned her head to look out the passenger window. The landscape in this part of the city reflected the harshness of an industrial section. Not the town's best foot forward for out-of-town visitors who had to pass this way from the airport. She reflected on the wisdom of the town planners as she and Sean headed toward an interstate highway surrounding the city.

As Kruger directed the Ford Explorer onto an on-ramp, she said, "I forget you've always had to deal with life and death situations. I've only dealt with financial decisions. Will we ever get to lead just normal lives, Sean?"

He flashed the smile she loved to see. "What's normal, Steph?"

She chuckled and returned the smile. "Yeah, what's

normal?"

***

JR regarded the automated warning message displayed on his left computer monitor. For the second time in as many days, someone sought information about Sean Kruger on the Internet. Whoever it might be did not stealthily conduct their inquiries. The clumsy attempts were conducted on a host of different web-based search engines. One search in particular allowed him to backtrack and determine the location of the individual. They were currently in a hotel in Creve Coeur, west of the St. Louis area. Once he knew the IP address of the computer doing the search, he downloaded one of his many hacking programs, and the contents of the computer spewed forth.

What he found, once he examined several of the files, caused him to reach for his cell phone. His call was answered on the second ring.

"Kruger."

"You have a new admirer out there."

"Aww, geez. What now?"

"Someone in St. Louis is stumbling all over themselves trying to find personal information about you on the Internet."

"How much have they learned?"

"Not much. She did find a CNN report with your picture, but beyond that, nothing."

"You said she."

"I did. Ex-military, amateur mixed-martial-arts enthusiast, and appears to be a loner."

"What do you mean, a loner?"

"I was able to copy the contents of her computer, and I don't find any references to friends or lovers, male or female."

"What's her name?"

"Goes by Amber Willis."

The call went silent for a few seconds. "Doesn't ring any bells."

"I haven't made any inquiries about her yet. Do you want me to?"

"Not at the moment, JR. Let me see what I can find out and, if I draw a blank, I'll let you run with it."

"Okay. I'll keep an eye on her whereabouts."

"I appreciate it. Thanks."

The call ended, and JR stared at the computer monitor. Too many people were looking for his friend. He opened a search engine he designed a long time ago and typed in the woman's name. The results confirmed his suspicions. Hunter Holden seemed hell-bent to make sure Sean Kruger paid for his transgressions.

He made another call.

"Hello, JR. This is a first. You normally send a text to have me call you."

"I need your opinion, Michael."

"All right. Go."

"I've discovered an ex-military, martial arts practitioner and suspect in various disappearances searching for info on Sean."

"What kind of info?"

"Mainly looking for a photo."

"Did they find one?"

"Yes, a CNN report I missed."

"Male or female?"

"Female."

"Do you know her name?"

"Amber Willis. Ever hear of her?"

"No, but that doesn't mean anything. Where's she from?"

"Best I can tell, Chicago."

"Is she still there?"

"No, she's in a hotel in St. Louis."

"Huh." Wolfe remained quiet for a few moments. "She's

from Chicago, is now in St. Louis, and has a picture of Sean."

"Correct."

"She's headed this way, JR."

"I believe that to be a safe assumption."

Wolfe grew quiet for a moment. "Got a picture?"

"Military ID."

"That works. Send it to me."

"Just did."

"Does Sean know about her?"

"I told him just before I called you."

Wolfe chuckled. "Let me guess. He didn't want you to do anything."

"I am sure he is checking with some of his contacts at the FBI."

"That would be a smart move. Can you track this woman?"

"As long as she keeps her cell phone on."

"Okay. If she leaves St. Louis heading southwest, let me know."

"Thanks, Michael."

***

After the phone call from JR, Kruger sat in his home office and stared out the window at the trunk of the oak tree. After about a minute, he searched his cell phone for a number and made a call.

"Charlie Craft."

"Charlie, it's, Sean."

"Hey, Sean. Good to hear from you."

"I need a favor."

"Sure, anything for you."

"Could you check the FBI database for a woman named Amber Willis?"

"Hang on."

Kruger heard the clicking of a computer keyboard and then silence. Two minutes later, Charlie said, "Uh, why are you asking about her?"

"Apparently, she is trying to find me."

"Let's hope she doesn't."

Taking a deep breath, Kruger let it out slowly. "What'd you find?"

"She's on a bureau watch list for questioning in the disappearance of an attorney in Georgia." He paused for a moment. "She has a history of being seen with people who disappear."

"Great. Do you have a mug shot of her?"

"Military ID. Will that work?"

"Yes, could you send a copy to me?"

"Sure. Usual method?"

"Yeah. Protect yourself first, Charlie."

"You got it. How're the kids?"

"Growing. How about yours?"

"Same. Hey, I gotta go, Sean. I'll call when I have a little more time."

"Thanks, Charlie."

The call ended and a minute later, he heard a ping notifying him of a new email. He opened the picture. To his surprise, she looked familiar. After studying the photo for a few moments, he remembered. She had been a suspect in one of his FBI investigations a number of years ago.

***

Using his access code, Kruger unlocked the entry door to JR's building at half past noon. He maneuvered through the maze of security doors and arrived at his second-floor office two minutes later. He noticed JR's door open, so, after placing his backpack on his desk chair, he walked over to the open door and knocked on the frame.

JR looked up from his computer monitor. "Didn't expect

to see you here today."

"Got a question for you."

"Okay."

"Do you remember during one of my futile attempts to retire several years ago when I tried to be a college professor?"

With a grin, JR said, "Yes, which attempt?"

"The time Jonathan Luna kidnapped one of my graduate students, Cora Nelson?"

JR nodded.

"As you remember, that little incident resulted in my return to the FBI. About a week later, the Christian County sheriff asked to meet with me in his office."

Raising an eyebrow, JR kept his attention on his friend. "And?"

"He had a problem and didn't know how to get the bureau involved."

"Let me guess. You helped him?"

"I did. I've always thought it wise to help out local law enforcement. You never know when they might reciprocate."

"Agreed."

"Anyway, he showed me a photograph of a woman taken by a security camera. The photo was our Amber Willis, although we didn't know her name at the time." He paused. "The picture was taken at a convenience store in downtown Ozark. The office of a prominent attorney just happened to be close by. The same day her image was captured, the attorney disappeared."

"Let me guess. They never found his body?"

"Last time I checked, no."

"Uh-oh."

"Apparently, he told his wife he had a client in Las Vegas and needed to travel there frequently. Once I looked into it, I learned he didn't have a client in the city. What he did have was a gambling problem."

"Where does Amber Willis enter the story?"

"That's the interesting part. Charlie found a picture of her and the attorney checking into the Mandalay Bay a day after he disappeared from Ozark. It was the last known photo taken of him."

"He's somewhere out in the desert, isn't he, Sean?"

"Yeah, I believe he is."

"Was she ever identified?"

"Not as Amber Willis."

JR frowned. "This doesn't sound like someone you want to mess with."

"It's not me I'm worried about now, JR. It's Stephanie and the kids."

CHAPTER 38

St. Louis

Amber Willis awoke with a headache. During the long night, sleep eluded her until a little after four in the morning. The answer to her question about leaving the country remained unresolved. Staring at the bedside digital clock did not help with the pain behind her eyes.

She poured water into the one-cup coffee maker and turned it on. The aroma from the coffee pouch provided by the hotel almost made her gag. As more of the colored water flowed into the Styrofoam cup, the stench increased.

After stumbling into the bathroom, she turned the shower on thinking the hot water might help the pounding in her head. Slipping off the T-shirt she wore, she stepped into the enclosure and let the jets of steaming water hit her in the face. She stayed in that position for five minutes as the water stung her skin. The headache eased, and she finished cleaning herself.

With the bathroom mirror steamed over, she wiped the moisture and observed her image. She barely recognized the person staring back at her. Her once-long brown hair, now worn short, only needed to be shaken after a shower. Bloodshot brown eyes surrounded by puffy pale skin gave her the look of someone fifteen years older. She left the bathroom and retrieved the now-cooling coffee. With a sniff and a frown, she took a sip. The bitter taste caused her to shiver.

Returning to the bathroom, she wrapped a towel around herself and returned to the hotel room desk. With the computer opened, she checked her balance in the Bank of America account. It remained the same as the previous evening.

The temptation to drive to the airport and fly to San Diego or Tucson overwhelmed her. It would be simple to then slip over the border and disappear. She knew of locations in both Tijuana and Nogales, Mexico, where passports could be acquired in a matter of hours.

With the decision made, she let the towel fall to the floor and dressed.

***

Kruger woke with a start. Stephanie's regular breathing next to him eased his racing heart. A quick glance at the clock on his nightstand revealed dawn to be several hours away. Taking a deep, calming breath, he closed his eyes again. But his mind slipped into overdrive. From past sleepless nights, he knew getting back to sleep would elude him.

Swinging his legs out from beneath the covers, he sat on the edge of the bed and took a deep breath. He let it out slowly. He repeated the process and relaxed, a little. He felt a hand on his back.

"What's wrong, Sean?"

"Nothing."

"The only time you sit on the side of the bed and breathe like you just did is when something is bothering you."

"Really."

"Yes. You haven't done it since you retired. So, don't lie to me. Just tell me what you're worried about."

"Hunter Holden."

"No surprise there."

"I'm worried about you and the kids. The man is vindictive, and a vindictive psychopath is dangerous."

"I have faith in the men Jimmie has watching the house."

"So do I, but I don't want to assume anything."

She rose, scooted next to him, and placed her head on his shoulder. "Do you have enough evidence to get the FBI involved?"

"Nothing a first-year law student couldn't shoot holes through."

Quiet fell over the couple as they sat in the darkness of their bedroom. Kruger placed his arm around her waist and drew her closer.

He whispered, "Thank you."

"For what?"

"Just being here."

She pushed him back onto the mattress and removed her nightshirt.

***

Standing in front of the ticketing counter at Lambert International Airport, her options for Tucson or San Diego were numerous. All made stops in either Denver or Dallas. The American Airlines options were the quickest. After getting in line to purchase a ticket, she felt a tightness in her chest. Closing her eyes, she tried to calm herself by breathing deeper and letting the air out slowly. Finally, when she got to the head of the line, she abruptly said, "Shit," and walked back to the waiting area. After standing still for several minutes, she followed the arrows pointing to ground transportation to the parking lot.

Fifteen minutes later, she steered her car onto south 270, headed toward the I-44 south exit. Once she merged into traffic on the busy interstate, Amber turned her cell phone off and placed the Honda on cruise control.

***

At the same time Amber Willis turned southwest onto I-44 heading toward Springfield, Sean Kruger gathered Jimmie Gibbs and JR for a quick meeting. When the door to the conference room closed, he said, "Guys, I was reminded this morning that we know more than Hunter Holden knows we know. Let's take advantage of this fact."

JR nodded. "It appears the woman in St. Louis is headed south. She turned her phone off before she got to Eureka."

Gibbs' eyebrows rose. "How long ago was that, JR?"

"About thirty minutes."

"That puts her into town in about two-and-a-half hours. Do we know what she's driving?"

"No. When I hacked into her computer, there wasn't a lot of personal information on it. Seems all she uses it for are Google searches and email."

The ex-Navy SEAL stood. "I'm going to get her picture to the guys I've got watching Sean's house. I also think I need to pull a few more to reinforce our efforts."

After Gibbs left the conference room, JR turned to Sean. "Don't you think it's time to have Stephanie and the kids take a vacation?"

Drumming his fingers on the table, he shook his head. "She and I had that discussion this morning. I want her to, but she reminded me that she, Alexia, and Nadia have to be available if Hunter Holden wants another meeting. I reluctantly agreed. She also has confidence in the gentlemen keeping watch over the house."

Jimmie returned to the conference room. "The guys know someone is on the way. I've called in two more teams, and they will escort Stephanie and the kids to and from school. One of them is going to audit her classes at the university so he can be close at hand. Another one will stay with the kids." He smiled. "Uh, Sean?"

"Yeah."

"Sandy and I have been talking about it, and we both agree we're going to pay the guys out of the operating fund you built up. We don't want you personally footing the bill for their help."

Kruger remained quiet for a few moments. He pressed his lips together and nodded. "Thanks, Jimmie. I appreciate it." He stood. "We need to be proactive so they don't have to do this forever."

Gibbs folded his arms. "I like proactive. What've you got in mind?"

***

Amber Willis' first pass by the Kruger residence occurred at exactly 2:14 p.m. The time was notated by two KKG employees sitting in an AT&T service van parked two doors down from the Kruger home. One of the two wrote the year, make, model, and license plate number of her car down while the other took a picture of her as she passed the van.

They also noticed her paying way too much attention to their vehicle. The driver said, "We've been burned, Bobby. Call Gibbs and tell him we have to move."

"Got it." Bobby Garcia made the call and waited for Gibbs to pick up.

"Did you see her?"

"Yeah, she looked right at us. We need to rotate out."

"Got it. When did she drive by?"

"Two minutes ago. We've got pictures, 2012 gray Honda Accord four door." He then recited the license plate.

"You guys earned your pay today, Bobby. Tell Rick to go ahead and leave the neighborhood. We'll swap out the

AT&T van for a Suburban. Email the pictures."

"Thanks, Jimmie. We're out of here."

***

Gibbs ended the call and looked at Kruger. "Gray 2012 Honda Accord, with Illinois license plates."

"That's probably her. Did they get pictures?"

"Yeah. She spotted the van and stared right at them as she passed."

"Good idea to move it. She might get suspicious if she goes around later and it's still there."

"You want me to send a team into your house?"

Glancing at his watch, he nodded. "Steph and the kids won't be home for a few hours. They can camp out in the bonus room above the garage."

With a smile, Gibbs said, "They'll like that. You've got a comfy sofa and big-screen TV up there."

"Make sure they don't get too comfortable. We don't know what the woman has planned."

"I'm kidding, Sean. These guys are pros."

"I'm not. We don't know her skill set, yet."

With a crooked smile, Gibbs chuckled. "That makes us even. She doesn't know what our guys are capable of, either."

"Jimmie, I appreciate your confidence. But my family is involved. I can't take any chances of them getting hurt or worse."

Gibbs placed his hand on Kruger's shoulder. "Sean, you forget, Sandy and I handpicked these guys. They're some of the best-trained operators in the business. They're not going to let anything happen to your family or you."

After a deep breath, Kruger let it out slowly. "I know, Jimmie. It still makes me nervous."

CHAPTER 39

Southwest Missouri

After the first pass of the Kruger home, Amber Willis drove around the surrounding neighborhoods to get a better sense of ways in and ways out. To the north of the house lay open undeveloped land with trees and underbrush on the northern border. To the south, well-tended suburban homes with yards averaging nine thousand square feet were the norm. The majority of these homes offered their owners a private backyard utilizing six-foot wooden fences. So, gaining access to those yards would be problematic.

Returning to the road north of the home, she parked the Honda on what appeared to be a seldom-traveled farm road and hiked toward the land behind Kruger's property. Willis found an abandoned silo, apparently left from when the land supported a farm. With a small halogen flashlight in hand, she explored the interior, but nothing inside allowed access to the top. Returning to the exterior, she discovered a metal ladder extending from ground level to the summit. Unlike the current trend toward metal farm-storage units, this particular abandoned silo consisted of interlocking cement slabs.

After testing the ladder, it seemed sturdy enough to hold her weight. At the top, she discovered an opening in the ceiling that allowed access to a platform overlooking the interior. Once on the platform, she found an opening with an eagle-eye view of the neighborhood to the south. Toward the southeast, trees obstructed the view of most of the houses. However, when she counted roofs, she determined there was a clear view of the back deck attached to the Kruger home.

Her plans on how to fulfill her contract changed as she studied the view.

***

JR watched from Kruger's office door as he loaded his laptop into his backpack. "You sure going home is the smart thing to do, Sean?"

Looking up from his task, the ex-FBI agent nodded. "Steph and the kids will be home in about thirty minutes. I don't want them coming home and finding the KKG guys upstairs without my presence. Kristin will understand, but Mikey won't." He resumed his packing. "The whole situation is starting to piss me off, JR. I don't like living under the threat of someone trying to kill me or my family."

"Understandable."

Kruger chuckled. "At least you didn't say I understand how you feel."

"I think the only one of us around here who would know is Alexia."

"Yes, I'm sure she does." Lifting his backpack, he slipped it over one shoulder. "Thanks for all your help on this, JR. I'm not sure the plan we have in place is going to do any good. The woman is a wild card. We don't know what she's been tasked with doing."

"We can make an educated guess."

"Yeah, there is that. I'll be at home if you need me."

With those words, he left his office and trudged down the stairs.

As soon as his friend disappeared from sight, JR returned to his office and sat staring at his cell phone lying on the desk. After several minutes of contemplating the call, he picked it up, found the number, and completed the call.

"The way you've changed your habit of making phone calls tells me something's wrong."

"Yes, Michael, there is. The individual we think Holden hired to kill Sean is here in town."

"I'll be at your office in thirty minutes."

"Thank you."

***

Wolfe studied the picture taken of the Honda Accord and the woman. "Has she been seen since this picture was taken?"

JR replied, "Not to my knowledge."

The retired Marine sniper remained standing. His arms folded. "What do we know about her?"

"Not much. Ex-military and proficient in martial arts. The FBI suspects her of several kidnappings but doesn't have hard evidence to prove it."

"Well, you've got Sean and his family surrounded, so I doubt she would attempt something along those lines."

"How else could she do it?"

"Multiple ways. Follow them and force them off the road."

"I didn't think of that."

"Another way would be to find a sniper hide and wait for the right moment."

"That would be hard to defend against."

Wolfe's mouth twitched. "It can be." He continued to stare at the monitor with the picture. "You live across from Kruger, don't you?"

"Yes."

"What's the neighborhood like?"

"Mostly one- and two-story homes, fenced yards, back decks, and trees. Why?"

"Just thinking. Any homes for sale around there?"

"Not that I know of. But I can check." He started typing. On his right monitor, a real estate website appeared. He studied it and then shook his head. "None at the moment."

"What about folks on vacation?"

"That would be hard to determine."

Wolfe rubbed his chin. "Check the post office. Sometimes people have their mail stopped when they're away from home for a while."

"That would take a little longer to determine."

"I've nowhere to be."

Fifteen minutes later, JR looked up from his computer. "Nothing there except a house three streets to the south."

"There would have to be line of sight for a sniper."

"Too many trees from that distance."

The retired Marine turned. "Let the watchers know I'll be driving around the neighborhood. I might see something others might miss."

JR grabbed his cell phone and punched numbers.

***

Wolfe drove around the neighborhood thinking like a sniper. This time of year, there were too many mature trees in leaf in the area. A sniper would find it difficult to get a line-of-sight position. He saw absolutely nothing possible to the south of the house. However, when he ventured to the north, the open land gave him pause.

When he saw the silo, he stopped his Jeep and studied the structure for a few minutes. While Kruger's house was not visible from where he parked on the farm road, this silo might offer an opportunity.

He chose to approach it on a circuitous path. Once there, he observed an opening to the inside. Next to it was a patch of disturbed tall grass. On closer examination, the disturbance appeared to have been made by the shoes of a human. Looking at the exterior ladder, he could see where bird droppings were missing from two parts of the rungs. Just like someone had recently climbed to the top. With a smile, he realized he had found the same location as the would-be assassin.

Taking his time, he walked back to the Jeep and could see where the intruder entered the field. Flattened grass still showed signs of someone having recently passed. When he came to the country road, he found tire tracks in the dust where she parked. Pictures of the tracks were taken with his cell phone and he attached it to a text message to JR. It read: *Found tracks. Are these tires from an Accord?*

Five minutes passed before a return message read, *Tread is consistent with tires used for that model.*

Now he knew where she would be. The problem remained when.

***

Jimmie Gibbs stood quietly as he listened to Wolfe describe the silo. "Makes sense, Michael. We have no information telling us if she is any good with a rifle. You think it's a seven-hundred-yard shot?"

"At least. Maybe more."

"I know most of the gun shop owners around here. I can ask around to see if anybody has recently seen her in their stores."

"That could take a while."

"Not really. There aren't that many."

"Not knowing her skill set worries me more than where she'll buy a gun. Who knows? She might have brought one with her. We need to consider that possibility."

JR spoke. "Gentlemen, her military file does not indicate she had long-gun training. Plus, all the missing person cases she's been a suspect in center around abductions."

Wolfe nodded. "Yeah, that may be the case, but why did she climb the silo?"

"I agree with Michael, JR. She climbed the silo for a reason. You've been on Sean's deck before. Can you see the silo from it?"

"Yes, I'm afraid you can."

Tilting his head, a bit, Wolfe asked, "Where on the deck?"

"Pretty much the entire space. He loves to watch storms come in from the northwest. His deck is positioned perfectly for him to do so. And the silo is right in the middle of his view."

"We have to assume she suspects people are watching over Kruger. If she doesn't, she's not as smart as I give her credit for. That's how I would do it. Take a long-distance shot, make your getaway, and disappear. I followed some of the roads north of the silo, and there are numerous routes out of the area."

JR nodded. "Yeah, that's what drew him to the neighborhood. It's practically in the country. There were horses grazing on those fields when they first moved in."

Turning to Jimmie, Wolfe said, "Can you have your guys keep him and his family off the back deck tonight?"

"Yes."

"I need a day to get in position."

"Where are you going to be?"

Wolfe stood. "It'll be a surprise." He walked out of the conference room toward the stairs.

CHAPTER 40

Southwest Missouri

Kruger remained silent as he listened to Jimmie Gibbs summarize the steps being taken to protect him and his family. When the retired Navy SEAL concluded his briefing, Kruger said, "I'm not hiding from her."

"Sean, we aren't asking you to hide. Just be mindful of where you are at any given time."

"Same thing. Steph and the kids are heading to KC tonight to spend the weekend with her sister. I'm staying to keep an eye on the house."

"We have a team planning to follow them."

With a nod, Kruger continued. "Has she been spotted since her initial pass by the house?"

"No. Wolfe thinks she scouted the silo behind your house as a possible sniper hide."

"That's a long shot."

"Yeah, 862 yards. We put a range finder on it from your back deck."

"Do we know if she's any good with a rifle?"

"JR can't find much about her except military records.

Nothing there about sniper skills."

"That doesn't mean she hasn't learned."

"We know." Gibbs pursed his lips. "Look, Sean, there's only so much we can do to protect you."

"I know. Maybe it's time to draw her out into the open."

"What've you got in mind?"

***

Amber Willis stepped out of her hotel room in Monett, MO. The proprietor of the Days Inn had accepted her offer of cash after she offered him a two-hundred-dollar nonrefundable deposit above the per night rate. All paid in advance. She recognized the man's accent as being from Afghanistan, but she did not engage him in conversation besides negotiating her stay.

She realized this probably wasn't the first time he rented a room to someone trying to stay off the grid.

Her plans for the day included the purchase of a Remington 700 at an estate sale. After engaging with the organizer, the previous day, she knew how much cash to have and where to go to sight-in the rifle.

After a quick breakfast at a nearby McDonald's, she arrived at the location of the sale, parked, and walked into the house. The actual sale would commence at noon.

"Good morning, Amber."

"Morning, Ms. Cindy. I've decided to get the Remington."

"Good choice, hon. Let me get it for you. I put it out of sight after our visit yesterday. Didn't want anyone to sell it out from under you."

While the event organizer ducked into the back room, Amber looked around and spotted a Sig Sauer P320 M18 in the gun cabinet with a price tag of six hundred dollars. It looked to be in pristine condition. This was the civilian version of the sidearm she carried as a military policewoman. When Cindy returned, she handed the rifle to Amber and said, "There you go."

She examined the rifle. "It's been well cared for."

"Yes. The owner was very particular about how he cared for his guns."

Pointing at the Sig Sauer, Amber said, "Can I see the Sig? It's the same style I carried as an MP."

"Sure, hon. By the way, thank you for your service."

Amber nodded as she accepted the pistol from the sale organizer. "What if I wanted to get both? Would you make me a deal?"

"Tell you what. The sale doesn't officially start until noon." She glanced at a clock on the wall of the living room. "You pay cash, and I'll let you buy them now."

"You've got yourself a deal." Amber started to hand the woman her driver's license.

Cindy held up a hand, palm out. "No need, hon. Since I'm not a licensed gun dealer and this is a private sale, no background checks are needed."

"Really?"

"It's a fact. Missouri doesn't require one if the transaction is private."

Amber knew this, and the reason she was now in Monett was due to an advertisement about the estate sale with several Remington 700s listed. "Yesterday, you told me about a gun range in the area. Could I get directions?"

"Sure."

At a few minutes past 6 p.m., Amber Willis returned to her hotel room. With the rifle successfully zeroed in and a complete box of ammo cycled through the Sig Sauer, she spent the rest of the evening cleaning both guns.

***

Wolfe trudged through the open field toward the grove of trees north of the silo. Using a handheld laser-mapping device, he recorded distances and slope angles. He knew the distance and down angle from the top of the silo to Kruger's back deck. He also knew the distance to the tree line north of the silo.

Kruger appeared out of a grove of trees and walked toward him. As the retired FBI agent approached, Wolfe asked, "What'd you find?"

With a finger pointing north, Kruger said, "There are two worn paths about half a mile that way. Underbrush isn't as thick as I thought it would be, and I believe a person using a night-vision device could navigate it with ease."

Wolfe made a note in a small notepad he held. "We're missing something, Sean."

"I've got the same feeling."

"Just because the silo is there, doesn't mean that's where she will set up a hide. Or even that is what she is planning."

Placing his hands on his hips, Kruger stared out toward the back of his house eleven hundred yards to the south. "No one has seen her drive by again for three days. But I don't think she's gone."

"I don't, either, but I would like to hear why you think so."

"First of all, Hunter Holden will not give up. Some of the most persistent criminals I've ever pursued during my career with the FBI were psychopaths. My bet is he's offering a lot of money for someone to come after me. Plus, he'll hold some of it back until the job is complete."

Wolfe remained quiet.

"Secondly, even though she hasn't been seen, she is probably in the planning stage and not in a hurry to get the job done. She'll take her time and wait for the right moment. What are your thoughts?"

"I have to agree with both your points. There's a third reason she hasn't been spotted again or given up."

"And that is?"

"While Springfield is a medium-size city, it really isn't

that big. Too many chances of being spotted. My guess is, she did a thorough job of scouting the area and is now in one of the surrounding communities getting ready. We won't see her again until she goes after you."

"JR believes she's using cash. He's monitoring her credit cards, and they haven't been used."

"If she's smart, and I believe she is, that's exactly what she's doing."

Kruger's cell phone chirped. He accepted the call. "What's up, JR?" He was silent as he listened. Finally, he said, "I'm with Michael now. I'll let him know." He placed the phone in his jeans back pocket, smiled, and directed his attention to Wolfe. "One of Jimmie's gun shop buddies called him and told him a woman matching the description of Amber Willis spent the afternoon yesterday sighting-in a Remington 700 with a Burris XTR II scope."

"Where was this?"

"Monett, Missouri."

Wolfe pursed his lips and directed his attention toward Kruger's house to the south. "The Burris XTR II line has several solid thousand-yard scopes, Sean."

"Then we aren't wasting our time, are we, Michael?"

"No, I don't think we are. Let's keep after it."

***

Amber Willis checked out of the hotel in Monett, Missouri at seven the next morning. Her trip to the firing range with a gun shop attached allowed her to zero in the scope on her Remington. However, one of the gun shop managers seemed to be paying way too much attention to her. It made her nervous at first, but she finished what she needed to accomplish. Her indecision about what to do next consumed her thoughts, resulting in a sleepless night.

Before leaving the parking lot, she consulted a paper map of Missouri bought at a Walmart across the highway from the hotel.

After studying the map for several minutes, she took a deep breath. The unusual attention she received from the man at the gun range continued to spook her. From her study of the map, she discovered a way to escape and disappear. Tulsa, Oklahoma could be reached in less than three hours. There, she could board a plane and fly to Tucson. From there, she could be in Nogales, Mexico by evening. Putting the car in gear, she headed west toward the Oklahoma state line.

CHAPTER 41

Minneapolis

The news from his bank in Paris brought a smile to Hunter Holden's lips. All the seed money for the investment in Stephanie Harris' venture stood ready to disperse. The only remaining task he needed to accomplish before the deal finalized would be to authorize the transfer.

He stood, gazing out the floor-to-ceiling window, his hands behind his back. A knock at the office door caused him to turn around. Dean Melton stood in the opening.

"Hunter, we have a huge problem."

Holden motioned his assistant to enter. "Close the door. What is it?"

"Stephanie Harris isn't who she says she is. She's the wife of Sean Kruger."

The CEO of Transnational Financial only stared at Melton. Finally, he said, "Son of a bitch." He paused and returned to face the window. "So, this whole charade is nothing but another scam."

"It would appear so."

"How did you find out."

"The individual hired to take care of Kruger found his address by tracing it through his wife." Melton offered Holden a piece of paper with an image printed on it. "If I'm not mistaken, that's a picture of her. Note the name: Stephanie Harris-Kruger."

Holden turned, accepted the paper, and studied it. "Where did this come from?"

"Website of a university in Missouri. She's a recent PhD and a tenured professor in the business school there. We now know why she disappeared from the business world."

The CEO's jaw muscles clenched as the veins in his neck bulged. He violently wadded the page and threw it at his office door. "Dammit."

Melton stood quietly as Holden's breathing accelerated and he turned back to glare out the window. The only sound in the office came from Hunter Holden's rapid breathing. After a minute, his respiratory rate declined. But he still kept his attention outside. Finally, he asked, "How many employees are here today?"

"Only six."

Glancing at his watch, he said, "Send them home."

"Yes, sir."

As soon as Melton closed the office door, Holden sat behind his desk and accessed his personal bank accounts. Once he had a handle on his assets, he sent an email to the company's bank representative in Paris, asking for an in-person meeting with him two days hence.

The reply arrived twenty minutes later.

Holden's next email went to a travel agency he used, requesting a first-class ticket to Paris. Finally, he engaged the services of a Realtor in Taiwan.

At this point, the emails multiplied.

***

Southwest Missouri

JR's monitoring of emails in and out of Transnational Financial detected a flurry of activity starting at noon. With each new email, his concerns about Hunter Holden being on the verge of leaving the country increased. If this was the case, it seemed to be a sudden decision. One neither he nor Kruger anticipated.

By midafternoon, there was no doubt something was going on at Transnational. He dialed Kruger's cell phone.

"Kruger."

"Where are you?"

"About a mile north of my house. Why?"

"How fast can you get to the office?"

"Twenty minutes. What's going on, JR?"

"I'll tell you when you get here."

Twenty-five minutes later, Kruger sat in JR's conference room listening to a summarization of the Transnational emails. When he finished, Kruger tapped his lips with a finger.

"Why now? What happened to cause this type of a reaction?"

"Don't know. That's the reason I called you."

The retired FBI agent crossed his arms. "The emails never mention his current financial situation. Yet, he's making arrangements to fly to Paris. Isn't one of their main banks there?"

JR nodded. "Yeah, BNP Paribas."

"He doesn't need to go to Paris to handle an investment transaction. He can do that over the phone or on the Internet. However, engaging a Realtor in Taiwan seems to indicate he's planning an extended stay."

JR typed furiously on his laptop. He stopped, read something, and then typed again. He looked up. "Something curious about the island of Taiwan, Sean."

"What?"

"It doesn't have an extradition arrangement with the US."

"How about that, JR." Using his cell phone, Kruger

placed a call.

JR stopped working on the computer and listened to one side of the conversation.

***

Somewhere In Northeast Oklahoma

In the vicinity of Vinita, Oklahoma, a building spans the Will Rogers Turnpike. At one time the largest McDonald's in the world, it can no longer lay claim to the distinction. It is, however, an oasis for weary travelers who wish to stop for a rest or something to eat without paying a toll to exit the expressway.

Amber Willis sat at a table overlooking the busy thoroughfare and watched semis, pickups, SUVs, and cars speeding northeast and southwest. She mindlessly munched on a double cheeseburger and cold French fries as traffic sped underneath the bridge connecting the north and south parking lots to the restaurant. This area contained the dining area for the fast-food behemoth. In addition to the dining area, a gift shop occupied a portion of the square footage. Within this store, travelers could purchase trinkets designed to remind them of a trip they did not enjoy.

Staring at the traffic passing beneath her, she could only think of the hundred thousand dollars she was leaving behind. An additional thought also occurred. She would be looking over her shoulder for the rest of her life if she did not finish the job. However long or short that might be.

A passing family of two girls and their parents drew her attention. The taller of the two girls said, "What do you mean I wouldn't be in trouble if I had told the truth?"

The mother, a tall blonde woman in her mid-thirties, gave the girl a patient smile. "Emma, all you had to do is tell your father and I, you spilled the drink. You didn't need to blame your sister."

"But…"

"Doesn't matter now. You lied to us and…"

The family moved out of earshot for Amber to hear the punishment the little girl would receive. She returned her attention to the window next to her table. Her burger and fries, cold and now forgotten, lay on the wrapper. A paper cup next to the food contained what the dispenser humorously labeled Coke. Gazing out over the flat, open Oklahoma countryside, she did not miss the concrete jungle of Chicago, the cold wind coming off Lake Michigan, or the smell it brought with it.

Taking a deep breath, she stood. Turning toward the north stairwell, she followed it down to the parking lot and her car.

***

Kruger ended the call and looked at JR. "Well, you heard what I had to say."

"Are they going to put him on a no-fly list?"

With a shake of his head, the retired FBI agent said, "No. They have no cause. Frankly, I think they would be relieved if he disappeared in Taiwan. One less possible headache being kicked down the road."

"Are you giving up?"

Kruger did not reply.

"That doesn't sound like you, Sean."

"Did I say I was giving up?" He shook his head. "I'm just getting started." He paused for a moment. "Were any of the names Holden recruited for investing in the fake company mentioned in his correspondence?"

"Only one. Frank Baxter. Holden sent an email telling him the deadline for investing was rapidly closing. Baxter replied, in no uncertain terms, that hell would need to freeze over before he invested in one of Holden's schemes again."

"Really. I wonder if Mr. Baxter would like to explain his reasoning." He paused for a moment. "There's probably a thousand Frank Baxters in the United States, JR."

"Actually, there are fewer than five hundred."

Shaking his head, Kruger closed his eyes. "How in the world do you know that, JR?"

"Google can be a wonderful source of information at times. However, we don't need to guess which of those five hundred is the one you want. The guy lives in Buckhead, Georgia, a suburb of Atlanta. His mansion is actually a short distance from the 12,000-square-foot condo residence of Elton John."

Kruger raised an eyebrow. "Elton John lives in Atlanta? You're kidding me?"

"Nope. Like I said, Google can be a fountain of useless trivia."

"So, what about this Frank Baxter?"

"His grandmother was the daughter of a Chandler. A direct descendant of Asa Griggs Chandler."

"Is that important?"

"Extremely. Asa Griggs Chandler is credited with starting the Coca-Cola company in the late 1800s after buying the secret formula from a pharmacist."

"Old money, then."

"Very old and very well-connected money. From what I've been able to determine, Baxter has invested with Hunter Holden before. Successfully a number of times, and catastrophically once."

"JR, can you get me the contact information for Frank Baxter?"

"Sure, why?"

"I'm going to take a day trip to Atlanta tomorrow and have a chat with the man."

"Want company?"

"Not this time, JR. I'm not going to be exactly truthful with Mr. Baxter."

CHAPTER 42

Atlanta

A little after nine in the morning, Frank Baxter appraised the man standing before him. Six foot plus, trim, age indeterminate, professionally dressed, and displaying identification as an FBI agent. "What's this about, Agent Kruger." His tone was defensive, his posture stiff.

"Hunter Holden."

One of Baxter's eyebrows rose. "What about him?"

"Do you know him?"

"Before I answer your question, answer one for me. Why is the FBI interested in Hunter Holden?"

Kruger smiled. "Mr. Baxter, you are not under investigation. We are seeking additional information on him from some of the individuals who may have invested in his company, Transnational Financial."

"That did not answer my question."

"I'm aware of that."

Baxter pursed his lips and took a deep breath. "I know the man."

Kruger sat in one of the leather chairs in front of Baxter's massive oak desk. He remained quiet, his legs crossed and hands on the armrest.

"My involvement with Hunter Holden has ceased due to lack of performance."

"It's the lack of performance we are interested in, Mr. Baxter. Were you aware he is planning to leave the United States on an extended stay in Taiwan?"

Baxter's eyes grew wide with this bit of news. "No, Agent Kruger, I was not aware."

"We have it on good authority he recently approached you and several other individuals about investing in a startup company. Those funds, amounting to well over one hundred million dollars, will be siphoned off and not used for their intended purposes. If that's the case, Hunter Holden will be in violation of numerous US Code Title 18, Chapter 9 clauses. All of which are felonies."

With a slight smile, Baxter said, "Hunter Holden has been violating Title 18, Chapter 9 articles for a number of years. Why the interest now?"

"Currently, he's out of the FBI's reach because he hasn't conducted business in the United States for years. We feel his pending move to Taiwan is in preparation for a major infraction. The US and Taiwan do not have an extradition agreement."

"My question remains, if you know all of this, why are you talking to me?"

"I need names of other investors he may have approached besides you."

"I would not…"

"Mr. Baxter, we know you were recently approached and turned him down. Others did not. We don't have visibility on those individuals. We can use their testimony to put Holden away for a long time. But we are fighting a deadline. If he leaves the country before we can get an indictment, he'll escape punishment once again."

Putting an elbow on an armrest of his office chair, Baxter

placed his chin on a fist. Once again, he appeared to be studying the man in front of him. Finally, he said, "Very well. Some of these individuals are very sensitive about allowing regulators to know where they invest their money."

"I understand, Mr. Baxter. Your name will not be revealed as a source."

Baxter smiled and leaned back in his chair. "How do you want the information?"

Kruger removed a business card from an inside suit coat pocket and reached forward. "Email the list to this address."

Taking the card, he studied it. "When do you need it?"

"Time is a commodity in short supply for this investigation. Within the next hour would be ideal."

"I can print the list out now if you want a copy, or I can email it."

"Doing both would be most helpful, Mr. Baxter."

***

As the HA-420 HondaJet streaked west after taking off from Peachtree Dekalb Airport near Buckhead, Georgia, Kruger called JR.

He answered almost instantly. "I've got the email from Baxter. Now what?"

"Send the info to Ryan Clark's personal email account. You still have it, don't you?"

"Did you really have to ask that question, Sean?"

"No. But one never knows."

"Done. Now what."

"I'll call him. We're running out of time."

"Got it."

The phone went silent. Kruger searched for another number. He pressed the call icon and waited. It was answered on the fourth ring.

Ryan Clark said, "What've you got for me, Sean?"

"JR just sent you a list of individuals who are about to

lose a considerable amount of money when Hunter Holden leaves the country for Taiwan."

"They have lost or will lose?"

"Will."

"How much are we talking about?"

"In excess of one hundred million."

"How many individuals?"

"Five."

"Twenty million each. You're right, that is a considerable sum."

"Just thought you should know."

"Does Holden have these funds currently?"

"Yes."

"I won't ask how you know."

"Probably best."

The call went silent for a few moments. "Would Charlie's team be able to find this info if they knew where to look?"

"Charlie would. Not sure about his team."

"Send him the info."

"Ryan, Holden has a ticket on an international flight tomorrow evening to Paris. Once he leaves the US…"

"Not sure we can get an indictment that fast, but we can have agents in Paris waiting."

"Whatever you need to do."

The call ended, and Kruger directed his attention out the window next to his seat. His concern about the woman seen driving by his house returned to his thoughts.

***

Amber Willis arrived back in the Springfield area late in the evening. Heading toward the downtown area, she passed a billboard for a historic motor lodge located on a section of the historic Route 66, a few blocks west of center city.

After checking in, she parked her car in an out-of-the-way section of the parking lot hidden from the street. Once she opened the door to her room, she rolled her eyes. The room resembled a hotel room from the 1950s. Other than reminding her of a movie set, it appeared clean with a state-of-the-art flat-screen television and Wi-Fi.

Having passed a Walmart on her trip into town, she returned and bought an inexpensive Chromebook. Back in her room, she created a brand-new profile and used Google Earth Street View to become more familiar with Kruger's neighborhood.

***

Arriving home at roughly the same time as Stephanie and the kids, Kruger fixed a snack for the children. Once they were done, he suggested they watch a little television while he spoke to their mother.

Kristin, even though she was adopted, resembled Stephanie in both eye and hair color. She also displayed her mother's quick intellect and a maturity beyond her seven years of age.

"What's going on that you don't want Mikey and I to know?"

With a fatherly smile, Kruger knelt down to be eye to eye with his daughter. "I need to discuss with your mother something I don't want you and your brother to worry about."

The little girl crossed her arms and tilted her head. A gesture she had picked up from her father. "I'm seven years old. I can handle bad news."

Stifling a chuckle, Kruger closed his eyes for a moment and nodded. "Yes, I know you can. But sometimes adults need to discuss matters in private. This is one of those times."

The little girl put her hands on her hips. "Father, aren't Mikey and I part of this family?"

"Yes, Kristin, you and your brother are a very important

part of this family."

"Then, we need to know what's going on."

Kruger stood and looked at Stephanie. She nodded.

"Very well, Kristin. Let's all sit at the kitchen table, and I will explain what's going on."

***

Amber Willis slept poorly. The hotel, originally built in 1929, consisted of multiple cottages, some with two rooms and others with a larger single room. The business had experienced various remodels. The latest one developed for nostalgic travelers of the original Route 66 pathway. Amber found the nostalgia hokey. She had never heard of Route 66 or the myth constructed around the legendary roadway.

She decided this would be the only night she stayed and left the hotel property just before dawn. With the cover of darkness and light traffic, she followed the path to Kruger's neighborhood memorized during her study of the city on Google Earth the previous evening.

With daylight still an hour away, Amber traveled the streets in front of her target's home and the ones south of it. On her second pass on the street directly south of Kruger's, she observed a man and woman, along with two teenage children, loading suitcases into the back of an SUV. She pulled to the curb six houses beyond and watched them with her rearview mirror. Checking the time, she noticed it approached five thirty.

Ten minutes after she started her vigil, the man closed the garage door, and all four got into the vehicle and drove away. Turning the overhead light switch to off, she slipped out of the car and kept next to the homes in the neighborhood as she approached the now-empty residence.

Opening the privacy fence gate into the backyard, she waited to see if any dogs would sound an alarm. The neighborhood remained quiet. Slowly closing the opening, she climbed a small set of stairs to the back deck. Looking behind it, she could not believe her luck. She had a clear view of Kruger's driveway and garage door.

By 2 a.m. the following morning, having made sure the family of four had not returned, she broke into the house through the back door and then secured her Honda in the garage.

From a window in a breakfast nook, Amber Willis could spy on the comings and goings of the Krugers without raising suspicions.

CHAPTER 43

Southwest Missouri

The morning of Stephanie and the children's trip to Kansas City saw the family rushing around to make sure bags were packed and specific toys and stuffed animals secured for transport. Kruger, after listening to the logic offered by Jimmie Gibbs, agreed to load everyone and everything into Stephanie's Ford Explorer inside the garage before raising the door.

He backed out of the garage and headed toward his office. Anyone watching or observing the house would not know who or how many individuals were in the vehicle due to the dark-tinted windows. When they arrived at the KKG office, two of KKG's most trusted operators, Bobby Garcia and Rick Evans, helped the family transfer luggage and the precious toys to a black GMC Yukon Denali. This would be the vehicle used to transport Stephanie and her children to Kansas City for a long weekend with her sister and brother-in-law. Promises of a trip to Worlds of Fun, the Kansas City Zoo, and The Nelson-Atkins Museum of Art helped both the kids enthusiastically agree to the trip.

As the big SUV headed east away from the office building, Kruger watched, his arms folded. Jimmie Gibbs stood next to him.

"They'll be fine, Sean."

"I know. I have a lot of respect for Bobby and Rick."

"Don't tell them I told you, but both are looking forward to the trip. Bobby told me he hasn't been to KC before and is looking forward to it."

"You ready for the next phase of this little experiment?"

Gibbs nodded. "I've never driven your Mustang before."

"You can drive a stick, can't you?"

"How hard can it be?"

"Jimmie?"

The retired SEAL chuckled. "Of course, I've driven a stick. I grew up in car-crazy California."

Kruger shook his head. "You're impossible."

"That's what Alexia tells me." He followed his friend to the Ford Explorer for the drive back to the Kruger house.

As they pulled into the garage, Jimmie grabbed Kruger's arm. "Not until the door is down."

"Got it." As he waited for the door to close, he looked at his friend. "Want some coffee?"

"Yeah, I'm not leaving for a little while. Make it look official."

An hour later, Jimmie asked Kruger. "Where do you want me to park your car?"

"Take it to your house. That way if anyone looks for it, they won't see it parked at the office."

The smile on Gibbs' face grew. "Uh, can I take the back roads?"

"I would prefer it if you did." He paused. "You think this will work, Jimmie?"

"It's how we trapped a group of Taliban rebels hiding out in Kabul once."

"That's reassuring."

Gibbs chuckled. "Will you be okay, Sean?"

"I'll be fine. You forget I spent a majority of my adult life living in a hotel room by myself."

"Call if you need anything."

"Sure."

"Remember, if you leave, be in the Explorer before you open the door."

"Got it. Stop being a nervous hen. I know how to take care of myself."

Gibbs left, and Kruger retreated to his office to see his Mustang drive up the street. With a sigh, he sat at his desk and answered emails.

***

Amber watched the Mustang back out of the garage and drive east. The wife's vehicle remained in the garage. If the Mustang did not come back by dark, she would enter the house, hold the family hostage, and wait for Kruger to come home.

Checking the time, she settled down for a short nap.

Traffic in the neighborhood at midnight consisted of the occasional car driven by one of the few residents who worked late shifts at the local hospitals.

Checking for lights in neighboring houses and cars driving by, Amber, dressed in all black, crossed the street a few houses up from the Kruger household. She stayed in the shadows until she reached the side yard of the retired FBI agent's home. She made a fast dash toward the back privacy fence gate. Opening it slowly, she slipped into the backyard and breathed deeply as she kept her back against the fence.

No lights could be seen in the back of the house. She climbed the steps to the back deck and listened for any movement within. After standing still for a few minutes, she tried the back doorknob. It was locked. She extracted a thin piece of metal and a tension tool. Working as quietly as possible, she unlocked the dead bolt first and then the knob.

Opening the door a few inches, she listened for any signs the occupants heard her activities. Only silence emanated from the interior. She entered the kitchen and silently closed the door. A night-light under the kitchen cabinets cast an eerie glow over the area where she stood. After orientating herself, she moved to her right into a large living area. Holding her recently purchased Sig Sauer in her left hand, she moved through the darkened house. As she entered a hallway, she looked to her left and saw the outlines of a desk and chair dimly illuminated by the glow of a street light outside a window behind the desk. By the illumination of a decorative lamp on a console table, she determined two additional rooms were on her left. At the end of the hall, she saw a closed door with a bright streak underneath.

Heart pounding, she felt like anyone in the house could hear her approach the closed door. Taking a silent deep breath, she turned the knob and burst into the room.

***

JR heard his cell phone vibrating on his nightstand and quickly grabbed it. He struggled to get his glasses on to see the caller ID. It was Kruger.

"What's happened?"

"I need you to call Sandy and Jimmie. I've had a visitor tonight."

"What's their condition?"

"Probably wishing they'd never entered my house at night."

"Any blood?"

"Not yet. But the potential is high."

"I'll be right there."

"Call the guys first."

"No cops?"

"No cops."

***

The large hand of Sandy Knoll applying pressure to Amber's back, she reluctantly walked into the kitchen and immediately turned toward the tall man already there.

"What are you going to do?"

Kruger tilted his head and smiled. "I think a better question would be, what were you going to do entering my house in the middle of the night with a gun in your hand."

She looked behind her at Knoll and Gibbs. "Who are these two thugs?"

"Those gentlemen are my associates. You should call them sir."

Knoll stood behind her, his arms folded, while Jimmie wandered around the kitchen to position himself beside the diminutive woman.

"What are you three going to do, rape me?"

"No, we're all happily married." He paused for a moment. "Why are you here, Amber Willis?"

Her eyes widened briefly, but she quickly returned to a bored expression. "That's not my name."

"Whatever, Amber. We know more about you than you realize." Kruger picked up the gun she had held. "We know you bought this at an estate sale in Monett, Missouri, and that you have been stalking this house."

"I don't know what you're talking about. I've never been to this Monett place, and I certainly haven't been stalking this house."

Kruger showed her his cell phone with a picture of her driving by the AT&T van. "Want to rethink your statement?"

She stared at the phone and then crossed her arms. "That proves nothing."

JR entered the kitchen from the back deck. "Her car's out front. Found it in the garage of the Fletchers. They're out of town for a few days. Looks like she made herself at home, too."

"Anything in the car?"

"Remington 700 with a really good scope on it."

"We'll let the police know you have in your possession a Remington 700 and a Sig Sauer P320 M18."

"Not against the law to own firearms."

"It is when you're a convicted felon."

"How do you…" She stopped, glared at Kruger, and then sat on a barstool. "I'm done talking."

"We know you were an MP in the military and have competed in numerous mixed martial arts events. You were convicted of aggravated assault in Illinois and sentenced to six years in prison. You only served three and then were paroled for good behavior. After your release, your employment records get a little sketchy, but you have almost half a million dollars stashed away in several accounts in the Cayman Islands. All of which could be seized by the FBI, if you don't cooperate with us."

She sat up straighter, and her glare intensified. "You have no right…"

Raising his voice, Kruger bent over to stare her straight in the eye. "You have no right to threaten my family, so don't get indignant with me."

Amber closed her eyes and seemed to shrink in size. "I was almost to Tulsa. I could have gotten on a plane and disappeared."

Knoll asked, "Why didn't you?"

She shrugged.

Standing behind her, Jimmie said, "Help us stop the guy who's paying you, and you can do just that, disappear."

Shaking her head, she spoke in a whisper. "And look over my shoulder for the rest of my life? No thank you."

Still at eye level, Kruger said, "Help us take his entire organization down, and you won't have to look over your shoulder. We can even help you change your name."

With a laugh, she locked eyes with Kruger. "How the hell can you do that?"

"Think about it for a moment. We knew where you were the entire time."

"How did you do that? I've only been using cash."

Kruger shrugged. "You help us, and we'll help you disappear."

She stared at him for a long time before shifting her attention to JR, Knoll, and Gibbs. After taking a deep breath, she asked, "What do you want to know?"

CHAPTER 44

Southwest Missouri

"The guy's name is Dillard. I've never heard him called any other name. He hangs out at the Lakeside Tavern north of the loop in Chicago. It's a dive bar. The clientele is mostly old burnouts who sit around all day drinking cheap beer and complaining about their lot in life." She paused to take a sip of coffee. She still sat at the kitchen bar. "He's the one who finds jobs for me once in a while."

Kruger sipped his coffee. "What does he look like?"

"Mid-fifties, maybe older. Thinning gray hair, hawk nose, squints a lot, raspy voice, and dresses like a tourist in Hawaii. You know, cargo shorts and an untucked bowling shirt."

Gibbs asked, "What do you mean, raspy voice?"

"Like he's smoked all his life. The few times I've been around him, he smells like a cigarette."

Knoll asked, "Do you know if he's been in the military?"

She nodded. "That's where I first met him. I busted him several times when I was stationed at Ft. Benning."

The big man frowned. "How long ago?"

After studying her coffee cup, Amber looked up. "Twelve years."

Knoll stood and went outside to the back deck.

Kruger took over the questioning. "Did this Dillard character ever tell you who you were working for?"

"No, not really. He sometimes hinted, but this time he did. He told me if I didn't complete my assignment, there'd be hell to pay."

"Had you ever heard of Hunter Holden before?"

The woman's answer was a shake of her head.

"Why do you think he told you this time?"

"Don't know. I guess he thought it would intimidate me. It didn't."

Knoll returned to the kitchen and smiled. "Master Sargent Robert Dillard. Goes by the name Robby D. Busted down to private after seventeen years in the army and a dishonorable discharge in 2013. He was at Benning during the same years I was there."

Amber raised an eyebrow. "You were at Ft. Benning?"

"Yeah. Army Special Forces."

With a frown, she studied the large man for a moment. "That's why you look familiar. You were a major, weren't you?"

"Yes."

Gibbs asked, "How did this Dillard fellow get ahold of you?"

"Through the bartender. If I accepted a job from Dillard, I'd give him a hundred-dollar tip."

"What about the opposite, if you wanted to talk to Dillard?"

"No need. Dillard goes there every day for lunch. They've got good burgers."

Sipping his coffee, Kruger stared out his back door for a few moments. He returned his attention to Amber. "What were your instructions after you fulfilled your assignment?"

A tear leaked from her eye. "Take a video with my cell

phone after I put a bullet in your forehead." She paused to take a deep breath. "And then give the video to Dillard."

Kruger's mouth twitched. "That's a little grim."

"Yeah." She hunched over, cradling her coffee mug with both hands.

"I think it's time for us to have a little chat with Robby D., Sandy. Call Stewart and have the plane ready. We can be there by noon if we hustle."

***

Sandy Knoll entered the Lakeside Tavern at 12:34 p.m. It took a few moments for his eyes to adjust to the gloom, but then he could see Robert Dillard sitting at a far corner table staring at him. Knoll made a beeline to the location. As he sat across from the disgraced soldier, he said, "Hello, Robbie D."

"What the fuck are you doing here, Major?"

"Came to pay you a friendly visit."

"Somehow I doubt that."

"Eat your burger. It'll get cold."

Clasping his hands in front of him, Dillard glared at the larger man. "I'll repeat myself. What are you doing here?"

Leaning over the table, Knoll growled. "You sent someone to hurt a friend of mine, Robbie. Not a real smart thing to do."

After taking a bite of his burger, Dillard said with his mouth full. "No idea what you're talking about."

Knoll held up his cell phone with a picture of Kruger standing next to Amber Willis. "Does this picture help your memory?"

The disgraced soldier's eyes widened for a split second before he regained his neutral expression. "Never seen either one of them before."

"You just confirmed something I heard at Fort Benning."

"What's that?"

"You weren't the sharpest crayon in the box." Knoll sent a text message, folded his massive arms, kept his gaze on Dillard, and sat back.

A minute later, Amber Willis, followed by Sean Kruger and Jimmie Gibbs, entered the tavern. The man sitting across from Knoll saw them immediately and stiffened.

Knoll leaned over again. "We can do this the easy way, or it can get ugly. Your choice, Robbie D."

The man stayed silent, even after Gibbs sat next to him and Amber placed herself next to Knoll. Kruger pulled a chair to the end of the table. "I'm Sean Kruger, a retired FBI agent with friends in high places. Care to tell me who contacted you to hire Ms. Willis over there?"

After a quick glance at Amber, Dillard turned to Gibbs. "Who are you? FBI?"

"Nope, the name's Gibbs. I'm a retired Navy SEAL."

Dillard shook his head and stared at the half-eaten lunch. "Shit."

Knoll growled. "Something you happen to be deep in."

"Look, Major, if I cooperate with you guys, can I walk out of here?"

Kruger and Knoll nodded.

"The guy's name is Dalton Hadley. He's a local fixer. I'm told he has connections to the Chicago Outfit, but I don't think he does."

Kruger said, "Why?"

"He travels to Minneapolis too often. If he's part of the Outfit, they'd never let him leave the city that much."

"If he doesn't work for the Outfit, who does he work for?"

"Some rich guy in Minneapolis."

Shooting a quick glance at Knoll and Gibbs, Kruger said, "Hunter Holden?"

"Yeah, I think that's the name."

Knoll leaned over the table. "Where can we find this Dalton fellow?"

"Don't know. He always contacts me."

"How?"

"Text message."

Kruger smiled. "Why don't you send him one?"

"Never tried."

"I think it's time you made the effort."

CHAPTER 45

Minneapolis

Hunter Holden fed documents into an industrial shredder purchased for just such an occasion—the liquidation and dismantling of Transnational Financial. Dean Melton deposited another white banker's box on the table where Holden worked.

"This is the last one from the archive room."

"Good. I'll start on the records in this room after I have that shredded."

"Hunter, I'm not sure I'm going to Taiwan with you."

"Suit yourself. You're not on the payroll after today. In fact, there isn't any payroll after today."

Melton frowned at the man he had served faithfully for two decades. "Any severance payments?"

Holden stopped and turned toward the man. "Dean, your bank account is flush with money. You've profited immensely over the last few years from decisions I've made. No, there will be no severance payments."

Melton left the room.

An hour later, with all the documents shredded, Holden

went back to his desk and searched it one more time to make sure nothing incriminating remained. Satisfied after the search, he stood, grabbed his cell phone from the desk surface, and walked out of his office for the last time.

Melton watched as Holden passed his office door headed toward the elevators. No sign of recognition. The man did not even look his way. Taking a deep breath, he surveyed his own office now stripped of personal and business documents. His next task would be to eliminate any remaining fingerprints with paper towels and a bottle of Windex.

Sentimentality did not exist in Melton's DNA. The grief he felt was for the end of an era where he made a lot of money and held power over people who would normally ignore him. Being the last person in the office and not hearing a goodbye from Holden had been expected. He had reconciled the relationship the two men held a long time ago. Convenience. Their association was based on Melton providing services Holden refused to do himself. At one time, each man needed the other, but those days were long gone. He gathered a bundle of files he kept locked in his desk and returned to Holden's office.

When finished in his ex-boss' work area, he returned to his own. After wiping down the surfaces of his desk and furniture, he then cleaned the outside of the Windex bottle and placed it in the waste basket, along with the used paper towels.

According to Holden, Melton's last official duty for the company would be to lock all the office doors on the last day. As he started to attend to this task, he snorted. "Fuck this." He left the office keys on the reception desk and took the elevator to the ground floor.

***

Dalton Hadley received a terse text message from Dean

Melton at 1:32 p.m. The word count on the message equaled the same as the fingers on a person's hand. *You're fired. No additional cash.*

"Asshole." Hadley returned the cell phone to his pocket as he watched three men and a woman exit the Lakeside Tavern. One he knew to be Sean Kruger. The others he did not recognize. All four entered a large SUV. Thirty seconds later, it sped away from the area. He waited five minutes and then crossed the street to the bar.

After entering, he spotted the man he needed to see, sitting by himself in the far corner. When he arrived at the table, he asked, "Who the hell were you talking to, Dillard?"

"Who's Hunter Holden?"

"The guy who paid you a lot of money a week ago."

"Well, I was just told he's the one who wants an FBI agent dead. Not a smart move, man."

"Who told you that?"

"Kruger and two very scary ex-military types."

"What'd you tell them?"

"I forget."

"Damn, you sold me out, didn't you?"

Dillard shrugged. "No more than you did me."

Hadley practically ran out of the tavern.

***

After a quick flight to Minneapolis, Kruger and Knoll rented a car and drove to the offices of Transnational Financial. Amber Willis, accompanied by Jimmie Gibbs, returned to Springfield. Barnett would fly back to Minneapolis the next day. When Kruger exited the elevator, the floor the former private equity company occupied was eerily quiet.

He turned to Knoll. "Check with the building manager. Something's wrong here."

"Got it."

After the elevator door closed, Kruger walked the halls of the floor and then returned to the reception area. With hands on his hips, he mumbled to himself, "Obviously, we're too late."

At that moment, Knoll exited the elevator and said, "The building manager said the lease is paid up through the end of the year. He wasn't aware they'd moved out."

"Let me show you something." When they approached the receptionist's desk, Kruger pointed to a set of keys. "Those keys are to each of the office doors. None are locked. Plus, I found Holden's office."

The retired FBI agent led the big man to a large room in the northeast corner of the floor. "This was his."

"How can you tell?"

"Look in the desk. Lots of correspondence addressed to him. None of it appears to be of major importance. My guess is he sanitized it and left the rest for others to clean up."

Looking up from the papers on the desk, Knoll asked, "You find anything useful?"

"No. Not yet." Kruger's attention remained on a section of the room occupied by a floor-to-ceiling bookcase. He slipped on latex gloves and handed a pair to Knoll. He then walked toward the shelves and read titles. After a few minutes, he pulled out a book and looked behind it. "Sandy, come here."

The retired major stepped over to where Kruger stood. "What've ya got?"

Kruger continued to remove books, exposing more of what appeared to be a panel. After removing half the volumes, it appeared the panel extended the full length of one shelf. "Huh." When the entire shelf was empty, the panel could plainly be seen. "I wonder what this leads to." He tapped on the center of the back board and heard a hollow sound. Pushing on the upper edge of the panel, it popped outward.

"Sandy, come witness this."

The big man watched as Kruger lowered the panel forward, revealing a stack of files. He removed one and handed it to Knoll who placed it on Holden's abandoned desk. In total, they retrieved a dozen file folders, each about an inch thick.

Sandy Knoll opened the first file handed to him and read quietly for a few minutes. "Hey, Sean."

"Yeah."

"We might want to put these back and call the FBI."

A smile appeared on Kruger's lips. "What's there?"

"These are the documents they need for an indictment."

Kruger pulled out his cell phone and dialed a number.

***

The original team of FBI agents searching the offices of Transnational Financial amounted to a half dozen members of the Minneapolis Field Office. When they discovered the hidden panel in Hunter Holden's office, the agent in charge stopped everyone and made a phone call. By midnight, additional agents, mainly from Washington, DC, including a man name Charlie Craft, swarmed over the abandoned office.

Charlie walked up to Kruger and Knoll who silently watched the procedure. "How did you know about the secret panel, Sean?"

"Your agents from Minneapolis found it, Charlie."

"Why do I not believe that?"

With a quick smile, Kruger nodded toward the elevator. Craft followed him, and they both rode it down to the ground floor. Once outside in the crisp late-night air, Kruger said, "We got the building manager's approval to look through the offices. He didn't know Transnational had already moved out. So, during our inspection of Holden's office, we found the panel. I immediately called Ryan Clark. Simple as that."

Charlie folded his arms and stared at his old mentor as a

smile came to his lips. "That's your story?"

"Yes."

"Okay. I get it. What's in the files?"

"Enough evidence for the FBI to get the indictment they need to arrest Hunter Holden."

"Did you see anything else in the offices?"

"Just plastic trash bags of shredded documents. Most of those were in the office you guys are searching."

A cell phone on Charlie's belt chirped. He answered it. After a few seconds of listening, he said, "I'll be right there." He ended the call and returned his attention to Kruger. "Seems they just hit the jackpot for evidence against Hunter Holden. Let's go."

***

Knoll once again stood next to Kruger as excited FBI agents scurried around the offices. The big man whispered, "Holden did a thorough job of shredding documents. Why do you suppose he forgot about the hidden panel in the bookcase?"

Looking at his friend, Kruger shrugged. "Too much of a hurry to leave would be my guess." He frowned and grew silent. "Unless…"

"Unless he didn't know the files were there."

"Someone planted them."

"That brings up a whole new set of questions."

"Yes, it does. Hold on. Here comes Charlie."

The lanky forensic expert did a fast walk up to Kruger and Knoll. Wide-eyed, he said, "Hey, Sean, didn't you get involved with Hunter Holden when the insurance company asked you to investigate a suspected jewelry heist at the Field Museum in Chicago?"

"Yes."

"We just found a file outlining the whole operation. Hunter Holden was the mastermind around it. There're even documents on where the diamonds were taken, cut down, sold, and for how much."

"Huh."

"I've got to let the director know." He hustled away.

Kruger turned to Knoll. "I think it might be a good idea if we make sure Holden misses his flight in the morning."

"Great idea."

CHAPTER 46

Minneapolis

Unbeknownst to Kruger and the FBI, Hunter Holden, at the last minute, switched his original travel plans to a direct flight leaving Minneapolis-St. Paul International airport at 7:40 p.m. earlier that evening. At the same time FBI agents gathered evidence for their indictment, Holden slept quietly in Business Class on a Boeing 777-200 on his way to Charles de Gaulle International.

With the remote assistance of JR Diminski, Knoll and Kruger located and entered the exclusive home of Hunter Holden at fifteen minutes before five in the morning. The minute they gained access, Kruger knew the house was unoccupied. He stood in the foyer of the grand home and said, "Shit. He's already gone."

Knoll turned and focused on his friend. "How can you tell?"

"There'd be lights on. He'd be preparing to leave for the airport by now."

"Yeah, you're right."

Without hesitating further, Kruger punched numbers into

his cell phone. When the call went through, he said, "Stewart, we need to be in Paris, like yesterday. How can we do that?"

Silence consumed the vestibule as he listened. "Yes." More silence. "Not sure, a day, maybe more." The retired FBI agent fell quiet again. "We can be there. Thanks." He ended the call. Turning to Knoll he said, "Stewart has access to a Bombardier Global 5000 that's currently in Wichita. It's got the range we need to get to Paris and can fly at .85 Mach. He'll need a copilot on an international flight. So, we need to be at the airport by ten this morning."

With a chuckle, Knoll said, "That quick?"

"You know Stewart. He can get shit done when he needs to. He's bringing Jimmie and grabbing our go-bags."

"Glad he's on our team. Who's the copilot?"

"Who do you think?"

"He might be handy to have around in Paris."

"Kind of what I was thinking."

***

Somewhere Over the Atlantic

Having spent the past thirty-six hours awake, Kruger slept fitfully on the plane. Where Gibbs and Knoll experienced no trouble catching a little shut-eye, the ex-FBI agent gave up five hours into the ten-hour flight. With nothing better to do, Kruger walked forward to the cockpit. He saw Stewart leaned back, snoring slightly, his arms folded. Turning to the copilot he said, "Thanks for doing this, Michael."

Wolfe's mouth twitched. "Glad to be of help. What are your plans when we get to Paris?"

"Are you familiar with the city?"

"I can get around. Why?"

"Before you two arrived, I got a call from Ryan Clark. He

told me even with the new evidence uncovered at Holden's office, they wouldn't be able to get an indictment signed by a judge until at least tomorrow."

"Holden could be long gone by then."

"Those are my concerns as well."

"You obviously have a plan in place."

"Not really, but I'm working on it. JR told me he's staying at the Four Seasons hotel a block south of the Champs-Élysées."

"I know where it is."

"His meeting with the banker is somewhere within the 8th arrondissement."

"That area of Paris encompasses the Arc de Triomphe on the western side and the Place de la Concorde on the eastern boundary."

"Somewhere within that area is where Holden has an appointment with the BNP Paribas representative."

"That could be anywhere. With Holden, my guess would be a fancy restaurant with a private dining area. Those types of places are all over Paris."

Kruger smiled slightly and returned to his seat. He pressed an icon on his phone.

"Yeah."

"Can you determine if there are any restaurants around the Four Seasons with a private dining area?"

"Do you want to wait, or should I call you back?"

"I'll wait."

Four minutes later, JR said, "There's a five-star restaurant a block south of the hotel. Fancy place, and they offer private dining rooms."

"Can you get access to their reservations?"

"Probably. Who would I be looking for?"

"Don't know, but he or she would be with BNP Paribas."

"Well, that might help. I'll call you back."

Ending the call, Kruger stood and returned to the cockpit. Wolfe said, "What'd you find out?"

"JR's checking."

"Sean, let's say he has a meeting. Traffic in Paris can be obnoxious. If JR can determine where the meeting is and it's close to the Four Seasons, my bet is he'll walk. If he does, we snatch him off the street and fly him back to the US."

Kruger tilted his head slightly and contemplated Wolfe. "You know, that's not a bad idea."

Keeping his eyes on the instrument panel, Wolfe nodded. "Not my first rodeo."

***

Located on fifty-three hundred acres, seven kilometers north of Paris, Paris-Le Bourget is one of the more congested business airports in Europe. With its three runways and parking areas, it can accommodate all types of aircraft. The Bombardier Global 5000 flown by Stewart Barnett and Michael Wolfe landed without fanfare at 5:18 p.m., Paris time, a seven-hour time difference from Minneapolis. As Barnett parked the plane in a designated parking area, he noticed it was one of five on the tarmac. No one would remember it.

With his fluent French, Wolfe was put in charge of renting a Fiat Ducato panel van from the local Europcar rental office. By seven that evening, Kruger, Knoll, and Gibbs were being driven by Wolfe toward the 8th arrondissement and the Hôtel Château Frontenac. Barnett chose to stay near the airport so he could have the plane serviced and ready to go when needed. By 10 p.m., Kruger and Gibbs were walking around the Four Seasons less than a block from their hotel.

"What do you think, Sean? Will we have time to do a snatch and grab?"

"Our timing is going to have to be perfect for it to work. JR said a Charlene Boucher with BNP Paribas has a reservation for two in a private dining room at 1 p.m.

tomorrow at a restaurant called Beefbar. The address is 5 Rue Marbeuf."

Gibbs turned to the south. "When Alexia and I got married here, Beefbar was one of the places we ate. It's that way."

Kruger smiled. "I forgot this is where you and Alexia got married."

"Yeah, in Notre Dame, before the fire. She cried for days when we heard the news."

They walked in silence toward the restaurant down Avenue George V, made a left on Rue du Boccador, and then another immediate left on Rue Marbeuf.

Kruger said, "This isn't going to work, Jimmie."

"Why?"

"I've been in Paris, and Rue Marbeuf is a one-way street going north toward the Champs-Élysées. We'll get hung up in traffic, and that will be it."

"Yeah, I see your point. When Alexia and I were here, there were cars parked on both sides and chaos between. So, what else..." Gibbs paused. "How long is Holden's reservation at the Four Seasons?"

"He's booked on a flight to Taiwan day after tomorrow."

"When does it leave?"

"His flight is on Turkish Airlines and leaves at 5:50 p.m. with a three-hour layover in Istanbul."

"So, he won't be getting up at four in the morning to catch a flight?"

Kruger shook his head. "No."

"Do you know what room?"

"Yes."

"We grab him from his room tomorrow night. Traffic will be lighter, and we can make it to the airport before dawn."

Kruger looked north on Avenue George V and remained quiet. A slight grin appeared. "We take him between 2 and 3 a.m."

"I'd suggest between three and four."

Kruger looked at his friend. "You're the Navy SEAL, I wouldn't pretend to argue with you."

Gibbs folded his arms. "That gives us a little over twenty-four hours to plan."

"Guess we'd better get started."

***

Kruger sat in a comfortable chair, his legs crossed, elbows on the armrests, and his hands making a steeple as he listened to the plan proposed by Gibbs. Keeping his thoughts to himself, he looked at Knoll. "What do you think, Sandy?"

"I think it's got merit. What about you, Michael?"

Turning to Kruger, Wolfe said, "Sean, you've mentioned that Holden is unpredictable, right?"

"Consistently."

"We know where he will be at one tomorrow afternoon. When he gets back to his hotel room, we lose the ability to keep tabs on him without drawing attention to ourselves. Once this happens, we are at a disadvantage."

Everyone nodded.

Gibbs said, "We'll need some type of ruse to enter the hotel and his room."

Wolfe smiled. "I still have a few contacts here in the city. I'll handle that part."

Kruger looked around the room. "Then everyone agrees. Jimmie will follow him, and Sandy will provide transportation. Michael and I will handle the operation inside the hotel."

CHAPTER 47

Paris

Hunter Holden felt relatively safe walking south on Avenue George V toward his meeting with the BNP Paribas representative. The cosmopolitan feel of Paris, one of his favorite metropolises, always amazed him. Trees lined the streets and shaded the sidewalks. Something foreign to an American city.

Taking a left onto Rue Marbeuf, Holden entered the Beefbar and disappeared inside.

***

A slender athletic man followed Holden as he strolled toward his meeting. Jimmie Gibbs crossed the street and sat in a small bistro across from the Beefbar. He pulled out his cell phone and typed out a text message. He pressed the send icon.

After putting his phone away, he ordered an espresso.

***

Kruger read the text message from Gibbs and nodded at Wolfe. Both men wore coveralls with the name of a local plumbing company emblazoned on the left breast of the garment. The previous night's discussion helped cement the team's decision on when to grab Hunter Holden. Paris traffic in this section of the city remained too erratic. If they got stuck in traffic, the chances of being arrested by Paris police increased. In addition, the idea of entering his suite at 3 a.m. for an abduction was discarded after Kruger reminded the team of Holden's sudden departure from Minneapolis. The man was too unpredictable.

The alternate plan they came up with seemed to have the best chance of success.

Situated on the eighth floor, Holden's suite contained twice the square footage of an average hotel room in Paris. When they approached the door, Wolfe held a small device under the RFID pad on the lock, and it clicked open. Both men slipped into the spacious area and silently closed the door.

Withdrawing his cell phone, Kruger pressed a name in his contact file.

JR answered on the fourth ring. "Are you in his room?"

"Yeah, the device worked as you advertised. Looks like we made the correct decision about doing this today. I'm looking at packed bags on the bed. What about the security cameras in the hotel?"

"There was one shot of you and Wolfe from the back. It's no longer there. Call me just before you leave his suite. I'll detour the camera feeds to my system for fifteen minutes. That way I can keep tabs on you. Will that give you enough time to get him out?"

"It should. Sandy will have the van parked out front, and we'll simply walk Mr. Holden through the front entrance and into the van."

"I'll wait for you to call me before I return the camera

feeds."

"If you don't hear from me, the whole thing will have gone south."

"I'll hear from you. What could go wrong?"

Kruger sighed. "Yeah, what could go wrong?"

***

At exactly 3:51 p.m., Holden emerged from the Beefbar and turned to his right to walk back toward the Four Seasons. When he turned right on Rue du Boccador, the slender man sitting at a table across the street stood and placed a twenty euro note under his espresso cup. He lifted a cell phone to his ear and said, "He's heading back."

Staying on the opposite side of Avenue George V, Gibbs kept his target in sight as they walked north. Holden crossed the street at Rue Pierre Charron and entered the Four Seasons.

Gibbs made another call on his phone. It was answered with silence and the retired SEAL said, "Just entered the lobby."

As soon as he ended that call, he pressed another name in his contact file.

Knoll answered. "Yeah."

"Holden just entered the hotel. I'll meet you in ten."

"Got it."

***

The door to suite 803 opened, and Holden turned immediately to his left to enter the bathroom. When he finished his business, he continued on into the living space of the room and stopped dead in his tracks. "What the hell are you doing here?"

Kruger sat in a leather club chair next to the door leading to the balcony. "The same question could be directed toward yourself, Hunter."

Holden stood in the center of the room, hands on hips, face growing crimson. "We're in Paris, Kruger. You have no authority here."

With his arms on the cushioned armrest of the chair, the retired FBI agent offered Holden a sly smile. "One could say I don't have any authority in the US, but here I am. You're going back with me to face an indictment for the Field Museum diamond heist and conspiracy murder charges."

"You have no proof."

"Afraid the FBI does. They found a considerable amount of evidence in a secret panel hidden behind the books in your office."

Holden apparently sensed someone behind him. He started to turn, but, before he could, Wolfe placed a hand on his forehead, leaned his head back, and plunged a needle into his carotid artery. The ex-CEO blinked once and went limp. Wolfe caught him under the arms and lowered him onto the bed.

"Good night, Hunter." Wolfe looked at Kruger. "It'll take about fifteen minutes before he'll respond to suggestions."

"Will he remember anything?"

Wolfe shook his head. "Once we get him on the plane, I can give him a little more, and he won't remember the flight."

"Where did you get that stuff?"

"An old acquaintance with the Mossad. Like I told you last night, I still have connections here in Paris."

"I won't ask any more questions."

"Wouldn't answer them if you did."

Kruger smiled and searched Holden's packed suitcase.

***

When the elevator door opened on the lobby floor, Wolfe exited first, followed by Kruger holding the elbow of Hunter

Holden. Having shed their coveralls, they were dressed similar to Holden. The former CEO of Transnational Financial wore sunglasses and a blank expression. He faced forward and walked in step with Kruger.

The hotel concierge stepped out from his desk near the front door, smiled, and asked in French, "Is Monsieur Holden checking out?"

Wolfe answered in kind. "No, he's not feeling well. We're taking him to a doctor."

"And who might you be, Monsieur?"

"Business associate. We were having a meeting in his room when he complained of a searing headache."

"I see, may I have your name, Monsieur?"

"Yes, Dean Melton."

"Very good. Hope you feel better, Monsieur Holden."

As they stepped out of the front entrance of the Four Seasons, a white panel van screeched to a halt and a door opened. Holden was hustled into the vehicle just before it accelerated away.

Knoll made a left onto Rue Pierre Charron and accelerated toward Avenue des Champs-Élysées. The van turned left and followed the internationally known street to the iconic Arc de Triomphe. It merged into the traffic circling the monument and disappeared into afternoon Paris traffic.

***

Robin Rodin, the Four Seasons tenured concierge thought it strange Hunter Holden had not spoken to him as he was being escorted out of the hotel. He went to the front desk and asked when Hunter Holden was to check out.

The young woman typed something on her computer and studied the screen. "According to this, Robin, he was leaving tonight."

"That is what he told me. Maybe I should check his

room."

Taking his pass key, Rodin rode to the eight floor and entered Hunter Holden's room. The chaos he found caused him to rush to the house phone in the room and ask for an outside line. When he heard the dial tone, he pressed the numbers 211.

***

Jean-Louis Fresnel with the Directorate of Territorial Security, or DST, Frances' equivalent to the American FBI, examined various pieces of evidence in the room of Hunter Holden. One piece in particular intrigued him, a hypodermic syringe and needle. He picked it up with his latex-gloved hand and sniffed. He detected the faintest hint of almonds.

After placing the object in an evidence bag, he made a call on his cell phone. A gruff voice answered. "What have you got, Jean-Louis?"

"I suspect someone has kidnapped the American millionaire, Hunter Holden."

Silence dominated the call for several moments. "That is interesting. We received a Red Notice on Holden from Interpol less than thirty minutes ago. Someone must have beat us to him."

"What shall I do here?"

"If Monsieur Holden has been spirited away, I say good riddance. We have less paperwork to worry about."

"Very well. I'll leave the room as I found it."

"If I were you, I would report it as a missing-person incident."

"An excellent idea."

***

Halfway Across the Atlantic

Kruger ended the call with JR and turned to Sandy Knoll sitting next to him. "The FBI has issued a federal arrest warrant for Holden and Interpol issued a Red Notice on him."

The big man smiled. "How do you want to handle it when we land?"

"Good question."

"Got someone you want to do a favor for with the agency?"

With a smile, Kruger nodded. "The SAC in Des Moines did us a favor. I think I'll return it. Ask Stewart to request a change in our flight plan to Iowa."

***

Special Agent Bridgett Nelson met the Bombardier Global 5000 on the tarmac near the FBO of the Des Moines International airport. The time was almost five in the morning when the plane braked to a halt. Kruger lowered the airstairs and she scrambled aboard.

He offered his hand, she shook it, and asked, "What's the surprise?"

Kruger pointed to the semiconscious figure of Hunter Holden sitting in the first seat of the cabin. "He's yours. Tell your boss you found him in a drunken stupor along the highway."

She smiled. "I can't say that."

"How much paperwork and how many doses of Tylenol will it cost you to admit he was handed over on the tarmac of an international airport.?"

Studying the groggy man, she contemplated the question. "I'll think of something." Returning her attention to Kruger, she asked, "Why me?"

He shrugged. "Why not, you?"

"I'll take that as a compliment."

"It was meant that way."

CHAPTER 48

Minneapolis

Dean Melton sipped coffee at a local Starbucks and studied one of the news links on his cell phone. The article detailed the arrest and arraignment in Des Moines, Iowa, of one of Minneapolis' richest individuals, Transnational Financial CEO Hunter Holden. The report stated Holden, in a drunken stupor, was arrested while wandering around an upscale neighborhood earlier the previous morning. He was under FBI detention and charged with conspiracy and murder.

A slight smile came to his lips, but the reality of the situation suddenly dawned on him. Holden would throw him under the bus in a heartbeat. Time to head south, away from the cold tundra of Minnesota. Using his cell phone, he checked his bank balance and decided he owned nothing more important than his freedom. He could afford to abandon his possessions. Getting out of town became far more urgent. He picked up his cell phone and started making calls. But before he abandoned the northern states, he needed to make a stop in Chicago.

***

Holden sat in an interrogation room, shackles on his wrists and his leg chained to a ring embedded in the concrete floor. With his hands clasped, he smiled at the two FBI agents sitting in front of him. "I'm not answering any questions without my attorney present."

FBI Special Agent Bridgett Nelson appraised the disheveled man in front of her. "We've tried to find Dean Melton, as you suggested. So far, he can't be located. Any comments?"

"No, other than to say any crimes committed by Transnational Financial would have been initiated by him."

She smiled. "We've interviewed other former associates of your company. They've told us you ran the office with an iron fist. Nothing happened without your consent."

"I have no further comment until my attorney is present."

Nelson stood. "I might mention, all of your financial assets in the US have been seized by the government."

"What do you mean, seized?"

"The files we discovered in your hidden compartment spell out those funds belong to clients, not you."

"I demand to see my attorney."

"So you've said. I was merely trying to keep you informed. Have a nice day, Mr. Holden."

She and the other FBI agent exited the room. Staring at the now-closed door, he pounded his fists on the table in front of him. "This is all Kruger's fault."

A knock at the door occurred and then a man in an expensive suit entered the room. Holden said, "About time you got here, Abbot."

Greg Abbot smiled and sat across from the ex-CEO. "Are you aware of the evidence the FBI has against you, Hunter?"

The prisoner shook his head.

The attorney continued. "I've seen a summary of the discovery documents. It does not paint a positive image of your chances of staying out of prison."

"It's all made up. Dean Melton probably planted it there."

"Signatures are all yours. From what I've been told, you have a unique signature, and it's on all the documents. I haven't seen them yet, but if that's the case, it's pretty damning."

"Find Melton. I'm sure he's the one who signed the documents."

"I hope that's not the case because it will make you look even worse in the eyes of the law."

"How's that possible?"

"That would raise conspiracy charges on top of fraud and murder charges. Bond is going to be tricky as it is. They have evidence you had an airline ticket to Taiwan. That would imply you are a flight risk. So, getting out on bail will probably not happen."

Holden struck the table again with his clenched fists. "Your job is to get me out of here."

Abbot leaned forward. "Your behavior isn't helping, Hunter. Now, shut up and listen to me."

"How dare you talk to me like that. I pay your firm a considerable amount of money each month to take care of issues like this."

"That may well be, but we are financial lawyers, not criminal attorneys. There's a difference. Right now, you need a high-priced attorney who has experience with these types of matters."

"Then find one."

"That will be difficult. The company's and your assets have been frozen. You are being considered a flight risk, plus your attitude sucks."

Holden closed his eyes. "If I give you power of attorney, can you use my house as collateral?"

"I could have. But your creditors placed a lien against it."

"What do you mean?"

"A group of your investors have filed fraud charges

against you and, last I knew, placed a lien against your house."

"Then what assets do I have?"

"None that I'm aware of."

"I have money in BNP Paribas in Paris. A considerable amount, I might add."

"Hunter, you don't. Apparently, you instructed them to transfer this money to an account in Taiwan. It never made it, but it's no longer in Paris, either."

Holden tried to stand, but his constraints prevented him doing so. "Never made it. How?"

"We don't know, we have an attorney working on it. It's not looking good though. You're basically broke, Hunter."

"Melton."

"Excuse me."

"Dean Melton. He's responsible. The FBI needs to arrest him."

"I've tried to contact him, but his cell phone goes directly to voice mail, and he has not returned any of my calls."

"The son of a bitch is probably hiding out."

"Well, until we can contact him, you are in this by yourself."

***

Southwest Missouri

Kruger raised an eyebrow. "What do you mean you have no idea where the money in Paris went?"

"Not sure how to explain it. Sean, it's gone."

"Holden was supposed to transfer it to a bank in Taipei. Did that not happen?"

JR shook his head. "Not that I can tell."

"Then where'd it go?"

"One minute it was in BNP Paribas and then, poof, gone. I was able to see the transfer, but the money never got to the receiving bank."

Kruger folded his arms. "Huh."

"Want to hear my theory?"

"I'm listening."

"The Mossad."

Kruger chuckled. "Why do you think it was the Mossad?"

"You said Michael reached out to them in Paris. I'm just thinking, maybe they decided to take advantage of the situation."

"If they did, more power to them. Saves us from having to worry about it."

"I've dealt with some of their IT guys. Would not want to go up against them."

"That good?"

"Yeah, Sean, they're that good."

"What's the latest on Holden?"

"Super quiet. You might have to call Bridgett Nelson to find out what's going on. Nothing's on the Internet that I can find."

"Now that is the best idea you've had today." Kruger pulled his cell phone out, searched for a number, and touched the screen. The call went unanswered. "Maybe she'll call back."

Two minutes later, she did.

"Kruger."

"Sean, it's Bridgett. Sorry I missed your call."

"No problem. What's going on with Hunter Holden?"

"DOJ made the case he's a flight risk and won. He's being held without bail."

"Smart."

"He's also claiming Dean Melton is the one responsible."

"Of course. Is he under arrest?"

"No, he's on the run. FBI has a national BOLO out on him. So far, no results." She paused. "Uh, Sean."

"Yeah."

"How quick can you get to Des Moines?"

"What do you need?"

"DOJ decided to grant a request from Holden's lawyer."

"Don't tell me Hunter Holden wants to talk to me."

"Afraid so. He says the only person he will talk with is you."

"Let me make arrangements, and I'll call you back."

"One other thing." Bridgett paused for a moment. "I'm not sure how to thank you."

"You don't need to."

"Yeah, I kinda do. I'm being promoted."

"Congratulations. Where to?"

"DC."

"Uh—oh. Be careful what you wish for."

"Why do you say that?"

With a chuckle, Kruger said, "DC can be a meat grinder."

"Should I turn it down?"

"Hell no. If that's what you want, go for it. It might not come around again."

"Okay. Hey, I have to run. But I will keep you posted on Holden."

"Thanks, Bridgett. Good luck."

The call ended, and Kruger took a deep breath. He let it out slowly.

JR asked, "What was that all about?"

"Bridgett got promoted to DC."

"Are you jealous?"

"No." He paused for a moment. "Not about going to DC. This little episode with Holden made me realize I still miss the hunt and getting bad guys off the street."

With a hearty laugh, JR shook his head. "You just did, Sean. Without you, Holden wouldn't be sitting in a jail in Des Moines. He can't hurt people anymore."

"That's the other thing. His lawyer made a request of the DOJ, and they granted it."

"Don't tell me."

"Yeah, he will only talk to me."

"Will that expose your assistance in bringing him back to the US?"

"Don't know. Guess I'll find out."

CHAPTER 49

Des Moines
Two Days Later

Bridgett Nelson escorted Kruger to an interview room within the Polk County Jail. He followed her as they entered and noticed Holden in a prison jumpsuit sitting at a table next to a man dressed in a suit.

No words were exchanged until Kruger sat across from the prisoner. The retired FBI agent tilted his head. "You wanted to talk to me, so talk."

Holden locked eyes with Kruger. "You honestly believe I'm the one who planned the Field Museum diamond theft?"

"What I believe is inconsequential. From what I've been told, the documents in your office pretty much spell out your role in this crime. My part in this was to counsel the insurance company on whether there was fraud involved."

"You need to talk to Dean Melton. He's the one who set it all up."

"And you had nothing to do with it."

The prisoner started to say something, but his attorney put a hand on his sleeve and shook his head. Holden yanked his arm away and glared at his new criminal lawyer. "This is important, Mr. Newman. I'm going to answer his question." He paused and returned his attention to Kruger. "I had absolutely nothing to do with it. Unbeknownst to me, Melton put all the wheels in motion."

Kruger smiled. "Right. You just took advantage of the situation. Is that what you want us to believe?"

The former CEO nodded.

Kruger stood. "I've been dealing with individuals like yourself for my entire career with the FBI, Holden. People like you can look your victims in the eye and lie without remorse or a second thought. You also like to play the victim card. I'm not buying what you're selling."

Holden looked up at him. "Do you really think I'm dumb enough to leave those types of files in my office? I assume you saw how I left it. Everything was shredded. Someone else placed them there after I left, and the only person still in the office was Melton."

Keeping his eyes on Holden, Kruger paused for a moment and returned to his chair. "I'll play your game for a moment. What was Melton's purpose?"

"To throw the blame on me."

"No, what was his purpose for having the diamonds switched out?"

"It should be obvious."

"Humor me. I can be a little slow sometimes."

Leaning over the table, the prisoner said, "To get me out of the way so he could take over the company."

"If that was his goal, he didn't quite have it figured out. Your company, at this moment, could technically be considered bankrupt."

"I still have money."

"Are you sure? The money you had in Paris is gone."

Holden's eyes grew as round as saucers.

Continuing, Kruger gave the man a half smile. "I know you were transferring it to Taiwan, but somewhere between here and there, it vanished. Also, that wasn't your money. It belonged to five clients."

"I'm telling you, Melton is behind the whole scheme, Kruger. Find him, and you'll realize I'm innocent."

Rolling his eyes, Kruger stood again and looked at Holden's attorney. "Good luck with your defense, Counselor." He then walked out of the room, followed by Bridgett.

When they were out of the jail and standing by their cars in the parking lot, she asked, "You believe him, don't you?"

"Unfortunately, he said something that actually makes sense."

"What?"

"He's a very intelligent man and made a good point about leaving those types of files behind. If I was a betting man, I'd say their defense will be centered around claiming the files are forgeries."

She folded her arms. "That's our whole case against him."

"Exactly. The only reason he wanted to talk to me today was to throw doubt on the authenticity of your evidence against him. He's clever, and, I would bet, a good chess player."

"Any idea where Melton is?"

"No, I concentrated on Holden. I paid zero attention to Melton."

"Well, that's where my focus will be until we bring him in."

Kruger offered his hand and, as they shook, said, "Good luck, Agent. You're gonna need it."

***

Returning to his office later in the afternoon, the trip to the airport actually took longer than the flying time to Des Moines. At the same moment he placed his backpack on the floor next to his desk, JR appeared in his doorway.

"Well?"

"It was a serious waste of time. Holden used the meeting to throw doubt on the files found in the secret compartment in his office."

"You're kidding?"

"Nope. It might just work if Dean Melton is never arrested," Kruger explained.

JR chuckled. "So, what are you going to do about it?"

"I am not going to do anything about it. It is entirely in the capable hands of the FBI. We are going to go back to our normal routine and pretend Hunter Holden doesn't exist."

"Do you really believe you are done with this mess?"

"No, but I have no authority to pursue it further. The insurance investigation is complete, and Holden is in custody."

JR leaned against the doorframe of Kruger's office and folded his arms. "What if I told you I might know how to find Dean Melton?"

"I'd listen carefully."

"What was the name of the guy who Dillard said was his contact?"

"Dalton Hadley."

"Yeah, that guy. He's the key. His cell phone would have Melton's contact info on it. If we had that? Well, I could follow him."

"Sounds like Sandy and I get to take a trip to Chicago."

"Let's hope it's just a day trip."

"Want to go?"

"Sure. I haven't strong-armed anyone in a long time."

***

Chicago

A cold wind blowing in off Lake Michigan, accompanied by ice pellets, graced the area surrounding the Lakeside

Tavern. The time approached twelve thirty in the afternoon as a rented GMC Yukon Denali, parked across the street from the bar. It contained three individuals. Sandy Knoll sat behind the steering wheel with Kruger next to him. JR occupied the seat behind Sandy, his laptop open.

Kruger pointed to a figure crossing the street, a black stocking hat pulled over his ears and his hands stuffed into the pockets of a navy peacoat. The figure trudged toward the front door of the establishment.

Knoll commented, "Damn predictable, isn't he."

Kruger kept his eye on the man as he swung the door open and ducked inside. "Very decent of him. Saves us from tracking him down."

From the back seat, JR mumbled, "Would you two get this over with so we can leave this icebox."

Kruger and Knoll opened their door at the same time and crossed the street. JR watched them disappear into the tavern.

Robert Dillard sat at the same booth in the back as he had the first time they met. Knoll sat across from him, and Kruger caused the man to scoot over before he followed suit.

With a smile, Knoll said, "Hello, Robbie D."

The man looked at Knoll and then at Kruger. "What the hell. Not you two again?"

"We're like bad pennies. We keep coming back," Kruger said with a frown.

"I have no clue where Hadley is. I haven't seen him since you guys were here last. So, bug off."

Knoll reached over and grabbed Dillard's cell phone from the table in front of him. "Then you won't mind if we check, will you?" He handed the item to Kruger who stood and walked out of the bar.

"Hey, you can't do that, I have rights."

"Sorry, Robbie D. We're not cops. All we want is a contact number for Hadley. That's all."

"I would have given you that. You didn't have to steal my

phone."

"You'll get it back. Unfortunately, I don't trust you, so to make sure we have the correct info, we decided to borrow it."

Dillard stared at the man sitting across from him. "Fuck you, Knoll."

"The sentiment is mutual, Robbie D."

Twenty minutes later, Knoll guided the Denali away from the curb. "Where to, JR?"

The computer hacker stared at his laptop screen and shook his head. "The last time Dillard spoke to Hadley was right after you two spoke to him. Nothing since."

Kruger turned in his seat to look at his friend. "Can you pinpoint Hadley's location at that time?"

"Not yet. The phone's been off the air since that phone call. Nothing since."

Kruger displayed a frown and turned his attention to Knoll. "What did you and Robbie D. talk about while I was gone?"

"He wasn't very talkative. But I did find out where Hadley lives."

Raising an eyebrow, Kruger said, "That might be helpful. Where?"

"That's where we're going now. Dillard heard he'd moved to an apartment building north of here called Lakeshore Lofts."

CHAPTER 50

Chicago

The buzzer to apartment twenty-five went unanswered. Kruger tried it one more time before he returned to the Denali.

"No answer."

"Doesn't mean anything."

JR looked up from his laptop and said, "The place is managed by a big conglomerate. There isn't an on-site supervisor."

Kruger turned to look at the computer expert. "Can you hack into the system and unlock the door?"

JR shook his head. "No." He typed a few more seconds. "But I just found Hadley's building and apartment access codes."

Knoll chuckled. "I believe that will work even better."

Thirty minutes later, the three men slipped into the apartment of Dalton Hadley. The apartment's interior revealed either a slob for a tenant or an extremely thorough search for something by persons unknown. Kruger said, "This doesn't look good. I'll check the bedrooms. You guys stay here."

When he returned, he held a cell phone in a latex-gloved hand. "JR, see if you can download this." He handed a pair of latex gloves to JR and Sandy. "Put these on. I don't want to leave any stray fingerprints. Once we leave, I'll call the police."

As Knoll put the gloves on, he said, "I take it you found Hadley."

"Yes. With a bullet hole in the center of his forehead."

"Close range?"

"Looks like he might have been asleep when it happened. And from the appearance of the body, he's been dead for a few days."

Looking around, Knoll asked, "Then what happened out here?"

"My guess would be whoever did this was looking for something."

JR held a small chip in his hand. "All I need is this SIM card, and we're good to go, Sean."

"Good. We need to get out of here. Take the chip, and I'll put the phone back."

"Won't the police check it out?"

Kruger shrugged. "At this point, I don't care. That might be the only way we can locate Melton."

Back in the Denali, Kruger asked JR, "Is there any way to call 911 without a SIM Card?"

"Yes, just take the card out and make the call. The call won't have any authentication codes associated with it."

"That's what I thought, but I wanted to confirm."

***

Melton approached the desk in the lobby of the DoubleTree and offered an American Express card.

The young clerk looked at the card. "How many nights are you planning to stay with us, Mr. Dalton?"

"Just one."

"Would you prefer two queens or one king in your room?"

"Two queens please."

"Very good. How many key cards?"

"One, thank you."

She handed him the plastic card and said, "Per your request, I have you on the ground floor."

"Thank you."

"Is there anything else I can do for you, Mr. Dalton?"

Melton smiled and shook his head. "That's all. Thank you."

Five minutes later, he turned on the TV in his room to see if any new developments occurred with Hunter Holden. As he listened, he spread the contents of a suitcase he had gathered at Dalton Hadley's apartment on one of the beds. As he sorted, four piles were needed. One for unimportant information, one for incriminating documents about Hadley's past, and another for the man's financial situation. The final stack would hold documents Hadley had accumulated concerning the Field Museum project. These were the ones he sought.

***

Southwest Missouri

The time approached five minutes past 10 p.m., and JR still remained at his desk. An unusual occurrence since the birth of his son, Joseph. With his concentration so total, he failed to hear the approach of someone to his office.

"You know, this late at night, you probably should have the security system on."

JR whirled around. "Oh, it's you. What are you doing here?"

"The same could be asked of you. Go home, JR. It's late."

"Well, every time you get us involved in one of these investigations of yours, I end up working late."

Kruger chuckled. "I went over to your house, and Mia told me you were still here. So, I thought I stop by and check. As a rule, you only work late when you're making progress."

"Want to know what I've found?"

"Main reason I'm here."

Pointing to his left computer monitor on his desk, JR said, "That is a readout of Hadley's SIM chip."

After putting his half-readers on, Kruger leaned over and studied the information. "Busy boy."

"Yes. It seems he had his fingers in several projects." He pointed to a number that appeared numerous times. "That particular item stumped me for a long time. Just before you showed up, I was able to identify it."

Straightening, Kruger looked over his glasses at JR. "Let me guess. Hunter Holden."

"Good guess. His cell phone is called more than others."

"Were you able to find one for Dean Melton?"

JR shook his head. "Not yet."

Returning his attention to the computer monitor, Kruger pursed his lips. "How do you know the number is Holden's?"

"It's a Verizon account paid for with a personal account belonging to him, not the company."

"Doesn't mean it's his personal phone, then."

Without a further comment, JR returned his attention to the monitor and then his hands to the keyboard. Data flashed on the middle monitor, and the computer genius swiveled his head back and forth from one screen to the other for several minutes. Kruger stood patiently behind him, watching.

"Damn, Sean. I'm getting slow. I didn't think of that. But you're right. Hunter Holden has at least five personal cell phone accounts spread around the three big carriers."

"How many are still active?"

"They're all still active." A smile grew on his lips. He

pointed to one set of digits. "But that one is the only phone still making calls."

"Would it be safe to assume that phone is being used by Melton?"

"I don't like assuming anything, but you're probably correct."

"Where's the phone now?"

"Bloomington, Illinois."

"That's just south of Chicago about 130 miles." He paused. "Why don't you put a tracker on it and go home. When I was there, Mia sounded worried about you."

***

The Following Morning

Kruger arrived early at the offices of KKG Solutions and found JR already bent over his computer in his office.

"I thought you went home last night?"

Looking over his shoulder, JR said, "I did, but couldn't sleep. I think I have a lead on Melton."

Having poured a mug of coffee, Kruger took a sip. "Really. Where is he?"

"The phone pinged a tower east of Davenport, Iowa about ten minutes ago. Then it disappeared."

"He's heading toward Des Moines."

"I believe that's a safe assumption."

The retired FBI agent pulled his cell phone out and checked the time. He then searched for a contact and pressed the call icon.

"Bridgett Nelson."

"Mornin', Bridgett. It's Sean Kruger."

"Good morning, Sean."

"Are you still in Des Moines?"

"Yes, I will be until they transfer Hunter Holden to Minneapolis. Why?"

"A source tells me Dean Melton may be enroute to your location."

She was quiet for a moment. "Should I ask who this source is?"

"Probably not. We're going to send some information to Charlie Craft. Hopefully, he will call you with more details."

"Hopefully?"

"I'm sure he will contact you."

"Thanks, Sean. I continue to rack up debt to you."

"A long time ago, someone paid me forward with assistance. This is my way of paying back the debts I owe."

"Thanks, Sean. I'll wait to hear from Charlie."

The phone call ended, and Kruger looked at JR. "Want to call Charlie Craft?"

"Sure. You planning a trip to Des Moines?"

"No, it's time I step aside and let the FBI handle it."

"That has to sting."

"JR, my friend, it does. But not as bad as I thought it would."

CHAPTER 51

Des Moines

Special Agent Bridgett Nelson stood outside the Polk County Jail, scanning the parking lot. She had agents strategically scattered throughout the complex. They each had a picture of Dean Melton and were checking all cars entering and leaving the facility.

At exactly 11:53 a.m., the handheld radio she held squelched. "This is Unit 9. I've got a white Audi Q5 entering the lot. Driver resembles suspect. Over."

Bridgett responded, "All units. Heads-up on possible sighting. Unit 9, keep us informed. Over."

"Driver is now confirmed to be suspect. He is parked in back row, north lot, five cars from exit row. Over."

She looked in that direction. "Units 10 and 11, cover the exit. Don't let him out of the lot. The rest of you, converge on the location. Over."

***

Melton realized his mistake too late to be able to do much

about it. As he sat in his parked car checking his cell phone, four FBI agents surrounded the vehicle. With guns drawn and pointed at him, he had no other choice but to put his hands on the steering wheel in plain sight and allow them to yank him out of the car.

With his hand zip tied behind his back, he listened as his Miranda rights were read to him. Afterward, he turned to the female agent who seemed to be in charge. "How did you know?"

"We're the FBI. We know things."

An agent who had the trunk open lowered it enough to see over it. "Hey, Bridgett, you need to see this."

Special Agent in Charge Nelson walked to the back of the truck and saw a suitcase with an ID tag on it. "You're kidding me."

"Nope, I don't think he thought we'd be waiting for him."

She went back to their prisoner. "Do you know a man named Dalton Hadley?"

"Never heard of him."

"Then why's his suitcase in your trunk."

Melton closed his eyes and shook his head. "Shhhiittt."

***

"There was a suitcase in the car with an ID claiming it to be the property of Dalton Hadley. And here's the main reason I called you. The suitcase contained a lot of evidence supporting Hunter Holden's claim he had nothing to do with setting up the Field Museum theft. It was in fact Dean Melton who set it up and used Hadley to hire the two burglars."

Keeping his silence, Kruger chose not to comment. He let Bridgett continue.

"The question we have now is, whose idea was it? Holden is claiming the entire affair was thought up and executed by Melton. On the other hand, Melton is claiming all he did was execute Holden's instructions. So, Holden's lawyer is now questioning why he is being held without bond."

"Has he been released?"

"Not yet. A new bond hearing has been scheduled tomorrow."

"If they let him out, he'll disappear."

"We are all well aware of that. We have DOJ and bureau attorneys scheduled to be in court that day. The director told me, whatever I need, just let him know."

"Bridgett, Hunter Holden is extremely manipulative. He'll need to be transported with great care."

"That's what Director Clark told me."

"Good luck."

"Thanks, Sean. I'll keep you up-to-date as best as I can."

The call ended, and Kruger pursed his lips.

***

United States Federal Courthouse
Des Moines

Hunter Holden smiled and shook the hand of his attorney. He did not say thank you but instead followed the bailiff to a holding cell until his bail could be arranged.

Bridgett Nelson watched him as he exited through the door. A bureau attorney named Barbara Lowe appeared beside her. "Sorry, Bridgett."

"It's okay, Barbara. At least they authorized an ankle bracelet."

The woman attorney, with twenty years of service with the bureau, smiled. "My guess is he will petition for the court to send him to Minneapolis."

"Will they grant it?"

"DOJ will fight it. But, as you can see from today's hearing, Holden seems to know how to manipulate the system."

"I noticed that."

"Hey, when you talk to Sean Kruger, tell him I said hello."

"You know Sean, too?"

"Yes, you'd be surprised how many friends he still has at the bureau."

"No. I wouldn't be surprised."

"I understand you will be joining the ranks of DC supervisors soon."

Bridgett smiled and nodded.

"Welcome to crazy town, and the best of luck to you." Barbara Lowe placed the long strap of her laptop tote bag over her shoulder, turned, and left the courtroom.

Bridgett watched her leave and then walked over to the bailiff and asked, "When do they expect Holden to be released on bail?"

"Couple of hours. Why?"

"Just curious. Thank you." She followed the bureau attorney and exited the courtroom.

***

For the past ten years, Hunter Holden had minions doing the mundane and boring day-to-day activities most of the population endures. He remembered how to do them but felt he remained above the fray. When he walked out of the federal courthouse, a free man, so to speak, in the company of his lawyer, he knew what needed to be done.

"How do I get back to Minneapolis, Kyle?"

Kyle Newman looked at Holden for a few moments and shook his head. "You don't. You are wearing an ankle bracelet that will keep track of your location. Any venture out of Polk County, Iowa, will violate the conditions of your bail, and you'll be back in there." He gestured toward the building they had just vacated.

"I don't live here. Where am I supposed to stay?"

"The court doesn't care."

"Where's my cell phone? They did not return it."

Newman frowned. "They didn't?"

"No."

Setting his briefcase down, he opened it and retrieved a file. After scanning several pages, he looked up. "You weren't in possession of one when you were arrested."

Holden closed his eyes. "Kruger."

"I beg your pardon?"

"Nothing. Back to where I am supposed to live. You need to petition the court to allow me to go back to Minneapolis."

"I already have. In the meantime, you're stuck here in Des Moines."

"And I am to go where?"

Glancing at his wristwatch, Newman picked up his briefcase. "I have another court date in thirty minutes. You have your wallet back. Find a hotel for a few days. I will try to expedite your transfer to Minneapolis."

He turned to walk back into the courthouse. Holden said, "What about a phone?"

Without turning around, Newman said as he approached the courthouse door, "I'm sure you can figure it out."

After the attorney disappeared inside, Holden looked around his surroundings. Across the street were numerous buildings with exterior placards advertising lawyers, bail bondsmen, and one shop selling prepaid cell phones. Apparently, other released individuals suffered the same fate when released—an unreturned cell phone. With a slow shake of his head, he walked toward the store.

***

Kruger pinched the bridge of his nose as he listened to Bridgett Nelson relay the news from the bond hearing for Hunter Holden. Finally, he said, "Has he been transferred to Minneapolis?"

"No."

"Where is he?"

"I have a few agents keeping an eye on him. He bought a cell phone and then checked into a Hampton Inn not far from the federal courthouse."

"I doubt he will be satisfied with staying there. How much money did he have on him when you arrested him?"

"Ten hundred-dollar bills, plus a few smaller denominations, and twenty-thousand in American Express traveler checks."

"Did he get it all back?"

"Yes."

"Any credit cards?"

"American Express platinum and a black Mastercard."

"So, he has unlimited spending with the credit cards."

"Yes, I would say that's a good assumption."

"Bridgett, I appreciate you keeping me up-to-date."

"When I get more information, I'll let you know."

The call ended, and Kruger rubbed his temples. "Damn." He stood and walked to JR's office. The lights were off in the computer genius' space. He glanced at his wristwatch and realized he needed to get home. Stephanie and the kids were probably already there after work and school.

Returning to his office, he picked up his backpack and placed it over one shoulder. He hesitated and withdrew his cell phone from his jeans pocket. He set the backpack down and returned to his desk chair to make a phone call.

CHAPTER 52

The Next Day
Des Moines

Chicago Detective Peter Barnes took custody of Dean Melton for his extradition back to Illinois for the murder of Dalton Hadley. With his hands cuffed behind his back, Melton sat in the back of Barnes' detective car and stared out the window next to him as they headed east on I-80.

Barnes said, "I guess you heard Hunter Holden is out on bail?" The detective glanced in the rearview mirror to see his prisoner's expression. Melton did not disappoint.

With a fierce glare, he said, "How?"

"Because you are the one being charged in the murder of Dalton Hadley and the mastermind behind the Field Museum heist. You're also being charged with conspiracy to murder in the deaths of Margaret Ross and her stockbroker."

"Bullshit."

"Just saying."

"I didn't kill him. He was already dead when I broke into his apartment. Hunter Holden and Hadley are the guys who put the Field Museum scam together, not me."

"Not what the evidence indicates."

"You mean the BS in the suitcase?"

Barnes chuckled. "Yeah, the suitcase you had in your trunk."

"Holden told Hadley to put all that together. The man always had a backup plan, even if he never used it. Those documents were his get-out-of-jail-free cards. I rarely talked to Hadley. It was always Holden." He paused for a moment. "You also need to talk to a computer hacker named Mollie Lewis."

Barnes stared at Melton's image in the mirror. "Who's Mollie Lewis?"

"She's the one who figured out how to coordinate the break-in and the security cameras being turned off."

"I thought that was done by the museum IT guy?"

"The Lewis chick did all the planning and detail work. The IT guy was a patsy used to throw you cops off. All he did was provide Lewis with access to the museum computer system." He looked out the window for a moment. "Do you really think I'm smart enough to plan out the intricacies of the Field Museum project?"

No comment came from Barnes.

"Well, I'm not. Holden had been looking for a way to take over Goldmax for a year. Ever since it merged with the lithium mining company. Walter Wagenaar outbid him, and it really pissed him off. So, he started working behind the scenes to steal Wagenaar's company. Holden can be a vindictive asshole most of the time."

"I've noticed." The detective paused for a moment, keeping his eye on the road and taking quick glances at Melton. "Want to get back at Holden?"

The prisoner shrugged and returned his attention to the cornfields flashing past the speeding car's window. After a few moments, he returned his attention to Barnes. "How?"

"Cut a deal with the Illinois attorney general. She wants Hunter Holden more than she wants you."

"Figures." Melton bit his lower lip. "How do I do that?"

"Leave the details to me."

***

Des Moines

"Can I get you anything, Anna?"

She looked up at the young intern. "No, thank you. I'm fine."

"I don't mind."

Anna Cole did not speak again. She sat by herself in the commons. An open space where patients were allowed to get fresh air. Normally, committed individuals were not allowed to be by themselves in this area. However, people just there for observation were allowed to do so.

Staffing issues dictated that individuals like Anna Cole were given less attention and more freedom. To a point. But Anna Cole knew something other patients did not—the six-digit access code to the exit gate for the commons.

She sat in a chair under a large oak tree and stared at the gate. When it was almost time to go back to her room before evening meal, she stood. Walking casually, trying not to draw attention to herself, she followed the wall separating the open area of The Iowa State Department of Mental Health facility from the outside world. When she arrived at the door, she placed her back to it, her hands behind her. She located the keypad and punched in the code. After hearing the lock click, she opened it and slipped out into the cool, crisp fall weather. She did not hesitate but walked calmly toward the parking lot. Once there, she casually tried doors on the parked vehicles. In the third row from the back, she found one open. Once inside, she crawled over the seats into the back of an SUV with heavily tinted windows.

No one knew she was missing until bed check. By then, the SUV she now drove headed north on I-35, approaching the Minnesota state line.

***

Southwest Missouri

"Thank you for seeing me today, Max."

Maxwell Kinslow energetically shook Kruger's hand. "So glad to see you again, Sean. What did you need help with?"

"A puzzle."

"I love puzzles. Particularly if they have to do with the human mind."

"Well, this one does."

Motioning to the table in his office, Kinslow waited for Kruger to sit across from him and spoke. "Please, explain."

"You've published a number of papers on CEOs and corporate leadership. What, in your opinion, is the main cause of a business leader losing his effectiveness?"

"Oh dear. There are many factors. Age, deteriorating health conditions, excessive drinking or illicit drug use, and marital problems, all are possible factors. But I don't think those are the ones you had in mind. Are they?"

"No. What about obsession?"

"Depends on the obsession."

"Revenge."

"Ah—revenge. One of the more basic emotions. Yes, I have seen a few CEO's fall to this condition. Their ability to think strategically diminishes. Then their obsession takes over and consumes most of their waking hours. This results in a slower response to day-in and day-out decisions. Sometimes even paralysis in their decision-making skills."

"Can an obsession push one of these individuals over the edge?"

With his elbows on the table, the professor made a steeple with his hands. "In my opinion, depending on the obsession, yes. But then, an obsession can push any one of us over the edge."

"I'm aware of that, Professor."

"Then what's your question, Sean?"

"In your opinion, can an obsession with revenge, by one of these individuals, push them to act in ways they normally would not?"

Professor Kinslow blinked several times but kept his focus on Kruger. "Act how?"

"Instead of directing others to do their dirty work, they do it themselves."

"Sean, you of all people, know the answer to this question better than I. You dealt with those types of individuals your entire career with the FBI."

With a slight shake of his head, Kruger gave the professor a sad smile. "No, I've never dealt with anyone possessing his level of intelligence and pathology, Max. He exhibits a callousness bordering on demonic. He is textbook narcissistic and possesses no interpersonal relationships I can identify."

Taking a deep breath, Kinslow looked toward the books in his in-office library. He started to stand but stopped and returned his attention to Kruger. "Without interviewing this person, I would be careless to offer a diagnosis. However, my opinion would be, if he experiences no relief from his obsession, he will rely on himself to act out."

Kruger smiled. "Thank you, Max. I needed a second opinion, and I value yours. You've confirmed my conclusion."

***

Southwest Missouri

Standing on his back deck, Kruger looked toward the northwest. Dark clouds rolled and boiled in the distance.

Dusk would occur soon, and the lightning would be more visible. A low rumble of thunder rattled the deck. He felt a presence. Stephanie moved up next to him.

She said, "When is the storm going to be here, Mr. Weatherman?"

"I imagine it's close to Stockton Lake. Sandy's and Jimmie's houses should be feeling the wind and rain by now."

"So, when here?"

"Thirty to forty minutes."

"You going to watch it come in?"

"Helps me think."

"About?"

"Hunter Holden."

"You mentioned he was transferred to Minneapolis."

Kruger nodded.

"How does that affect you?"

"Anna Cole escaped from the mental facility they had her in for observation."

"Does that mean you're going to Minneapolis?"

"What do you think?"

She put her arms around his waist, and he placed his arm over her shoulder. "Can I ask why?"

"The FBI thinks Dean Melton planned the entire Field Museum heist. I don't think he has the mental horsepower to do it. The more I think about it, the more I'm of the opinion Hunter Holden became obsessed with owning Goldmax. It took him a year to put it together, but he obtained his goal. JR found information indicating Anna Cole helped. When I asked her about him, she nonchalantly said, 'Oh, him'. She then told me she had been helping him for years."

Stephanie looked up. "What did Dr. Kinslow say?"

"He confirmed my theory."

"So, when are you going to Minneapolis?"

"As soon as a certain detective in Chicago agrees to meet me there."

CHAPTER 53

Southwest Missouri

JR knocked on Kruger's doorframe and then leaned against it. Without turning around, the office's occupant said, "Is the coffee done?"

"About ten minutes ago."

Kruger stood. "I'm getting a cup. Want one?"

"Already got it. Are you interested in something I found on Dillard's phone?"

The retired FBI agent stopped and concentrated on his friend. "I'm listening."

"Are you in a bad mood this morning?"

"Concentrating. What'd you find?"

"An interesting GPS location at about the same time Dalton Hadley's autopsy indicated he died."

Raising his eyebrows, Kruger said, "Dillard was there?"

JR nodded.

"Doesn't prove anything."

"No, but it does support what Melton told your detective friend in Chicago."

Returning to his desk, Kruger picked up his cell phone.

While he waited for the call to connect, he said, "He'll ask how we got access to Dillard's phone."

"Ignore the question."

With his eyes glued to JR, Kruger said, "Peter, Sean Kruger. Got a second?"

"Sure, what've you got?"

"Dillard's cell phone's location places him at Dalton Hadley's apartment at the same time the man died."

Silence prevailed on the call. Finally, the detective asked, "Should I ask how you got this information?"

"No, but if you subpoena his phone records, you'll find it."

"So, that would corroborate Dean Melton's story."

"I believe it would."

"I can use his testimony to get the authorization."

"That's how I would do it."

The call went quiet again for a few moments. Finally, Barnes asked, "Have you heard of a computer hacker named Mollie Lewis?"

"Her real name is Anna Cole. She was in FBI custody but escaped while under psychiatric evaluation."

"Damn."

"Why did you bring her name up?"

"Melton claims the IT guy at the museum was a nobody. He just gave this Mollie Lewis character access to their computer. He claims she's the one who coordinated the cameras and locks being manipulated."

"The woman you identified as Mollie Lewis has worked for Hunter Holden for years, Peter."

"Shit."

"When can you get to Minneapolis?"

"Are you going to meet me there, Sean?"

"Yes, and I'll bring an up-and-coming FBI supervisor with me."

"I can get all the paperwork done by tomorrow. Will that work?"

"I'll make it work."

***

Minneapolis

Anna Cole, aka Mollie Lewis, arrived at Hunter Holden's mansion just after midnight. She picked the lock on the back door and slipped inside. The SUV she carjacked in Des Moines was abandoned and pushed into Lake Marion just south of town, the owner bound inside the vehicle.

After exploring the residence, she determined the owner had been away from home for an extended length of time. She took a hot shower, made herself a cocktail, and settled in to wait for the man to come home.

She would not have long to wait.

***

The Uber driver dropped Holden off in front of his home. The early morning flight from Des Moines International to Minneapolis got him back to town a little before 10 a.m. His home detention authorized for his own residence while he awaited trial. His case would be transferred to the federal courthouse there in Minneapolis.

He unlocked the front door and stepped inside. His plans did not include being available when the trial started. He would be long gone. He shut the door, locked it, and turned.

In the middle of his foyer, a middle-aged woman with wild, disheveled hair greeted him with a Smith & Wesson 1911 pointed at his head.

"Put the gun down, Mollie."

"So, you recognize me?"

"Yes."

"Where's my money?"

Holden chuckled. "What money?"

"The cash you promised me for helping you rob the Field Museum."

"Didn't you hear? Those diamonds were fake in the first place."

Her mouth twitched. "Not my problem. You promised me a million bucks for my assistance."

"I don't remember that. Who told you a million?"

She pulled the hammer back on the big gun.

"Do you know how to use that thing, Mollie?"

"Well enough to blow your head off."

He scoffed. "Since you think I owe you a million dollars, will blowing my head off assist you in getting paid?"

"Shut up. You're always trying to make me think you're smarter than I am."

He inched a little closer to her. "But I am smarter than you, Mollie. I always have been." He took one more step toward her.

She backed up and smiled. "I'm smarter than you think. I knew where you lived all along. You didn't think I knew who you were. That moron Dean Melton thought I was dumb, too." The smile disappeared. "Don't get any closer. I know how to use a pistol."

Holden stopped inching toward her and frowned. "Okay. What are your intentions, Mollie?"

"My intentions are to get my million dollars and then disappear."

"That will be difficult. I'm confined to my home for the foreseeable future."

Her eyes narrowed, and she displayed a slight grin. "You think old school, Holden. All you have to do is give me an account number, and I'm out of here." She paused. "But not until I have confirmation the money is in my account."

His expression turned sour. "I don't know if I have a million dollars available, Mollie. I've had a few expenses lately."

"You have it, Holden. I've been here since midnight, and

I found all of your available accounts." She paused for a moment. "You son of a bitch, you're trying to cheat me while I'm pointing a gun at you. I wonder if the federal government knows about all of them. Some weren't in this country."

Holden took several deep breaths, and his jaw clenched.

The woman continued. "To answer the question, you asked earlier about if I blow your head off, I won't get my money? Well, the answer is, if I shoot you right here, I'll get more than a million dollars. So, the question is, how much is your life worth, Hunter Holden?"

"Now, Mollie..."

"My name is Anna Cole. People have been under-estimating me my entire life. No more. Do you know that a man named Sean Kruger, Chicago detective Peter Barnes, and FBI agent Bridgett Nelson are en route to your house?"

Holden stiffened.

"Oh, I guess you didn't know, did you? The reason I know is while I waited for you, I gave an old friend of mine—" She stopped. "Well, he's not actually a friend. More like a mentor I didn't like. Anyway, I gave him access to the laptop you had hidden in your bedroom. They now know the whole story."

"You didn't."

"I did. You see, Holden, they didn't know the truth. You did a good job throwing doubt on your part in the diamond heist. They thought you were innocent. What they were going to prosecute you on was the investment fraud. By the way, what happened to all that money?"

"What money?"

"The hundred million dollars you were sending to Taiwan?"

He shook his head.

"You really don't know, do you?"

"No."

She laughed. "The Mossad grabbed it."

"How…"

"They're good, Holden. Very good."

"Did you have anything to do with it?"

"Me? No. Remember, you're smarter than I am."

With the angry cry of a wounded animal, Hunter Holden rushed toward the woman holding the Smith & Wesson. She pulled the trigger as fast as she could.

EPILOGUE

Southwest Missouri

Kruger sat on his back deck sipping a Boulevard Pale Ale. His across-the-street neighbor sat next to him.

JR said, "Do you believe they will ever find Anna Cole?"

Taking a quick glance at his friend, Kruger shrugged. "You know her better than I do. What do you think?"

"Well, I know I totally underestimated her. And no, they will never find her."

"Why?"

"The information she sent me from Holden's personal computer pretty much showed she was the individual who planned and scripted the entire operation from the beginning. Holden only supplied the capital. If she was able to plan something that intricate, she can surely plan a disappearance."

"Is she better than you?"

"She has a more devious mind, but I'm still better on a computer." JR took a sip of beer. "What happened to Hunter Holden's money?"

"Bridgett Nelson told me they suspect Holden had over

seventy million dollars stashed in various accounts around the world. They recovered around twenty, but the remaining dollars they can't find."

"Anna?"

Kruger nodded. "That's the prevailing theory."

"What about Dean Melton?"

"He cut a deal with the DOJ and is exposing Holden's empire. Which, according to Bridgett Nelson and Peter Barnes, was more extensive than anyone imagined."

"Really."

"Looks that way. Peter sends his thanks for the tip on Dillard's cell phone. He's been indicted for the murder of Dalton
."

"So, what about you, Sean? What's next on your agenda?"

"I've got two fraud investigations for Tucker, Neal and Spencer, Incorporated waiting on my desk as we speak."

JR chuckled. "That was fast."

"Yes. Nathan told me they had a lot of work for us. Fortunately, the ones they have don't possess the intrigue the Hunter Holden affair possessed. But then again, they aren't as lucrative, either."

"I haven't heard anything about Hunter Holden's condition. Did you, Sean?"

"When I spoke to Bridgett Nelson, she also told me he was out of critical condition. The funny thing is, he's being transferred to a federal medical center during his recovery."

"No, surely not?"

Kruger chuckled. "Yep, he's being transferred to the one here in Springfield."

ABOUT THE AUTHOR

J.C. Fields is a multi-award-winning and Amazon best-selling author. His Sean Kruger Series and The Michael Wolfe Saga have been awarded numerous gold, silver and bronze medals in the Reader's Favorite International Book Awards contest. In March of 2020, his book, *A Lone Wolf* became a #1 Best Selling Audiobook. The second book in the series, *The Last Insurgent*, gained Amazon's #1 New Release status in January 2021.

As one of the featured authors on the highly successful YouTube podcast, *Fear From the Heartland*, hosted by Paul J. McSorley, he offers a variety of original short stories penned specifically for its listeners.

He lives with his wife, Connie, in Southwest Missouri.

Made in the USA
Coppell, TX
27 January 2023